ALSO BY JANUARY BAIN

City of Lies

No Good Deed

NO ORDINARY MAN

NO ORDINARY MAN

JANUARY BAIN

ROUGH
EDGES
PRESS

No Ordinary Man
Paperback Edition
Copyright © 2024 January Bain

Rough Edges Press
An Imprint of Wolfpack Publishing
1707 E. Diana Street
Tampa, FL 33610

roughedgespress.com

Paperback ISBN 978-1-68549-611-1
eBook ISBN 978-1-68549-610-4
LCCN 2024937382

NO ORDINARY MAN

CHAPTER 1

If you are going through Hell, keep going
—Attributed to Sir Winston Churchill

"MY GOD, SEAN, LOOK AT THIS! I DON'T BELIEVE IT. BEYOND amazing—beyond *anything* I've ever seen." The incredulous voice of John Whitmore, fellow lab tech and partner in crime, broke through the haze of what Sean Jamison was now certain stacked up as the official worst hangover of the twenty-first century.

"Could you keep it down," he mumbled. Even his eyeballs ached. He pried open an aspirin bottle, knocked three into the palm of his hand, and threw them into his mouth, crunching hard. Bitterness flooded his mouth relieved by a quick slug of water. The walls were closing in on him this morning, the tight confines of his workstation triggering his anxiety.

"Told you to stay away from mixing tequila shots and beer."

"Not helping," Sean said. "So, what's the big deal?"

"Well, if this is to be believed, then this guy. Who *exactly* is this guy?" He glanced at the name at the top of the page. "Jackson Banks. Appears to be a one-of-a-kind homosapien. Check this result." John thrust the report at him.

Sean looked at it, his sunglasses making the text hard to read. Frustrated, he pushed them upward to rest on his spiky hair.

"*Holy shit!* Is this for real? Are those gene sequences active? That's not possible, is it? That's junk DNA. What the hell! Really? You're fucking with me, aren't you?" Sean glanced at his partner. John shook his head in the negative, his expression dead serious. "But you'd have to be an alien for these readings to be even possible."

"I didn't believe it at first either, but I've already run it twice. Time to alert the big guys. This is cosmic—a game changer. I wonder how it happened. Are we going to be seeing more of this or is it a one-off thing? Man, I would love to meet this guy face to face. I wonder what he's like? If he knows? What can he do different than the rest of us?" John got to his feet and swept his hands over his already tidy hair and straightened his tie. He could drink with the best of them and still look like everyone's idea of a dictionary bureaucrat.

"Hey! Wait a minute."

Sean grabbed John's arm. His heart rate soared uncomfortably with the intensity of the thought. Ambition burned bright. He licked his dry lips.

"I have a better idea. Can you say Nobel Prize?"

CHAPTER 2

YEARS AGO, OR MAYBE YESTERDAY, A PSYCHOPATH SET FIRE to the house. Tonight, a similar noose tightened around Jackson Banks's neck, squeezing, lurking in the darkness. A scorching Santa Ana wind whipped up the debris on the street, making him blink. Someone or something was sending him a warning.

"Nice tits on that one," Bob said, interrupting. He was nodding toward an uncovered living room window. "Not as large as the ones I was banging—"

"Shut up. Did you hear that?" Jackson asked.

Bob Russel, the partner he was tied to tonight from the local chapter of the LA Neighborhood Watch, was an asshole. Not that he didn't like a nice pair as much as the next man, but this creep made an art form of the proclivity. Jackson liked women. Never having met the right one didn't mean she wasn't out there, right? And he didn't want to be just another prick when he found her. Though what woman would want him in his fucked up and scarred state was another question.

"What? I don't hear anything."

Jackson shone his flashlight at the bus shelter doorway, moving it along the outside structure as he walked closer. Bob shambled along behind him, his unnecessary tactical boots clopping on the cement. A new poster gleamed in the light; a photo of an innocent face followed by a short description. Another missing girl. His stomach roiled.

A thin black cat slunk out of the shelter and took a chance, pressing against his pant legs.

Jackson bent down and patted its sleek head then rubbed behind its ears. The cat purred, and his cell phone buzzed. He stood up and pulled it from his jacket pocket, checking caller ID. His chest tightened and his throat constricted. Finally.

"Leia," he said into the phone. Breathe. Just breathe.

"Jackson! It's me. I'm in trouble for real this time. Ya gotta help me! Please!"

A loud crash. The outside world vanished as he focused all his attention on his sister's voice. "Where are you?" he demanded.

An uneasy moment of silence followed by the splintering of wood. His heart hammered, a cold sweat breaking out all over his body. *God, please keep my little sister safe until I can get there.*

"Tony's," Leia whispered.

The line went dead.

Fuck.

He thrust the phone back into his pocket.

"Gotta go."

He didn't wait for an answer but ran full bore down the street to his house and into the backyard where his GMC half-ton sat, his boots crunching on the fresh gravel he'd laid down to fill potholes earlier in the day. He unlocked the vehicle and opened the driver's door. Tony's dump was fifteen minutes away in the seedy suburbs of East Hollywood, where dreams went to die. *My god, Leia. What have you gotten yourself into this time?*

He thrust the key in the ignition and turned it over, wincing at the grinding sound of the misfire signaling the pending demise of his starter. When the engine cooperated and turned over on the second try, he let out a hiss of breath and drove down the back alley. When the narrow fence-lined corridor ended, he cranked the steering wheel to the right to turn onto the side street.

He navigated the few blocks to the Santa Monica freeway. *When had it all gone so wrong?* He'd taught her to walk. Holding her small trusting hand going trick-or-treating. Bringing her a final glass of water before bedtime. Standing on the street corner watching their house burn to the ground, knowing what had happened inside. Yeah, that was it, the catalyst for all the shit that followed. Fucked by genetics, by life, and unlucky twists of fate. That was the Banks clan. Or at least what was left of it.

Minutes later, he jerked the steering wheel to the right, barreling straight for Tony's seedy bungalow, the tires squealing loudly in protest. His foot sunk into the floorboards, bringing the truck to an abrupt halt. He opened the glove box and took out his semi-automatic pistol, clicked off the safety, and tucked it in the waistband of his jeans, the cold metal reassuring against his warm skin. He surveyed the yard as he jumped out of his truck. No obvious evidence of foul play. No authorities either. He had to get her out. *Fast.*

The screen door squeaked on rusted-out hinges. The inside door refused to open, and he banged on it, pounding loudly.

If those bastards hurt her, they'll fucking pay. All of them.

The door burst open.

"What's your fuckin' problem, buddy?" the Neanderthal asked with a snarl, his shaved head and leather cut a dead giveaway. One of Tony's minions. The sweet, sickly odor of drugs and sweat wafted from the guy's dirty clothes, the fumes stinging his sinuses. He sniffled a sneeze. He didn't want his vision blurring.

"My sister Leia Banks just called from this house. Said she needs a ride home. I've come to get her."

"Never heard of her," he said, trying to force the door closed now that he knew he wasn't about to make money selling drugs. The asshole was far shorter than his own six-foot frame, built like a boxer with thick biceps swathed in tribal tattoos. Most likely outweighed him by a good thirty pounds too. It was a crap shoot as to who would win a fistfight. He didn't intend to find out.

Jackson slammed the door hard against the man. His victim grunted, caught unaware. It bought him time to push past him and into the kitchen. He pulled his gun and leveled it at the guy. He gestured briskly with the loaded semi-automatic toward the doorway. "Take me to her."

The asshole gave him an angry look, but he skirted around Jackson and led the way down the hallway and into the living room.

Fuck.

She was cowering on the floor of the small, cramped room, her arms over her head, her eyes tightly closed. A slew of disgusting shit littered the puke-green rug. The stench of drugs and BO was stronger in here. His stomach clenched in protest. It was all he could do not to run to her, but it was a move that would end badly. Faint sirens keened in the distance, speaking of more trouble to come. Two men were holding court over a man tied with a length of rope to a kitchen chair.

"What the fuck do you think you're doing here?" one of the thugs asked, catching sight of Jackson. His face was livid with anger and bloodlust, a knife clenched in his right hand. *Tony.* The man tied to the chair wasn't faring well, blood oozing from several cuts, one eye swollen shut.

"I've come for my sister. Let her go, and we'll be on our way." He gestured with the gun.

"No can do. Her shit-bag boyfriend owes me big time." Tony's expression darkened. "Got to be done. Nothing personal." He shrugged like he was talking sense to the converted, his crazed eyes glazing over. *Just fucking great. Drugged and ready to kill, a lethal concoction. God, please help me find the right words.*

"What do they owe you? I'll pay. You know I'm good for it."

"It's not just about the money—though I'll take it. It's about what's right. Time's run out for this motherfucker. Gotta send a clear message."

"Looks like you've already done that," he said. This was worse than last time—far worse. A drumbeat began to echo in his brain.

"Put the gun down and we'll talk," Tony said. Code for he was *never* going to let them go.

"Ya heard what he said," Neanderthal man said, backing up his boss. The guy's dubious job as bouncer had to suck. Scars crisscrossed his broad face. Jackson had no doubt he and Leia were not leaving here—not upright. He hated what he was being forced into with every fiber of his being, a far harder thing than an honorable tour of duty in Iraq.

"I only came for my sister," he said, darting a quick glance her way. He willed her to get to her feet, but she appeared too frightened or too intimidated or too drugged to move. A shiver of apprehension snaked down his spine. He blinked, diluting the sting of sweat dripping down his forehead and into his eyes.

"Ben here dragged your sister into this. Blame him if that makes it easier. But there are three of us—all armed. I just can't let you come in here and order us around. That would be very, *very* bad for business." Tony said the words softly, making the menacing message all the more chilling.

The gun bulged under Tony's sweat-stained tee shirt. There was no way he was getting Leia out of here alive. The die had been cast. Dread filled him. He would have to break his sacred oath.

Unthinkable. The thing he had sworn never, *never* to do again. The thing that had caused such devastation. Such pain. And ripped their lives apart. They had never recovered. Why was he being called upon to bring it out into the light of day again? *Why?*

Only for Leia, sweet baby Leia, could he do what must be done. Heartsick. No choice now as Tony announced his lethal intentions with a slight flick of his eyes at his own guy.

Everything unfolded in slow motion, the deadly knife pointing straight at Jackson's heart.

Jackson closed his eyes. He had only a split-second to turn this ship.

Focus.

He drew on all his power. Split it three ways, sending it into his chosen victims, his body vibrating, humming with the effort and intensity. Pain and torment sluiced through him. Memory sickened him to the core for what it had caused the last time the insane ability was unleashed. Revenge. And death.

Time suspended even further. Each second a single beat. Flashes of bright light broke across his vision. The dull beige walls and disgusting green rug shimmered, the room fading to near invisible for one too bright a moment. Strangely familiar. Horribly familiar.

His vision cleared, the light vanished, and the room came back into view.

Tony had stopped in his tracks, a few scant inches from stabbing him, his expression bewildered. Unbelieving. Stunned to the core. A twinge of sympathy shuddered through Jackson.

The blade dropped from Tony's fingers and thudded to the carpet, the razor-sharp edge gleaming wickedly in the harsh light.

Screams of agony. The acrid stench of sulfur seared the lining of his nostrils. What was burning?

All three men clutched at their chests, their faces grimacing in pain, their eyes wild.

Jackson dragged Leia to her feet. She stumbled against him.

She looked up at him with dread, then at the men moaning pitifully on the floor, suffering an agony. She pushed her disheveled hair back with a shaking hand, swaying dizzily. Jackson put his arm around her pitifully thin body, her shoulder blades bony and delicate like a bird's. His heart squeezed tightly, wanting to protect her.

"What—what about Ben?" she asked, her voice wavering in and out.

"The fucking pain!" Tony moaned, clutching at his chest. He tore at his tee shirt, ripping the fabric, making a large gaping hole.

The victim tied to the chair stared at the spectacle unfolding on the dirty living room rug with his one good eye so open the white circling the deep-brown iris was visible.

Move.

Jackson rushed to Ben's side. He tore off the ropes that tied him to the kitchen chair. The sirens were closing in. Time's up.

"Can you walk?" he asked, pulling the thin young man to his feet.

"What the fuck's going on? What did you do to me?"

Jackson didn't answer. He half carried his sister with Ben lurching behind them from the living room to the kitchen. Out the back door. She clung to him as he tried to get her into the passenger seat while Ben leaned against the fender, blood dripping from his mashed-up face. The insistent sirens were only a block or two away now.

"You hurt, sis?" Jackson asked.

She shook her head.

"We gotta go. Now!" He hated pressuring her, but needed her cooperation more.

She broke into a fresh flood of tears. Black mascara streaks under her blue eyes that exactly matched his were renewed. He swallowed hard, pressing his lips together to keep a feral scream deep inside. Her fear-ravaged face and scraggily pink hair that had once been gleaming brunette and a longer version of his own had weakened his defenses. He was looking at a ghost of his once-beautiful sister. The sirens blared, too close. He bit his lip, helped her into the truck and buckled her in like a toddler, all the while whispering in his rough voice, "It's okay. It's okay, sweetheart. You're safe now. I won't let anyone hurt you. Shush. It's okay, sis. We're going home."

He helped Ben into the back seat of the crew cab and jumped into the driver's seat. Slamming the truck in gear, he drove out of the back lane just as the police car raced past the front of the house. Figures, in East Hollywood, where no one gave a fuck. Ever.

CHAPTER 3

HECTOR TORRES SLUMPED IN THE BEDSIDE CHAIR, memorizing the sleeping face of his bride. His newest treasure. He compulsively turned the heavy gold wedding ring that matched hers round and round on his thick finger. Elena, his shining light. *God, why does she make me hurt her?*

His cell phone buzzed in his shirt pocket. He checked the number and padded out of the room to answer it. He never discussed business in front of women, especially one feigning sleep. It was a man's job to keep his woman safe.

He turned to look out an office window at the back of the house where one of the stable hands was busy putting his new favorite, White Star, through his paces in the paddock. The noble lines of the animal stirred his imagination. The stallion pranced with amazing spirit and grace in the slating rays of sunlight, his gleaming black coat a testament to good breeding and endless care.

Behind the view of the plains surrounding his hometown of Ojinaga, Mexico, the municipal dump was already spewing out plumes of toxic black smoke high into the air. The image of himself as a child running through the trees desperate to find his father, and then finding him hanging from the branch of a tree, burned to death on the banks of the Rio Grande ate at his soul. Meant to. The sickening stench still stark in his memory, a reminder of his own mortality. Kept him sharp. Knowing. And why he lived where and how he did.

He was not the first *padrino* to head Los Knights and run heroin from the Sierras to the Rio Grande and then north into the US, and he would not be the last. A deadly family tradition. Ambition burned hot in him this morning, as it did all mornings of his life. He wanted to lead the cartels. The recent objections from his first lieutenant did not faze him. He would press forward and make them into a corporation that would take over the manufacturing and distribution of the drug trade in all of Mexico. Fuck the Sinaloa assholes, thinking they owned the Golden Triangle.

The phone buzzed again. He sighed and straightened his shoulders.

"Hector." He grunted his name with a fierce determination that spoke of years of being in command. The men called him Torres the bull behind his back and he didn't discourage it. And now, with recent developments, he needed the edge more than ever. Developments that needed dealing with in the old way required loyalty. And loyalty was only bought with fear. A lesson learned at his old man's knee.

"It's George. We've got trouble, my *padrino*, I'm sorry to say. Garcia is right out of his fucking mind! Talking some crazy bat shit and refusing to listen to reason."

George Lopez was his best lieutenant. Not easily upset. One of the reasons he'd chosen him.

"What kind of crazy shit?" he asked, frowning, the view vanishing as his mind refocused.

"About his brother-in-law. You remember Tony Hernandez? He married Teresa, moved to LA—runs the shitty east side. Tony says he was teaching a deadbeat low-rung asshole a lesson. Garcia was helping him. The stupid *pendejo* had been bragging he was ripping Tony off. Guy name of Ben Carson. Real fucking idiot. Then this other guy showed up out of the blue."

"So?"

"It's what happened that's got him all fired up. Something this other asshole did to him and his guys before he rescued the sister and deadbeat."

"Okay. So what happened?"

"You need to hear this for yourself, boss. Some weird *vudú* shit. Talked about everyone having a heart attack brought on by something this guy did to them."

Hector sighed. The superstitions of his crew were a godsend when it worked to his advantage, but at times like this, they were a royal fucking pain in his ass.

"A man creates his own luck in this world. I'm on my way," he said and ended the call. Excuses didn't cut it with him. Only results.

He stomped to the hall closet and jerked his bullet-proof vest off the hanger with a noisy clatter, the wire hanger falling unheeded to the floor. Amid tensions with the upstart Templars at an all-time high, he couldn't afford to take chances. He texted his driver and bodyguard.

His mother hurried down the hallway toward him.

"Mamá, you should still be in bed," he said, chastising her gently. She was dressed in a simple black housedress, her hair in a tidy bun, the small gold cross necklace she always wore hanging around her neck. She handed him a stuffed paper sack.

"You must eat, mijo. Your wife, she sleeps late like *es chiqueado*. You should not have married a beauty queen."

Her scathing tone was filled with scorn for his still sleeping wife.

He bent and kissed her deeply wrinkled cheek. She was his adored mamá. Though he admired her dedication to raising her four children after his father was murdered, sometimes her hard attitude made his life more difficult.

"She's adjusting, Mamá, give her time."

"You work too hard," she said, reaching up and touching his cheek.

"For the family, always for the family, Mamá."

The sound of the garage door opening alerted him. Time to move. He kissed her cheek again and exited the house.

He slid into the passenger seat of the armored vehicle and glanced over at his old schoolmate, who had been his bodyguard for many years. Thomas was a serious man, his body heavily muscled by hours spent weight training. His shaved head and wary eyes made him an adult version of himself as a child on the playground. Exactly the kind of man he wanted by his side if things went south. And things always had a way of going south.

"Too early for this shit. I'm needed at the warehouse," he said.

Thomas nodded. "Sure, boss."

Ten minutes later, Thomas stopped the vehicle in front of the low riding cement storm structure. It was built like an iceberg, ninety percent unseen.

"Wait here," he ordered. He got out and opened the heavy steel door to the vast underground network located on the back of his holdings. He shivered; the cool moist air inside instantly dampened his clothing.

"Okay, tell me what happened," Hector demanded of his lieutenant.

"Mornin'. Sorry I had to pull you away from your

new bride so early in the day," George said by way of greeting, running a hand over his short-cropped steel-gray hair, his eyes dark with worry. "Want some coffee first?"

"No. Let's get this over with. Where is he?"

"In back."

Hector walked across the cement floor and pulled open the door. Garcia sat on a stone bench, his hands dangling between his legs. The man nodded a respectful greeting, his normally tanned complexion waxy and pale. Garcia worried for his life, as well as he should. No one brought him bad news without repercussions.

"What happened?"

"It was crazy, *padrino*. One minute we're fine, the next dropping to the floor. All three at once. Like we were all having a fucking heart attack. The guy did something to us. Worst pain ever, but I flew down here right away to report. You always say you want bad news in person. I ask your forgiveness for having to tell you this—for having to be the messenger of bad news." Garcia licked his lips, beads of sweat standing out on his forehead though the cement bunker was freezing cold.

Hector grunted as he rubbed his whiskery chin. He had not taken the time to shave this morning, preferring more time with his bride.

"And the debt owed?" he asked.

"Man said he'd pay it," Garcia answered.

"And has he? Made things right with Tony?" he asked.

Garcia shook his head in defeat. Licked his lips one more time. "Not yet. But promises have been made."

"Bad news," Hector said in the flat tone he used to calm and control his vast empire of workers. "I will send more committed men in your place. Men who won't fall to the floor when another man enters the room. You bring much disgrace on us acting like such pussies." His expression changed to one of derision as he gave Garcia a cold look. Of all the excuses he had heard for business gone bad, this was the worst.

Hector walked up to Garcia, made the sign of the cross on the man's forehead, and pulled out his prized silver pistol from its side underarm holster. The one given him by his men as a wedding present only days before.

"Make your peace with God."

Garcia began to pray. "Our father, who art in heaven…"

He shot him right in the center of his sweaty forehead. The man slumped sideways in his seat as blood and bits of white brain matter ran down the cinderblock wall, dripping into a pool of glossy red on the floor. The sickly odor of shit assaulted his nostrils as he took a deep breath. Fucking shame, death.

He turned to find George watching him from the doorway. The look in his dark eyes giving nothing away.

"I want you to go to LA and take my nephews with you. They need toughening up. Make sure that mother-fucker Ben Carson pays."

George nodded. Just business.

CHAPTER 4

JACKSON WORMED HIS WAY THROUGH THE FRIDAY NIGHT crowd at *Johnny G's*, dodging waitresses laden with heavy trays of drinks and people reeking of desperation, looking for a good time. He spied his friend at a back table well away from the seething humanity. Good choice.

Rand Givens was the only guy he'd bother to join for a drink at a bar on a weekend night. He'd used blackmail to do it, threatening to send round a strip-o-gram to his house. He'd been trying to get him out for weeks, said they were long overdue to tie one on. He rubbed at the tight scarred skin on his chest. He knew Rand only wanted what was best for him even if he kept reassuring his longtime friend that staying home was his default option.

Rand gestured to a waitress as Jackson sank into the other chair at the small round bar table.

"What can I get you, Jackson?" the waitress asked, favoring Jackson with a smile.

"Bourbon neat. Willett if you got it, thanks," he said, returning the smile.

"Add it to my tab," Rand instructed.

Jackson nodded his thanks.

"Coming right up," she said. Jackson watched her walk away, hips swaying as she made her way through the crowd, her blonde ponytail swinging in time with the throbbing beat of the bar band.

"You should ask her out, bro. Justine's got a thing for you," Rand said.

Jackson ignored the comment. One look at him with his shirt off and it would be game over. He waited until Justine placed the drink in front of him. He took a sip and eyed his friend, noting Rand was a few drinks ahead of him.

"So, anything new?"

"Same old shit," Rand said, frustration and resentment barely concealed.

"Want to talk about it?" They were each other's release valve when politics at work had them tied in knots, though Rand's job with the DEA was far more fraught with political landmines than his own working as a Special Investigator for US Customs.

Rand ran a hand over his thick brown hair, clipped shorter at the sides, his dark eyes thoughtful as he took another swig of his beer.

"Current operation's being blocked by the suits. This crap gets so old. Fighting over jurisdiction again. We have the resources, the manpower, *and* the knowhow, but we can't get them to see reason. Shit, we've done this kind of thing many times. We're the ones with the protocols and connections to keep our crew reasonably safe when in foreign countries. And men like Hector Torres are laughing at us as we fight it out on our home turf. At this rate, Hector will be an old man before we get our act together."

"Hector Torres?" Jackson asked. The warm smoky liquor slid down his throat, soothing after a hell of a week. He gestured at Justine to bring him another.

"Head of Los Knights. He has a ranch somewhere in northern Mexico. He's hard to pin down. A slimy bastard. And ambitious from all reports. He raises prize winning racehorses and has his finger in lots of businesses, some laundering his money. Trying to figure out which were created as a cover for his activities is one of our chief concerns. He's far too fucking good at covering his tracks, not to mention the people love him for providing jobs. Means they'll put up with all the other shit that drug running entails, I guess. Fuck!" Rand shook his head.

"People wonder why the top people rotate so often. I've observed there's a good reason," Jackson said, giving him a casual look.

"Yeah, so, what do you think it is?" Rand asked as he diligently worked to tear off the label on his frosty beer bottle.

"Those in charge and baby's diapers are changed for the same reason."

His fingers stopped their fiddling as he broke out in a belly laugh. "Hey, no fair, buddy! The one-liners are my jurisdiction."

"Had a problem of my own the other day with Leia," Jackson volunteered, his tongue loosened by the alcohol and a need to share his worries. It was a well-honed ritual with them.

"Shit, sorry to hear that. She okay?" Rand knew all about his dealings with his sister. Had often offered advice. But three stints in rehab had not dinted the disease consuming her.

"Her boyfriend, some asshole named Ben Carson, welshed on a drug debt. He was tied up and tortured by some guys in East Hollywood and Leia was there. Thank Christ she was able to call me from the bathroom. I got to the house barely in the nick of time."

Rand waited until Justine set the second drink in front of his friend.

"You guys want any food?" she asked. Her pretty face lit up with another smile. "Hot wings on special."

"Sure, why not bring us a couple dozen," Rand said. Justine sashayed away to place their order.

"Leia okay?" he asked.

Jackson shrugged as he dragged his eyes away from Justine's retreating curves to give his friend a quick glance before staring at the golden nectar in his glass again. "She's okay. Scared straight at the moment."

"How did you manage it?" His eyes bore into his and he had to look away first. Swallowed hard. Took another sip to wet his parched throat.

"They gave me no choice."

"And?"

"I *had* to use. It was close quarters and they meant business. A stray bullet could have hit Leia." He shuddered at the thought. "What choice did I have?"

The happy free-for-the-weekend crowd reached a crescendo at the front of the bar. A large group of women were celebrating somebody's upcoming nuptials judging by the bedraggled veil perched on one of the women's heads.

"I'm sorry. I know you've vowed never to do that. What it cost you last time—" Rand winced, sympathy clear in the lines of his face, his eyes filling with concern. "Did you know any of the men? What about blowback?" he asked, pinning him down for an answer.

"Yeah, well, maybe Tony Hernandez."

"I'll do some digging on Tony. I've heard he's been expanding his operations. The word on the street is he's got some powerful new connections in Mexico. Wants to prove something. There might be a problem."

"What are the guys going to say? That some guy disarmed them by giving them simulated heart attacks? Who's going to believe that?" Jackson pretended nonchalance.

"Maybe."

The hot wings arrived with another sweet smile and a flip of the ponytail. Someday, when his life made more sense, he'd ask a girl like Justine out. *Maybe a nice girl like her could see past my scars?*

"I know how reluctant you are to use it—how it brought tragedy," Rand said in a quieter voice that acknowledged the past. "And I know you didn't ask for the responsibility and the price you paid for it, but if you hadn't used it on me over there, I'd be long dead. Your ability can be used for good as well, remember that. It doesn't have to be a curse."

Rand's words sent him a flashback of the day when thousands of volts of electricity had coursed through his flesh, leaving him scarred, the skin on his chest shiny and stretched thin, networked with mottled areas from the skin grafts. Then the life affirming moment of restarting his friend's heart in Iraq after the incoming shell had badly damaged their Humvee. The fear of holding Rand in his arms, praying over his lifeless body, and then sending his power into him and seeing him shudder back to life, a moment that could not be fully understood or explained.

"Drink up," he said, just wanting to forget. No way was he going to face the most painful memory of all. Why his monster of a stepfather sat on death row. "I'm buying the next round and more wings."

"*Damn*, there's Catherine," Rand said, his expression tightening.

"We can leave," he suggested. Catherine was a living nightmare.

"Nah, not going to let her drive me away from a good time with my best friend."

Of course, like a furry moth to the flame, Rand's ex had to prance over to their table, her face red and sweaty from partying. Her trademark bright auburn hair gave off sparks, matching her personality too perfectly.

"Well, if it isn't my charming, unable-to-commit boyfriend and his faithful sidekick."

"Catherine," Jackson said. He kept his tone neutral though he had to suppress the urge to shut down the emotionally unstable woman who had stalked his friend after a disastrous break-up.

When Rand had hooked up with her, he had either been desperate or drunk. Maybe both. And definitely off his game after losing Loretta, the one he had fallen in love with only to discover she had an unforeseen unfaithful side. The biggest problem with Catherine was she got too possessive, too soon, and his friend wasn't ready. Just poor timing. He felt an unexpected twinge of sympathy for her. Life was all about timing. So far his own sucked.

The expression in her eyes, nothing but toxic death rays, made Jackson break out in a sweat, worried for his friend. She wobbled in her high heels, her disheveled mane partially hiding her face. She was one of the pre-wedding celebrators, blatantly declared on the rectangular plastic badge, *Team Sara*, pinned crookedly to her blouse. A woman helping another woman celebrate her success at landing a man was bound to be less than charitable to the big fish she had coveted. And she'd had more than a few too many. *Just fucking great.*

She pointed a sharp fingernail at Rand's chest, stabbing him as she punctuated her remarks, slurring her words. "You and me, we had a good thing. And then you just had to shut me out. Like I was nobody to you. Just freakin' shameful. You should go to jail for breaking my heart—that would show you!"

She failed to mention she had been hauled into a police station and charged after all of Rand's tires had been slashed. She'd been caught on video surveillance. Drunk. Got a suspended sentence and community service. And a court order to stay away. Which she broke whenever it suited her, like now. He never reported her, too good a guy. Just more proof she was the wrong one for him.

"I'm sorry, Catherine." Rand was wise enough to say no more than the sincere-sounding words he had been offering up since the break-up. Only Jackson knew he was grinding his teeth.

"Well, you should be! You missed out on the best thing that could have happened to you—you bastard! Don't think you can get me back with fake apologies." Straight back to the finger pointing, but it was less threatening as Rand's words took away her ammunition.

They sat and waited her out, giving her nothing to feed on. Good training in conflict resolution was the key, according to his friend. Jackson's own nemesis rotted on death row awaiting his face-to-face with the devil. *To hell with conflict resolution and letting things go.* He'd promised himself he'd be there to witness it, to make certain the bastard died for his crimes.

"Catherine, we need you! Come back here!" a slurred voice shouted from the bride's territory across the room.

Catherine looked undecided for a moment. Then she did the unexpected, fueled by alcohol. She leaned down and gave Rand a big sloppy kiss before toppling forward. He lurched backward, caught unaware. The chair jarred at his sudden movements to avoid her, the scrape of the chair legs as they tore into the hardwood flooring loud to Jackson's ears. Shit. Catherine grabbed at Rand, clutching at his shirt front and tearing the buttons off. They pinged onto the floor, scattering like popcorn.

"I'm sorry, babe," Catherine was babbling as she pawed at his friend, trying drunkenly to embrace him.

Jackson jumped up to pull her off. She scratched at his face with her long nails drawing blood as he struggled to get her back onto her feet, freeing Rand who jumped up and pulled his torn shirt over his chest.

"Leave us alone! It's your fault we're not together. You two are too freakin' tight! Just 'cause you saved his life doesn't mean you're his bum buddy forever! He'd see how good we are together if you'd give him some space. Why don't you just leave us alone!" Catherine screamed.

Jackson ignored her. Bit his tongue and marched her back to her table with an iron grip on her arm. He gave the bouncer who was about to come to his aid a nod off. The man halted, watching them.

"Leave him the hell alone," he hissed into her ear, ignoring a twinge of sympathy. "Take her home," he ordered the group. The designated driver, the only sober one at the table, nodded and got up.

He watched the pair leave, Catherine's expression still murderous and worrisome to Jackson. He could smell future trouble with a capital T.

"You okay?" he asked Rand as he rejoined him at the table.

"Sure," he said, giving him a wane smile. "Must be the new deodorant I'm wearing."

"You wear deodorant?" Jackson cocked an eyebrow at his friend who returned the grin, if shakily.

"Yeah. It's called 'desperation.' You want me to bottle it so you can enjoy the benefits too?"

"Thanks, but no thanks."

"Your loss."

He finished his beer in a few gulps. "I need to take a leak."

Jackson watched him weave his way through the crowd that had regained its previous momentum. His cells phone vibrated from an incoming text. *Leia.*

CHAPTER 5

"I DON'T THINK IT'S A GOOD IDEA," LEIA SAID, BALKING. She watched Ben pace the floor. With Jackson gone for the evening, they had the place to themselves, and she had hoped for some quiet time. Not running out to score blow to sell. "I'm giving up the shit anyway. If you loved me, you'd get that."

"Sugar, *you know* I love you. But I got to make a living for us. We can't sponge off your brother forever. Don't sit right by me. I want to provide for my woman. Our future. You're everything to me, you know that, right, baby?" Ben stopped pacing long enough to fall to his knees in front of her where she perched on the sofa, putting his arms around her waist. "I need you by my side. You give me the strength to want to do right by us."

She scooted closer to his warm body. He leaned in for a kiss, his thin face so achingly familiar and heartbreak-ingly bruised. At least both his eyes could open. He had shared that he saw his bruises and knife slashes as marks of the warrior. She melted against him. She could never resist him for long. He completed her.

"But Jackson's working on getting a second mortgage.

If you wait a few more days, you can repay the money and start over. Fresh. Maybe we can quit it for good this time, baby," she pleaded, reaching up to brush the lank hair back from his eyes.

"You know I can't do that. I need to provide for us. Pay it back. The only way I know how. I've got no other training, sugar. No other way to make a living. Maybe, after I've got enough socked away, we can find another way. But these guys—they want to meet right now. Advance us enough product to help us pay back our debts. It's all set up. You gotta strike while the iron's hot. That's not just words. Besides, if anything goes wrong, your brother will step in. *Fuck*. Look what he can do. It's a safe bet, sugar. A real win-win for a change."

Though she'd heard the promised words too many times before, the sound of Ben's reassuring voice lulled her into submission. He had kept her warm and fed, provided for her habit this past two years after the car accident had messed her up so badly that she had developed a heroin addiction to replace the opiates the doctor prescribed. Cheaper. And Ben needed her. Her body vibrated wanting its fix. She licked her dry lips. Maybe they would allow a small test of their product. Just a little, enough to get her by. Clear her head.

"Okay," she said.

"Good." Ben was all business as he pulled away and stood up, leaving her bereft. "The meeting's set for midnight at Sunset Tower Plaza off Santa Monica. Text your brother and let him know."

––––––––––

"I'LL DO THE TALKING," Ben warned before knocking three short bursts, a pause, and then two more loud ones on the hotel room door. She wished the meeting was on a lower floor, preferably street level, easier to bail if things went wrong. Her stomach tightened into painful knots. *Where is Jackson?*

"Come in." A short stocky younger man opened the door and carefully patted them down.

"Can't be too careful," he said by way of explanation as Leia shrank more within herself. The man had a trendy haircut with the sides shaved and top lock tied at the crown of his head like she'd been recently noticing on a television show about Vikings. It looked good and she thought it might look better on Ben than having his hair always hanging in his eyes.

She self-consciously raised a hand to her own hair. It desperately needed attention. The drug dealer's eyes had said it all when he gave her a once over, dismissing her. It hurt. She used to be considered pretty, even beautiful at times. What had happened to her? Drugs. Illness. Neglect. Shame scorched her soul, making her tremble. She glanced around the room, wishing the deal was over with so she could escape to a better, softer world.

Another man came over to join them. He looked about the same age as the Viking guy with a similar haircut except the coal black thatch was left free to stand up on top of his head making him look like an eraser head. She almost giggled aloud and had to press her lips together to avoid being noticed.

She moved further off to the side wishing she could just disappear, put on a magic invisibility cloak like from the fantasy stories she loved to think up in her head. A third man came into the room drying his hands on a towel. He was older with bristly gray hair. She bit her lips as she watched him warily. He was the dangerous one though; he gave off the fresh clean odor of soap that belied his dark intentions. She kept her eyes downcast, only giving him a twitch of her lips by way of a greeting.

"Ben, I'm George." He didn't offer his hand but stood with arms crossed over his barrel chest, the younger men flanking him. "I hear you've come to pay your debts. Pay back the money you swindled from Tony."

"Ah, not quite my understanding of the main purpose of this meeting." Ben's expression was faintly confused, then eased as he gained confidence. "But, if you advance some product, I'll be able to pay you back in no time. Plus, her brother"—Ben nodded in Leia's direction and she wanted to sink through the floor—"will pay all the money in a day or two when the bank releases the funds. He's a stand-up guy, Jackson Banks. Works for US Customs—a big shot. Some kind of special investigator. Check it out."

George's face remained noncommittal, but a speculative gleam from his dark eyes as Ben told him about her brother's job worried her. "And what guarantee do I have *you* won't rip us off again?" Though he spoke softly, the hackles rose on the back of Leia's neck. Panic built in her. *God, I need a fix. One last bit of peaceful bliss to help me through, settle my mind, take the craving away.* Sweat poured from her armpits. She sniffed, smelling herself, reeking of fear and desperation.

"I can't say how sorry I am. Some business problems got in the way. I made some bad decisions, but it's all sorted now. I can guarantee it will *never* happen again. You have my word."

"The word of a junkie doesn't count for much where we come from," the Viking said with a sneer.

"Manuel," George corrected the younger man.

"Okay, here's the deal. I believe your intentions are aboveboard and that our money is in transit. We're going to take you for a little drive. A safe place where the product is stored. You take it, sell it for profit, get your brother to pay what is owed within the week"—he nodded at Leia—"and everyone is happy."

Leia's system flooded with endorphins. Sweet release. They weren't going to die today. Of course not, Ben was useful to them. He was good at keeping his supply network humming. Good at business when he wasn't snorting and coming up with pipe dreams of making one perfect score. Good when it was just the two of them against the world. She'd help him see the light now. Keep him on track. Maybe crack the habit for good this time. Soon as she had one more hit. Buoyancy and relief lightened her step as she followed Ben into the Sunset Tower's broad hallway, the men right behind them.

CHAPTER 6

JACKSON CHECKED THE TIME ON THE DASH. FIVE MINUTES after midnight. Shit. Traffic had been a bitch and he'd gotten Leia's text late. *What the hell had Ben been thinking?* They could have handled this alone, kept his sister out of it. Anger made him punch the steering wheel, the tires of his truck screeching on the hot pavement. He pulled into the underground parking garage and jumped from the truck before he headed for the elevator.

Halfway there, he swung his eyes around the space for a second time to check for any activity. Leia and Ben were walking briskly with a trio of men a hundred yards to his left. He raced across the pavement to catch up. They were just about to climb into a vehicle when Jackson caught their attention.

"Leia! Ben! Wait up!" he shouted.

Everyone swung their heads around and Jackson noted the telltale bulges under their suit jackets. Packing heat.

The men turned to face him as Leia took a few steps in his direction and gave him a big hug. She was damp from sweating and her face was shiny. He could smell the fear.

He hugged her back and set her aside, blocking her from the men's view.

"I'm Jackson Banks. The guy who's going to pay off Ben's debts."

The older man of the trio stepped forward and offered his hand. Jackson shook it. Sized him up. Dark intelligent eyes, short cropped gray hair, and a strong handshake. Built like a tank. A formidable opponent with killer written all over him.

"You're the guy that Tony blames for messing with his crew. You interrupted justice in the making."

"When *justice* interferes with my baby sister, Leia's, life, it's my duty to become involved." Jackson's heart was racing as adrenaline flooded his system. They were here to kill Leia and Ben; he could see it in their eyes. Maybe keep them for a few days until he paid the debt in full, maybe not. They obviously needed to send a message more about double crossers than keep them alive to be earners. And Ben didn't appear to have a clue. Going along with whatever scenario they'd laid out for him. Seduced by drugs and profit.

"You're welcomed to come along with us," the man said smoothly as if it were a walk in the park. More like a walk to a shallow grave in the desert.

"I would take my sister home first. Then, and only then, would I consent to meet up with you later."

"Can't do that. Our schedule's too tight."

"It's okay, Jackson. We've made arrangements to fix everything. They're going to accept repayment—no problem-o," Ben interrupted. He was obviously trying to smooth things over, his eyes overly bright, his ambition surfacing.

"I don't think these men see it like you do. They're not going to let you get away with what you did. There's going to be an added cost," Jackson warned, trying to buy time. He knew Ben's attitude was partly his fault. He'd bailed him out once, the evidence still livid on his face, expected him to have his back again. *And what choice did I have?* Fuck. He didn't want to. And yet the hand of fate was pushing him again. Hard.

He tried another tactic. "How about we go back upstairs? Talk about this and have a drink together," he suggested.

"How did you mess them up at Tony's? Are you some kind of hypnotist?" one of the young men asked earning a quick frown from George.

"No. Let's just say Tony had a change of heart."

"Really?" George said, his tone skeptical. "Doesn't sound much like Tony or Garcia to me."

"Jackson had them on their knees just by looking at them," Ben bragged, making Jackson cringe. Last thing he needed—a macho driven showdown. He swept the area looking for movement, but the car park was still devoid of life.

"Is that right, Jackson?"

"Yeah," he muttered. He was being pushed into a tight corner. Or maybe he should've felt sorry for the trio. He didn't want to do it almost more than life itself, but he didn't want the next group of men sent by whoever was in charge coming after his sister either. How in the hell was he going to stop this? He was working blind. How big was the octopus's reach lurking behind these men?

"Who do you work for?" he asked, stalling.

"Nice as this little conversation has been, we gotta go now. You understand, right?" George opened his jacket slightly to show his gun.

He warred within himself. Could he just let these men take Ben if they could be persuaded to let Leia go? Lord knows he deserved it for putting Leia in harm's way again. But Leia loved him, and the young man was deserving of a second chance. Everyone was. Maybe except for him. After years of ignoring the past here it was staring him down. And it was killing him. All over again.

"Anything I can do to make this go away? Pay a twenty-point premium on what this asshole owes you?" Jackson asked, running out of options.

"Very generous. Maybe we could be persuaded to let your sister go, being family and all, but Ben—he goes with us."

"Sure," Ben said, obviously relieved about the solution though he gave Jackson a dark look for the asshole descriptor that was likely going to be carved in stone too soon. The drugs had left fucking Swiss cheese-sized holes in his brain. Jackson wanted to shake him, jar some sense loose.

"No! I won't let them take Ben!" Leia screamed as she moved unexpectedly out from behind Jackson. He tried to stop her, but she was fast, like a slippery eel. She was in Ben's arms before he could grab hold of her. Ben smirked.

Fuck.

No choice now.

What kind of shit would rain down on their heads for what he was about to do? If only he could have reasoned with them. Paid the debt off and got the pair to treatment. After a decade vowing never again, the hand of fate had made him choose twice. In a matter of days. And it hurt bad. So fucking bad.

Resigned, he focused on the trio, brought the energy up from inside him where it hovered in the dark, an unwanted passenger. An entity he had tried to freeze out. Never wanted to acknowledge. Wished would die off even, starved of life's vital oxygen. And at this moment had become essential.

It only took a split-second to tap into the beast. To pull the chains apart. Set it free. The odor of sulfur assaulted him, making him want to gag. Bright light once more shimmered across his vision, obscuring the scene, before vanishing into a haze of white smoke.

A look of complete, unadulterated surprise when the pain took root darkened his victims' eyes, the pupils enlarging. George clutched his chest first, his expression changing to one of agony as he dropped to his knees. The younger pair joined him a split-second later.

"Get in the truck!" he barked at Ben.

Ben hesitated. Then followed him as Jackson picked up Leia and ran.

"They weren't going to hurt us," Ben whined as he got into the back seat of the truck. "Now I've got to find new contacts."

Jackson had had enough. "You stupid bastard! You almost got Leia killed! Those men were *never* going to let you out of this alive."

"You can't talk to me like that!" Ben insisted, his face reddening with anger, obviously seeing profits slipping away from him.

"You want to go back and be with them—be my guest. But Leia goes home with me," Jackson said tersely, turning around in the driver's seat and giving Ben an angry glare.

The man who was still a boy shut up, his mutinous expression saying it all.

His cell phone rang as his prayers were answered by the GMC springing to life under his touch, starter replaced. He pulled it from his pocket. Rand. A city worker wearing a distinctive striped-yellow vest caught his attention crossing his line of vision, hurrying over to the trio they'd just left on the ground. The worker bent over the men before pulling out a cell phone from his pocket. Time to go. He pulled out of the parking space while answering the phone.

"Yeah," he said, turning the wheel with one hand, the phone clutched in the other.

"I know who your guy is—the supplier behind Tony's fast rise." Rand's voice was vibrating with crackling energy. "We need to talk. *Now*."

CHAPTER 7

"Fuck!" HECTOR DIDN'T BOTHER TO CONCEAL HIS ANGER AT his lieutenant's news. "And you're still at the hospital? What did the doctors say?"

Not being able to control the situation was intolerable. George's news grated at him, made him want to hit something. He looked out across the paddock toward the hazy distance. The wind was blowing the wrong way today and the odor of stinking garbage wafted on the breeze. Disgusting. He'd need another shower. He hated dirt and always went to his Elena clean. *She does not appreciate my thoughtfulness.*

"No sign of heart problems. It's got the doctors baffled. What do you want us to do next? Please tell me it's finish off this Jackson Banks guy 'cause I want to be there to take the fuckin' bastard down. What he did to us —that *vudú* shit, it was wrong, Hector."

Hector made an instant decision. "Do nothing. I want to check the guy out further. And stay put. I'm coming to you. Get us a room, the best suite in the hotel. I'll be bringing my wife. She's been complaining about no honeymoon." She was also good cover for entering the states. And this Jackson's supposed *vudú;* he wanted to know more before they finished him off.

"Let me know when arrangements are made."

"Of course, *padrino.*"

Hector set his phone down on the dresser. He could hear Elena in the bathroom with the water running, preparing for bed. The comforting sounds of the house surrounded him, yet the white noise left over from the day haunted him. So much was out of his direct control. He needed to tighten things up. Never enough hours in the day. He sighed as he removed the heavy gold chain from around his neck, adding it to the carved wooden tray that held his personal items.

Elena came into the room, her long cotton nightgown effectively hiding her body, head to toe. She looked far too much like a schoolgirl for his tastes. He wanted a woman who understood how to be a woman, a woman who came to him freely. Why couldn't she understand that?

He frowned. "I told you, I want you to wear the new things I've bought for you. What's the matter, don't you like them? I'll buy you more, whatever you like," he said, angry that she had defied him yet again.

She shrugged, not looking him in the eyes as she slid into bed, pulling the covers up to her chin.

"I don't want the bruises to show."

"Then don't make me angry," he said, gritting his teeth. Why was she so difficult? He swallowed his pride and tried to get her to understand. "You know I just want to love you, Elena. Have you come willingly to our bed."

"*Never* will I dress the slut for you," she snapped back at him. "You bought me, paid my family off, and all that I have left is who I am. I will *never* give that up."

Blood-red rose up behind his eyes and colored his view of the bedroom. His veins scorching with bitter anger, his hands visibly shaking, he considered what his mamá had advised only that morning. Babies were best conceived with a gentler hand.

"You're flying with me to LA in the morning."

He noted a modicum of interest in her guarded expression. Such a beautiful face with her soft golden skin, whiskey brown eyes that a man could get lost in topped by a tawny mane of silky hair. She was the envy of the other women in his employ. He loved to gather the thick strands in his hands as he kissed her. His mind turned to darker thoughts as he studied her carefully, thinking of all he was planning for this night.

"For real?" she finally asked.

"Yes, we're booked into the honeymoon suite of a fine hotel," he boasted, happy to see a rare smile break through her cool surface. No point in sharing which hotel. Women have loose lips. And lips he now wanted to enjoy, his groin thickening as Elena's eyes came alive with the idea of escaping the ranch for a few days.

HECTOR GOT up from his marriage bed, unsettled. He pulled on his clothes and holstered his gun. He needed something more. Something to let out his pent-up rage on and he knew just the place. Where his presence was welcomed. Within twenty minutes he had driven over to the motel-like lineup of single-story adobe buildings discretely hidden away on his property. The whorehouse was a luxury he maintained for his men and he was revered for providing the service. Tonight was his turn. He knew *exactly* what he wanted.

"Si, the new girl she arrived today—barely eighteen," the madam they all called Big Rosy said. She nervously added, "But, Señor Torres, I have a much better girl for you. One that already knows how to please a man. These new girls, they are like gringo. All innocent and no knowledge."

"Sofia will do fine," he grunted, eyeing the young beauty in the lineup of women paraded for hire in the main room of the hacienda. Big Rosy always said the same thing, and always he turned away from her advice and chose the newly arrived. He knew why, and she knew why. His mood darkened. He gave the obese woman with the frizzled hair untidily pulled into a topknot a cold look.

Big Rosy nodded at the dark-haired young girl to join them.

"See to Señor Torres's needs, Sofia. He is our *padrino*, our benefactor. We owe him everything."

"Si, Madam," she said, respectfully stumbling over the unaccustomed term of address attesting to the barrio she had been born and raised in.

Hector's blood heated as he followed the willowy young figure clad only in skimpy lingerie through the darkness to the outermost room on the edge of the complex. It was always kept ready for him. Elena, being the future mother of his children, bought her some respite, but when he paid for his pleasure, he would not be denied. Anything.

"What do you like for me to do, señor?" she asked in her sweet voice. She stood near the only furniture in the room. A large bed equipped with built-in restraints.

Without a word, he tore the nightgown from her body, drinking in her fresh young curves. He cupped a perfect breast, pinched the dusty nipple hard, savoring the bird-like trembling as she winced. The nipple quickly budded under his thumb and forefingers rough manipulations. He gave the other firm young breast the same treatment.

Watched her eyes widen with surprise at the suddenness of his attention.

He threw her onto the bed.

"Give me your hand," he demanded and pulled it tightly into a cuff and snapped it shut around the slender wrist.

"Now the other."

When she was firmly locked in place, he tore off his clothes. His cock jutted from his body. He eyed the naked beauty, her flesh so perfect she appeared to be carved from the finest marble.

She watched him warily. Fear danced across her lovely face. Good. She needed to know her place.

"I am not ready," she pleaded, her nervous breathing making her breasts jiggle.

He thrust his hand between her legs. Dry. Too dry to enjoy.

He bent down, positioning himself mere inches from her face. "If you ever breath a word of what I'm about to do to anyone—I'll kill you. Do you understand?" he asked, watching her face carefully for clues. Close enough to breathe in the fresh fragrance of her flowery shampoo.

She nodded vigorously, her dark pool of hair spilling out over the mattress.

"Say it."

"I won't tell anyone anything or you will kill me." Her voice trembled as she spoke the promise, but he saw the truth of fear in her dark eyes. Good.

He positioned himself to arouse her with his mouth, pinning her to the bed. The night was just beginning, and he had an arsenal of pent-up frustrations to unload. He was going to enjoy this encounter to the hilt for he was best at it, teaching a whore how to be a whore. He was the very best at it. He took up his belt that he'd discarded early on the floor and turned to the beauty still collapsed on top the bed. Now the games could really begin.

———

"RAMONE'S READY TO STEP UP," George announced with a grunt, chewing on the prerequisite toothpick as he stood alongside Hector.

They were watching the vet give White Star a checkup inside the barn. The horse snorted and jerked at the tight rein his handler had on his bridle looking for any excuse to escape. And for good reason. The stallion had taken an instant dislike to the equine veterinarian.

Hector was feeling good this morning and watched proceedings with a casual eye. After a night of carnal pleasure at Big Rosy's, he'd been pleased that Elena had been excited this morning at breakfast, joining him for once and planning her wardrobe for the trip. His mamá was right. Women needed softer handling. He'd take his frustrations more out on the whores from now on. That's what they were being paid to handle anyway.

"Fine, give him this name," Hector said, pulling the slip of paper from his pants pocket. The first order of business to be allowed in the Los Knights was proof of the warrior ability to carry out a hit to exact specifications. And he knew exactly who he wanted taken out. The newly elected chief-of-police had been a thorn in his side for the past few months. Declaring himself unable to be bribed, he'd only managed to make himself a marked man. Hector smiled with satisfaction. This was indeed shaping up to be a fine day.

George unfolded the slip of paper and glanced at the name, then pursed his lips.

"Perhaps we should speak outside, *padrino*," he said

with grave respect as he crumbled the paper, thrusting it into his jacket pocket.

The endless sounds of large bodies in constant motion made the floorboards creak incessantly as they strolled past the horse's stalls and out into the early morning sunshine. Hector took a deep breath, enjoying the fragrance of freshly cut hay sweetening the air. The sun's rays glinted in a starburst pattern off the roof of the barn, momentarily blinding Hector. He turned his back to it and gave his lieutenant a level look.

"You have a problem, *mi hermano*?"

"Perhaps I'm in the wrong here, and I beg your forgiveness if I overstep, but I worry about the timing. Many things are in play. Perhaps Ramone could take out a lesser target to prove his meddle," he suggested, his demeanor meant to defuse the situation.

Hector's gut tightened. He disliked his authority questioned. But he had to consider the advice of a trusted *teniente*. Anybody but George who had seen him through unspeakable things would be suspect.

"I will think on it," Hector said and heard him let out a woosh of breath. The man was not unaware of the precariousness of life. He knew it was important to let the men have their say. But as per no repercussions toward the naysayer, that was a whole other story.

CHAPTER 8

"WHAT *THE HELL* WERE YOU THINKING?" JACKSON LET BEN have it with both barrels as he watched his nemesis come into the kitchen and begin rummaging around in the refrigerator. Probably looking for something sweet. Addicts were so predictable. And Ben had turned even more surly since he'd dragged the pair home. Jackson was too worried about Rand's information on the Torres cartel, ratcheting up the noise in his head and souring his gut to feel the need to be overly sensitive to the addict's feelings. "Do you realize who Tony's connected to? Who most certainly will be coming after us now?"

"Yeah, so," Ben snarled, coming up with a jar of jam dug out from the back of the refrigerator. He twisted the lid off and threw it in the sink, dug his fingers deep into the jar and scooped up the sweet strawberry nectar into his mouth.

"Hector Torres."

"Who the fuck is he?" Ben asked, his lips sticky with red syrupy jam. Disgusted, Jackson took a deep breath. What did Leia see in this mutt?

"Hector Torres is the Mexican Mafia kingpin of the

Los Knights cartel. He supplies Tony and a hundred others like him."

Ben shrugged. "Mexican drug lords are a dime a dozen. Always coming and going. Why should he care about my paltry debt? Once it's paid, all will be forgiven. Trust me."

Never trust anyone who says *trust me*. A hard lesson learned from his stepfather's fist. And there was nothing *paltry* about the debt. He was taking out a second mortgage on the house to pay it.

"Didn't you learn anything the other day? If I hadn't pulled you out of there—you'd be dead." Jackson was more than ready to toss Ben out on his ear. Only the knowledge that Leia would bail with him kept him from doing it.

"You don't know that for certain. They seemed reasonable. It was your coming that made them turn on us. Until then, we had a deal," Ben accused Jackson.

Jackson rubbed his temples, the headache that had threatened all day burst into full bloom behind his eyes as his brain overheated trying to reason with a moron. The stabbing pain made him nauseous, and he swallowed bile. Ben's eating habits weren't helping. He took a deep breath.

"My DEA guy Rand filled me in on Hector today. The DEA, FBI, customs, the United States government—they *all* want him stopped. Right now, there's an ongoing investigation into all his activities. He's on a special list. You don't want to be pulled into this, Ben. *Trust me*."

"So, now that you've used that voodoo thing on them, they're coming after us?" Ben said with thinly disguised disgust that it was all Jackson could do not get up and slug him.

Maybe keeping Ben safe had been the worst idea. Ever. He could have gotten away clean with Leia and left his punk ass behind. He chewed on his bottom lip trying to decide what to say next. How to persuade Ben of the danger they were all in and what they had to now do to try to escape this precarious situation?

"Hey, my favorite guys, what do you think?" Leia breezed into the kitchen and twirled in a full circle. It took a second for Jackson to realize what she was showing off with his mind churning.

"You look very nice, Leia," he said, earning a big smile from his newly restored, much healthier looking little sister. Her pretty black hair swung on her shoulders, free of the gaudy pink streaks, and her makeup was expertly applied. She bent down and kissed his cheek.

"Thanks. My friend Lori did it. She just finished a course in hair styling. In a couple of years, she wants to open her own shop. Maybe I could take a course in something? Learn a new skill."

"You can be anything you want to be, sugar," Ben cooed as he took her into his arms for a big hug.

Yeah, right. Then why did this asshole ply her with drugs? He was far too good at saying what Leia wanted to hear.

"What do you think, Jackson?" Leia turned to him again, licking the strawberry jam from her lips from the sloppy kiss Ben had left behind. Jackson's head throbbed harder.

"You can do anything you put your mind to, Leia. You know that," Jackson said. His manic-depressive sister was on a high and he intended to keep her there for as long as possible. When she was like this she often didn't need to use. He also had to fix the situation with Hector's men. Get Leia away from Ben. And get on with his life considering that there might not be much left of it after this.

"Jackson's got us in a heap of trouble using that mojo

of his," Ben said, earning a murderous glance from Jackson.

Leia looked bewildered. "I thought it was all planned. We pay them off and we're good."

"Tony's connected to a man we don't want to mess with, sis, that's all. But we're going to make it work out. You have my word on it. Ben's volunteered to help us. Right, Ben? You want to keep your woman safe, right?" Jackson wanted to puke at needing to appeal to him. He dared the little shit to say the wrong thing.

"Yeah, sure, anything for my sweet Leia," he said, his virtuous expression marred by the jam staining his thin slash of a mouth.

Ben's phone beeped. He took it out of his jeans pocket, gave a strange smile, and sauntered out of the room.

Secrets. They were killing him.

Jackson's phone vibrated in his shirt pocket. A quick glance. He got up, gave Leia a reassuring smile, and walked out the back door into the yard.

"Yeah," he said.

"Jackson Banks. I think it's time we met." The disembodied voice came over the line, rough and low-pitched, fueled by a dangerous power. Or was that because of what he now knew about the man, thanks to Rand.

"Tell me where and when."

―――――――

JACKSON KNOCKED on the penthouse suite door, a shadow falling over the peephole. He was being scrutinized. The door opened and a beefy guy who looked like he'd just stepped down from a recruitment poster for bodyguards greeted him. His shaved head, scarred face, and flat dead eyes would give anyone with half a brain pause. Maybe he should have brought Ben after all. Used him as cannon fodder. Then again, even slime balls deserve second chances. Or was the expression fool me twice shame on me more appropriate?

The man gestured for him to turn around. He expertly patted Jackson down and took the heavy briefcase from his hand.

"The *padrino* will see you now," he said, ushering him into the larger living space beyond the foyer. The man he took to be Hector Torres was resting confidently on a plush white and silver sofa dressed all in black except for an oversized silver buckle on his belt, an engraving of a man riding a bucking bull on full display. His matching black hair was slicked back above a crooked beak of a nose, strong chin line, and intelligent deep-set eyes. He must have had a bad case of acne as a child because the scars were still visible. An intimidating face. His arm was slung along the back of the sofa and half-draped over the most beautiful woman Jackson had ever seen making him almost forget the man was in the room.

She took his breath away. Skin like honey, eyes the warm golden brown of a fawn's, and a wild mane of multicolored strands of blonde and brown that defied description as it flowed around her beautiful face and down her body with a life all its own. Who was she? Could she really be connected to a man like Hector Torres?

"Jackson Banks, I presume," the man said pleasantly enough as he got up off the sofa and offered Jackson a handshake. Jackson dragged his gaze away from the woman and they shook hands. Hector's grip was strong. He gave Jackson the once over. They were about the same height and build.

"I'm Hector Torres and this is my new bride, Elena," he said. She stayed put and only nodded. Married. Too bad. She looked timid which made him wonder. A woman who looked like she did should be brimming with self-confidence. Men should be falling at her feet.

"You're one lucky man," Jackson said with a nod toward Elena. Her name fit her perfectly. She had to be at least twenty years younger than her husband, her perfectly smooth skin without a line or blemish. Probably twenty or twenty-one. More than ten years younger than himself.

"What can I offer you to drink?" Hector asked as he sat back down, gesturing for Jackson to do the same on the sofa directly across from the pair.

"Bourbon if you got it. Neat." Best to appear friendly. Delicate negotiations lay ahead.

Hector nodded at the bodyguard. "If you wouldn't mind, Thomas?"

"Would you like a refill?" he asked his wife. She nodded, and Jackson wondered if her voice sounded anything at all like she looked. Because if it did it, she would sound like an angel. Might be better if it was too high-pitched and squeaky like a cartoon character or that annoying put-on baby voice some actresses assumed on camera.

Elena accepted the glass of white wine from Thomas and murmured her thanks. Yeah, the voice of an angel.

Thomas handed him a wide-bottomed crystal glass half-filled with bourbon.

"*Salute,*" Hector said and everyone took a drink except for Thomas. He remained standing, a silent sentinel.

The bourbon was of excellent quality and tantalized Jackson's taste buds as it slid golden and fragrant down his throat.

"My wife would like to visit a nightclub while we're

here in LA. Any that you can personally recommend, Jackson?"

He stole a glance at Elena and immediately wished he hadn't. Those Bambi-like eyes tore into his soul, their expression touched with profound sadness and a hint of innocence.

"Uh, I'm sorry, but I don't get out much. Hit a couple of local joints. Work takes up a great deal of my time."

"What is it that you do, Jackson?" Hector asked, though Jackson sensed he knew *exactly* what he did for a living. The man was a predator. A psychopath. As dark a presence as Elena's was light. Her being with such a man more than rubbed him the wrong way. If he wasn't careful, it would rub him raw.

"I work for US Customs as a special investigator."

"Impressive," Hector said. "I sense the hand of fate at work here. Do you believe in fate, Jackson?"

"Perhaps." He knew what was coming. Business. The premium on the debt owed. Better this than the other.

"Elena, my dearest, if you will excuse us, I would like to talk in private with Jackson."

She immediately got up, a beautiful goddess in a golden dress. The fabric swirled and rustled around her long slim legs though she was petite in stature, perfectly proportioned. She held a graceful hand out to Jackson.

"It was lovely to meet you, Jackson," she said as her slim hand slipped into his far larger one. Her touch was warm and electrifying, stirring something deep inside himself he thought long dead. He had to let her go, and a second too late, they broke contact. But not before he observed a bruise expertly hidden by makeup on the lovely curve of her cheek. His stomach clenched.

She left the room without another word. He heard a door close softly. Had this man done the unthinkable? Harmed a woman? If so, he was an even worse fucking monster that he'd imagined. He took a deep breath and let it out, his mind in turmoil.

"You married, Jackson?" Hector asked casually, his dark eyes focused on the far distance as he looked away and toward Thomas. The bouncer stood implacably by the wet bar, his hands crossed in front of his massive body, arms as thick as telephone poles.

"No. Not much luck with women. Though perhaps better than my friend." He immediately regretted the comment. Rand had to stay out of the conversation. Any connection to the DEA had to be avoided at all costs.

"Your friend having woman problems?"

"Let's just say his ex-girlfriend makes most exes look like angels."

"A woman scorned can be a force to be reckoned with. Your friend has my deepest sympathy."

Jackson nodded and waited, biting his tongue.

"We've been hearing strange things about your unusual ability to make people think they're having a heart attack." Hector came right out with it. A vision of a live rattler dropping onto the white rug right in front of him, hissing, fangs dripping with venom.

Tread softly. This man can have you killed. Worse, can have your sister killed.

"I take full responsibility for my actions," he began. "My sister was in grave danger."

"Family's important. When they're threatened—one does what's necessary," Hector agreed. "But what happened? What caused the men to think as they did?" he pushed harder, his deep-set intelligent eyes never leaving Jackson's as they pinned him to the sofa. Fuck, he'd kept it all hidden and bottled up inside for so long he didn't know where to start. He stalled for time.

"I've paid off the debt owed to Tony and brought a

bonus." Jackson nodded at the briefcase sitting on a sideboard to stall for time.

"Yes, tribute is appreciated and paying Tony will ease this thing. But I am far more interested in your strange ability. How do you do it?"

"I don't know what to call it," he said, licking his lips, his eyes darting around the room.

Vudú! Thomas accused from across the room, making the sign of the cross on his broad face and upper chest, his lips downturned with disgust.

"Voodoo," Hector deciphered the word. Jackson sensed one chance to explain.

"Many years ago, I was doing routine maintenance on a transformer when I worked a summer job for the city. Not realizing my boots were wet, I got jolted by thousands of volts of electricity. I passed out. It burned my flesh and I suffered some kind of brain trauma. I was young enough my brain rewired itself, is my best guess."

He rubbed his chest remembering the unbearable pain of that moment. "Later, after I got out of the hospital, I began to experience strange things. When I get angry, and focus my anger on someone, the emotion seems to get out and cause some kind of electrical misfiring in the other person. I can't explain it any better than that. Even a damn watch gives up ticking on me."

"And you use this power a lot?"

"*Never*, unless there's no other choice. I only used it to keep Leia safe from harm."

"Why don't you use it more?" Jackson could tell by his expression that if the ability were his he'd use it a hell of a lot more.

"I agree with your man—it's a curse. I've vowed never to use it unless there is no other choice." Jackson swallowed hard against the sense of impending doom. He shook it off with great difficulty. He had never spoken of the worst day of his life and what his cursed ability had caused his family. The information had come out during the trial, but it was a long time ago and the public has a short memory. The odd, impossible-sounding accusations against him had only made his stepfather look guiltier.

He took a deep breath and continued. "I'm here to make things right. And perhaps do you a favor with customs as premium on the debt even though it might mean my job." Jackson hated to make the offer, but his back was pressed to the wall and this thing had to end. Now. Even if it meant he had to start all over. Find a new profession. "But using my ability ever again, with all due respect, it's off the table. I didn't even use it in war to stop the enemy." He didn't mention that it could be used for good, this asshole had no right to know that.

Hector remained silent for a long moment. Jackson meant what he said. His conviction enabled him to give back as steely a stare as his host was currently throwing his way.

"I do believe you, Jackson. And I believe as well the hand of fate is at work here today. But my men have endured much pain and suffering and for that there must be much compensation. Do you have a plan on how we can make this right?"

CHAPTER 9

"OKAY, IT'S SAFE FOR YOU TO GO HOME NOW. I'VE TAKEN care of things," Jackson said. He was itching to get rid of Ben. The last few days with him in the house had tested him nearly beyond endurance. "But I think if you're a real man—a stand-up kind of guy—you will talk Leia into staying here where she's safest."

Ben's face flushed with instant anger. "Are you saying I can't take care of my woman?" he demanded.

Jackson sighed and prayed for the strength. "No, I'm not saying that. I'm saying you should care more about Leia than exposing her to any more danger. The world you live in, it's rife with danger. Then you go and make it worse by ripping off Tony. What were you thinking?"

Ben flushed even redder, his fists clenched at his side. "I'm not going to do that again, okay. But Leia and I, we belong together."

"There is one way you can have my blessing," Jackson said.

"Yeah, how's that?"

"Go into treatment. I've researched a place in Oregon called Good Hope that specializes in addiction. The pair of you, together you could support each other through it. I'll even pay for it. Get you both the help you need." It might stretch his finances thin, but it would be worth it.

"Then what?" Ben's lips curled up with disdain like he smelled a whiff of skunk. "I'll still need to make a living when I get out. I'll just be sober *and* broke. No." He shook his head adamantly. "It's not going to happen. Leia belongs with me."

"What did you want to do with your life? You want to die a drug dealer? Is that the epitaph you want on your gravestone?"

"What else is there?" Ben shrugged with the fateful and fatal existentialism that only the very young and ignorant can manage. "I didn't finish high school—no good at school. No one's going to hire me for more than peanuts. I can't take care of Leia on minimum wage."

"Leia has a health condition that needs managing. Do you see to it that she takes her meds every day?"

"I help Leia out all I can. She's better now, anyway. She thinks she probably doesn't need it anymore. She's been feeling so great lately."

"Leia will need that medication the rest of her life, Ben. This is serious. When she feels good is when she needs our help the most to keep on the lithium. Have you ever seen her sick—have an episode? Seen what happens?"

Ben shook his head. "Not really. But Leia's very smart, she knows what she needs," he insisted.

"Leia does not always know what's good for her," Jackson said, his anger threatening to spill over as he enunciated the words carefully. He drilled his fingers on the kitchen tabletop, barely hanging onto the itch to lash out.

"Okay, if you let me take you to Oregon for treatment, I'll see to it that you get a decent-paying job when you get back. Something where they'll let you train on the job. You both can stay here and save up for a place." The last idea cost him the most, the thought of having him underfoot every damn day. "You'll never get a better offer than this. I'd take it if I were you, because the way you're going, you'll be dead inside of six months if you last that long."

Ben looked conflicted. Good. Hope flared. Maybe, just maybe, he would do what was best for Leia.

"You see these tats," he said finally, flexing his arms. "They give me strength. Like this one." He pointed at a large fire-breathing dragon that stared defiantly at the viewer from his forearm. "Prometheus. Leia named him. Told me the whole story about how he stole fire from Mount Olympus to give to mankind. And how he was tortured for it. She knows a lot about history and literature. She's book smart, like I said."

"She needs your help to stay on track. She lives in her own world which can lead to complications. Please Ben, help her by being the bigger person here," Jackson pressed and instantly regretted it when Ben shook his head angrily.

"No can do. Rehab's a trap. Regular life's a fucking trap. Got to live the warrior creed man." He got up abruptly, the chair squawking as its legs grated the surface of the floor and stomped from the room.

An incoming call tore Jackson's mind away from his dismal failure with Ben.

"Jackson?"

"Yes."

"I want you to be a guest in my home."

"You know my thoughts on all this." Jackson's heart began to pound. Did Hector understand his position? And what about Elena? How could she be with such a man? Did she not know what he was? Could that even be possible?

"I'm not asking you to betray yourself or your family. Only to visit. To allow us to get to know one another better. You and I, we're special men—more powerful than most. We should be allied."

"Okay." The word popped out; Elena's beautiful yet sad face filling his mind. And then it was too late to take it back. He clicked to end the call. Was this was going to be the worst mistake of his life? But, in a life filled with mistakes, what was one more?

————

"WHY THE HELL would you go onto his turf? Bad idea," Rand said, his expression even more serious than normal. "And is this the right time to be getting involved in such a thing—you know—with what's coming up?"

Jackson ignored his veiled reference to the execution scheduled for later this month. That was filed away in a separate compartment in his mind and would not be thought of until that day. Only way he knew to stay sane.

They sat in Rand's living room. The room had a sterile bachelor look with the newest, largest, baddest big screen TV money could buy and black leather theater seating for the mostly sports games shown. Best place to talk in confidence, and root for your favorite team.

"I would think you'd be pleased. Look, have you been able to get an informer into his compound? This is the ideal opportunity to find out what's going on there. Check for weaknesses."

"You're not trained for this." Rand shook his head, his mouth tightening in a grim line.

"I don't like it any better than you do."

"Then why go?"

"Because I want Leia safe."

"I thought you made a deal? That you'd paid what Ben owed Tony?"

"I did. But he wants more. He wanted to use me—you know—what I can do, but I turned him down flat." He swallowed bile, his stomach churning.

"We can put Leia into a safe place if you think he's still going to go after her," Rand offered.

"I tried to get Ben to agree to that. Send them both to a treatment facility in Portland, Oregon, a place called Good Hope. No such luck. He can't see a future outside the drug business. Thinks minimum wage is beneath him."

"Democracy, it's near the finish line with thinking like that. Hell, we're already forty years past the average length of one. From our forefathers trying to escape bondage to provide liberty, we've got this newest generation voting themselves money from the public tit. Ben's only part of it in the headlong rush to screw up our way of life. Within a couple of generations, they'll see what their selfishness has wrought. A dictatorship always follows on the heels of a great civilization."

"Yeah, while I can't do much about his shitty attitude, except maybe change his diaper." Jackson was in no mood for discussing the bigger picture though he agreed with him. "But even if Leia can be persuaded to go by herself, she can't stay there forever. I need to find a way to make Hector Torres leave us alone for good."

"Maybe you both need to drop out of sight for a while. Move to another state. Give that white hat of yours a rest, buddy."

"No. I won't be driven from my own home. My work is here—my life is here."

"But going down there—it's a crazy idea. You would

be further exposed. You gotta know you'd be taking a deadly risk." Rand paused. "Something else going on?"

"Nothing." He was suddenly defensive.

Rand gave him a thoughtful look.

"I've heard his new wife is very beautiful, though he treats her like shit. One of the agents had some intel on her. Elena Cortez. Shameful way for a man to treat a woman. Did you meet her?"

"Yeah," Jackson said reluctantly.

"Is she really as beautiful as they say?"

"Yeah, she is." Images of her exquisite face and body lit up the interior of his mind.

"You know you can't save them all, right?"

"Look, I'm only going to Mexico to see what I can learn. I'd think you'd be thanking me, not trying to stop me. Won't it help your investigation? Whatever I learn would be helpful, right?"

"I don't want anything to happen to you. These are dangerous men in dangerous times. No room for error on this one."

"He's not going to do anything to me. He sees me as too valuable. I have contacts, contacts he wants to exploit. My going there will build up trust. Lay the groundwork to go after these guys."

"And if he insists on you using what you don't want to use?" Rand's eyes accessed him.

"He's agreed it's off the table. Nonnegotiable." Jackson took a large gulp of his bourbon.

"I think we need to give this more thought. Come up with a better plan. I have connections."

"Too late. I'm flying there tomorrow. Taking a few vacation days. Work's been trying to get me to use up some holiday time for years, so everyone's happy. Will you look out for Leia while I'm gone?"

"You know I will, but I'm not happy about this," Rand

said. "I think it's a huge mistake. But I will admit you got one thing going for you," he said with a rueful grin.

"What's that?"

"You look like one of them with your black hair and tanned skin. If you got brown contacts for those baby blues of yours, you'd be a perfect fit."

Jackson grunted. Leia had gotten the fair skin in the family, or maybe it was because she avoided the sun like a nocturnal creature. "Look, I'll try it my way first. Hector's a real family man. Wants me to be more on board by wining and dining me at his estate. That's all there is to this. When I come back, then we'll see. I don't want our government using my curse any more than Hector."

"No guarantee of that either way. Anything you do ups the possibility of your being exposed. Be very careful, that's all I'm asking."

"You know it."

"Did *you* know that last year apparently 2,338,157 people got married?"

"Yeah, so?"

"Shouldn't that be an even number?"

Jackson snorted and clapped his friend on the back. "Someone must have been in love with themselves."

"Well, I've heard it said if I could lick your own balls, you'd never leave the house."

CHAPTER 10

THE DRIVER STOPPED AT THE TIGHTLY CLOSED GATES, BUZZED down his side window, and spoke into the intercom. The compound was solidly walled with cement bricks, a gated compound more suited to Beverly Hills than somewhere in Mexico. Jackson had not been told exactly where he would be staying. It had been explained it would be for the best, that anonymity was always better when doing business in Mexico.

The drug trade had to be more lucrative than he'd even imagined. He took in the expense as they drove up the paved driveway. No wonder even the smaller players like Ben had a hard time letting go. He sighed, earning a quick glance from the driver. The man had picked him up at a private airstrip not fifteen minutes ago and had made quick work of getting him straight to the plantation. The tentacles of the octopus just got thicker and longer and stronger.

"It's a short distance to the main house, *señor*," he said politely.

The man had been eyeing him cautiously since first laying eyes on him. Probably thought he was about to use *vudú.* He grimaced at the memory he had been outrunning for so long. The image of long ago, and greedy flames burst to life behind his retinas. Seared. He forced them away with great difficulty, his skin damp with perspiration. Maybe someday in the distant future he'd find a reliable therapist. Or maybe not. Why drag up the past? A man gets on with the business of living.

A mansion with broad white pillars propping up the second story came into view reminding him of Tara in *Gone with the Wind*. Behind the house, a vast padlock labyrinth featured a modern barn connected to the maze-like structure. A stallion was being put through its paces in one section of the corral, its dabbled coat gleaming in the late afternoon sunlight, its sharp hooves spitting up little poofs of dust as it pranced in a circle, long tail swishing from side to side. The trainer was directing the horse's every movement with a firm grip of the reins. Even from the distance, the battle of wills obvious.

"That one—he has the devil's heart," the driver said as he pointed out the stallion, then made the gesture of the cross on his body as if the word devil itself were tainted.

The corral vanished from view. The man stopped the vehicle on the cobblestone driveway in front of the mansion. A large overhang shadowed the wide front doors. He popped the mechanism for the trunk and jumped out, retrieved Jackson's duffel bag, and handed it to him as Jackson climbed out of the front seat. A rush of burning air greeted him. A lone grasshopper landed on his jeans; the snapping sound of its insect body dry as the desert that surrounded the property. He brushed it off, the heat pressing in on him from all sides.

"Welcome to *Grand Torres*, Señor Banks."

"Thanks," he said, taking the bag from him. Jackson climbed the steps to the impressive white house. Lifted and dropped the large door knocker fired in the shape of a scorpion against the steel plate a couple of times, the sound echoing. Appropriate symbol.

"Si?" A middle-aged woman answered the knock, her black clothes and white apron immaculate, her hair locked into a bun threaded with gray.

"I'm here to see Hector Torres. I'm Jackson Banks."

"This way, señor," she said, her English heavily accented, her expression constrained.

Jackson followed her stiff figure through the foyer, his boots ringing on the black and white titled floor. It was an impressive entrance with a grand central staircase leading up to a second floor graced with wrought-iron railings. Nothing like he'd expected. He had envisioned a sprawling ranch-style house, a traditional hacienda.

She led him to the left of the staircase, past an unusual room where Jackson caught a glimpse of pews with an altar and a huge ornate wooden cross before entering a massive library. The walls housed hundreds, if not thousands, of books. Framed maps of the world adorned the walls and heavy brown leather chairs with gold studded detailing provided generous seating room. Each had its own convenient light source. Was it for show or did this family take education and reading this seriously? Again, nothing like he'd expected.

"I take your bag now?" she asked.

He handed it over and watched the woman march off with it. *What is he doing here?*

An older woman, her wrinkled face beaming with a broad smile, got up from a chair to greet him. For a split second before she spoke, she seemed startled by his appearance. But it was quickly concealed by good manners. "Welcome to our home," she said. "Please, sit… sit."

Jackson took the nearest chair and waited. The woman looked like Hector.

"You must be wondering who I am?" she said in a gracious tone. "I'm Señora Maria Torres, Hector's *mamá*. What can I offer you to drink, Señor Banks?"

"Please, call me Jackson. Bourbon if you have it," he said. It was after five o'clock somewhere.

"Of course," she said, filling two crystal glasses with a liberal amount, handing one to him. She sat down across from him, raised her glass, and toasted, "Salute."

He nodded and took a sip. A fine vintage. It slid down his parched throat and warmed his insides.

"Hector tells me you're working together. He thinks well of you and your abilities." Her dark eyes missed nothing gleaming with the same kind of sharp intelligence as her son's.

"Yes, we've had business dealings together." *If you could call it that.*

"I like to meet Hector's friends. Welcome them personally to Grand Torres," she said before taking another sip from her glass. Check them out was more like it.

She was Hector's hostess. Why not the wife? Elena came to mind, her vision burning brighter than the image of the flames he shrunk from. *Fuck, she is the one I am here to see. I must be insane.*

"Is Hector or Elena at home?" he asked, ignoring his dire assessment of recent actions.

"Hector will be home shortly for dinner. A little thing came up that he had to take care of first. And Elena—well—she's Elena. Likely busy with *former* beauty queen business." She shrugged, her tone scathing. She took another sip from the glass as if to burn away distastefulness from her mouth. The glass was nearly empty. Why did she not think well of Elena?

Her being a beauty queen should have enhanced her position. Weren't such pageants revered in Latin America? The memory of Elena's obvious sadness in LA squeezed his heart.

"Can I freshen your drink?" she asked.

He shook his head. "No, I would like to shower before dinner."

"Of course," she said smoothly, though he detected a hint of regret in her tone. She obviously enjoyed drinking and conversing with guests as the lady of the manor and most likely wanted to loosen his lips to find out more about him. She'd go hungry on that score. He was rationing his liquor until he got safely back past the border. This was the kind of woman who could make anyone's life a living hell if she set her mind to it. Probably already had.

In the guest suite he found his bag waiting. He pulled out fresh clothes and headed for the bathroom.

Dressed in a light cotton shirt and dress pants, Jackson slid open one of the glass doors off the balcony, stepped outside. The heat embraced him, less intense than an hour earlier, but sufficient to break out a light sweat. His room overlooked the stables. There was no activity now. He leaned on the railing and rubbed at his chest. *What the hell am I playing at?*

A brisk knock at the door broke his reprieve.

"Señor Banks, cocktails are being served in the library." It was the same woman as earlier. He gave her a polite smile.

"Thank you. I'll be right down."

He braced himself, then descended the staircase and strolled into the library. Never let them see you sweat.

This time Hector greeted him, all wide smiles and brimming with enthusiasm as he pumped his hand.

"It is good to see you again, Jackson. Come in. You've

already met my mamá and my wife Elena," he said and proceeded to introduce the other people in the room.

"This is Alonzo and his wife Aviva. He manages our trailer facilities. We produce the finest horse trailers in all of Mexico," he bragged.

Two men got up to shake his hand. The first man was a few years younger than Hector with slicked back hair, appearing less cunning than his older brother. Mid-level management. The other was younger with curly long hair framing an almost feminine face. Prettier than most women, reminding him of the actor from *Game of Thrones*.

"My brother Jesús heads the family's funeral business. It is why our home is so grand and welcoming. We allow mourners into our home for each funeral and also build custom coffins. It is half charity, half business—the best way to operate in Mexico to encourage loyalty. We charge no more than any family can afford. Jesús—he's not married yet, but we're working on it." Hector grinned broadly at his little joke, his arm around his slighter brother. Jesús was a somber young man, only nodding when shaking Jackson's hand. At least his grip was firm.

"And this is my beautiful unmarried baby sister, Teresa," he said as a young dark-haired girl of about eighteen dressed in a skin-tight electric-blue dress sashayed her way over to him, making sure she was showing off her ample curves to exacting advantage.

"Good to meet you," Jackson said, giving the sister a brief handshake. He glanced back to catch a glimpse of Elena perched like a marble statue on one of the leather chairs. She was dressed in a lush red dress that brought out all the golden highlights in her long hair as she sipped on a cocktail. Her face was a beautiful subdued mask, though her eyes could not hide her sadness. A loneliness that mirrored his own. *Yeah, that's why I'm here all right.*

"What's your pleasure, Jackson? I've flown in a crate of Kentucky's finest bourbon in your honor."

"Bourbon's fine," Jackson said.

Hector poured a drink from a portable cart outfitted with a variety of liquors and crystal glasses. He handed it over. Watched Jackson closely as he took a sip.

"Very nice, very smooth," Jackson complimented him, knowing it was expected.

"Good—good. Drink up. Dinner always tastes better after liquor."

Jackson ended up seated next to Elena. He gave her an encouraging smile.

"I hear you were a beauty queen," he ventured.

"Came in *second* during the Miss Universe finals. Let all of Mexico down," Señora Torres said, her face pinched with jealousy.

"Impressive," Jackson said, as Elena's lovely golden-brown eyes shining with a liquid intensity briefly met his. She remained silent.

"Who remembers who comes in second?" the plain-faced Aviva chimed in.

"Well, I happen to think that's an accomplishment to be proud of," Jackson said, earning a frown from the mother-in-law. He took a large swallow of his bourbon to wash his disgust away.

"What was your talent?" he thought to ask.

"Singing," she said with a hint of a smile.

"Dinner's served," the housekeeper announced from the arched doorway of the library.

"Teresa, please escort Jackson into dinner," Hector commanded as everyone stood.

Teresa rolled her heavily lined eyes at her brother's words but laid her hand on the crook of Jackson's arm and directed him to their place in line behind Hector and Elena. Señora Torres led the group on the arm of her

youngest son, Jesús, leaving Alonzo and Aviva in the
rear.

The huge dining room was softly lit with candles, the
crystal stemware and gold-rimmed china dinnerware laid
out on a bed of snowy white linen. Shallow bowls of dark
red roses were spaced every couple of feet on the massive
old wood table that looked like it had been in the family
for generations. Jackson envied them the family tradi-
tions all too aware his had been ground to dust by the
actions of a madman.

Jackson was seated between the matriarch and Elena.
He breathed in a whiff of the perfume Elena was wearing
as his eyes locked with hers, his senses bombarded as her
fragrance struck a chord deep inside him. Orange blossoms
with sweet musky undertones rushed into his lungs and
seemed to fill up all empty spaces he had been unaware of.
Until this exact moment in time. Her brief glances were so
evocative it was as if they had an entire conversation, one
of such intimacy he must be imagining it.

He downed a glass of water earning a frown from
Señora Torres.

"If you will do the honors, little brother?" Hector
asked from the head of the table.

"Our Heavenly Father, we thank you for the bounty
of our table and for the blessings of family and friends.
We ask that you watch over us in our hours of despair
and allow the world around us to live in peace. In the
name of our Lord, Amen," Jesús said, his voice gentle
and convincing.

A waiter came in bearing plates of steaming soup.
When the group was served and Señora Torres had
picked up her silver soup spoon, everyone followed her
lead.

Why was Hector allowing his wife to be eclipsed by

the old fossil? It irked Jackson. The meal tasted of ashes though he should have been hungry. Conversation flowed around him as he tried to imagine how Elena endured their company. *Why?*

The question pressed on him. She was too young for Hector, and he obviously did not make her happy.

"What do you do for a living, Jackson?" Señora Torres asked. Her gruff voice released him from his inner turmoil, making the hackles stand up on the back of his neck. Stay sharp.

"For the past eight years, I've worked for US Customs. I'm an SI—special investigator," he said and drank more water.

He watched mother and son exchange a glance. Teresa eyed him speculatively from across the table.

"Do you like your job?" Teresa asked. She twirled the stem of her glass in her fingers, seeming to admire the red wine it contained like a connoisseur at a pompous tasting.

"Yeah, I work hard at it. There are always a lot of new regulations coming down from the FDA to learn and apply. I find it fascinating, but I would imagine most people would cross their eyes with boredom," he said with a small self-deprecating shrug.

"Well, I think it sounds interesting. Do you like to ride horses?" she asked next, her eyes lighting up at the mention.

"Can't say I've had much opportunity. But, yes, I've ridden a few times in the past."

"You can ride with me anytime, Jackson," she said with a sly smile.

Great.

"Let Jackson choose his own activities," Hector said, earning a pout from his sister. "Only go riding if it's to your liking," he advised Jackson, drying his lips briskly on a napkin having finished his soup.

Jackson said nothing. A slight movement by Elena brought her body closer to his and her warm thigh brushed up against his. Electrifying. His brain zeroed in on the subtle touch. His groin thickened. Unnerved, he clenched the napkin on his lap between his fingers.

Course followed course and Jackson could barely choke it down. Might as well be a bowl of dirt.

"Do you ride, Elena?" he asked softly. Hector and the mother were in a debate about the value of a real estate property Hector was considering buying and the others seemed preoccupied for the moment.

She nodded emphatically. "Yes, I love to ride—the sense of freedom when you become one with the horse. Nothing else even comes close."

"Maybe you and I can go out together?" He kept his voice low, pleased to have gotten such a confession from the reserved woman.

"Perhaps," she said. Her expression warmed him as her golden-brown eyes softened.

He smiled at her with encouragement before taking up his water glass to wet his parched throat. *I'm fucking insane. But damned if I can stop myself.*

———

"I APPRECIATE your coming all this way to meet my family," Hector said, sipping his bourbon and watching Jackson. He'd invited his visitor for a nightcap after the rest of the family had excused themselves for the night. Time to get to know him better, though he found himself preoccupied imagining Elena preparing for bed. Sliding that red dress off her creamy shoulders. What had made her finally wear it? He'd been pressing her to wear such clothes for some time. Was she finally seeking his approval?

"You have built up a dynasty," Jackson observed from his leather chair seated across from him in the library. It was Hector's favorite room, a room built for quiet contemplation. And a good room to disarm people.

"Family's everything." Hector agreed, looking into the fireplace he'd had the housekeeper light for effect. He'd found flames to be mesmerizing and soothing to guests, but it was as if Jackson disliked it, purposely turning away from the view. Strange.

"My only family's my sister."

"It's no wonder you're protective. It's unfortunate she was pulled into another's regrettable actions. My sister— she's been a handful at times, but that's in the past. The internet and technology have allowed our young people to become too self-indulgent. Me. Me. Me. I'm sick at heart as to where it'll all end."

"Perhaps we've not set the best example," Jackson said.

Hector grunted and drank more of his bourbon, his thoughts grim. "Perhaps not, but we do what we have to," he said. "How do you really like your job?" Jackson proved himself a hard worker. He'd shared it was his first vacation in years, his coming to Mexico. There was much about this man that fascinated him.

"I'm good at it," Jackson shrugged. "Like I said earlier, it interests me."

"Forgive me for asking, but how have you kept your special ability unknown to your own government and country? I would think a man like you—they'd want to use your power." This was the sixty-four-thousand-dollar question. A man with such a gift, surely it should have been put to use by someone in charge by now. It defied belief.

"I've been careful and not given anyone the opportunity to observe it—and I don't intend to use it in the future unless my family is threatened." Jackson looked ill at ease, his steely glance said that part of the conversation was ended.

Hector nodded sagely, searching his brain for a new conversational thread to ratchet down the tension in the room.

"It's damn hard to get cargo containers into the states these days and not have them caught at the border," Hector mused, swirling the liquor in his glass.

"Yeah. Good customs agents and drug dogs are hard to beat. Changed things on the ground for us." Jackson's expression shifted.

"I've heard of all kinds of crazy shit that people pull trying to hide the odor. Hard to mask the distinctive odor of cocaine. You have any stories to share?"

"Craziest stunt I've ever heard pulled was a guy who used camphor wood soaked in human *urine* of all things."

"Yeah, hard to believe," Hector said with a small snort of surprise.

Jackson let out a soft chuckle. "Apparently the dogs didn't pick up on it."

Hector finished the dregs of his drink.

Jackson looked over at the books lined up like soldiers on their shelves.

"Read much?" he asked, curious.

"Not much time anymore. Mainly books on business and the odd thriller. You?"

"I enjoy biographies. Stories about people and how they became who they are. Also books on addiction. And yeah, thrillers," Jackson said.

"Each person has a unique journey to live," Hector

agreed. "But using drugs—hell, that's been around since before the birth of Jesus Christ. Think it's going away anytime soon? And you want to make it worse? Go ahead —ban it. *Pfffff.*" Hector blew out air forcibly between his pursed lips in disgust, warming to the subject. "Prohibition has been proved over and over not to work. And yet, what's the first thing wanna-be-elected politicians spout on about that seeks the popular vote—let's get the drug traffickers. Isn't that the definition of insanity? Expecting a different outcome when doing the same thing?"

He could tell Jackson never expected a philosophizing drug kingpin. Hector enjoying surprising people. They always expected drug lords to be complete blood-sucking Neanderthals.

"Are you saying we're just supposed to give up? Quit trying to help the addicts?" Anger crossed Jackson's face. The man was naïve, but well-meaning in wanting to help his sister.

"Individual addicts are another thing. Never give up on family."

"I don't intend to," Jackson shot back. "But does it ever bother you—the human tragedies that occur because of what you do for a living?"

"It's not a black and white world, Jackson, never was —never will be. People are free to make their own choices."

"Personally, I think we've strayed far too far into it's a 'shades of gray' world," Jackson said, obviously not overly worrying it he upset his host. Hector appreciated a man who was unafraid of speaking his own mind. He was getting jaded to the toadies that surrounded him. Sure, it cost a man to disagree with him, should it not?

"You must have been a big western fan," Hector said, his mind drifting away to a vision of his own bedroom.

He pulled himself back on track. He needed Jackson on side.

"Yeah, I suppose I was—am. I enjoy movies like *Dances with Wolves*."

"My tastes run more to *Goodfellas*, *Scarface*, or *American Gangster*."

"I would have guessed that." Jackson raised an eyebrow with a half grin as he swallowed more bourbon.

"We are who we are. Can't change that. When a man is asked to step up, that's the only time he has a choice. He can choose to accept the torch or tuck his tail between his legs and crawl home."

"A man has to step up for what is right," Jackson agreed. The man had cajones. And a glorious ability he coveted. Worth the time and trouble to get him onboard. And he already knew his weak spot. *The sister*.

"But enough philosophizing. It's been a long day. You must be tired."

Jackson nodded.

"Then I bid you goodnight, Jackson Banks."

Hector headed into his private wing of the house, mulling over the day. Then forgot all about it as he saw Elena lying in his bed, covers tucked to her chin feigning asleep. He quickly took off his watch and the heavy gold chain from around his neck. Tugged off his clothes and threw them on a chair. He climbed into bed tugging the covers away from her frozen body. She wore a heavy cotton nightgown.

"Elena, you looked very lovely tonight in the red dress," he said as if he didn't notice her eyes were closed. His fingers worked the top buttons on the nightdress and she stirred to pull away.

"No, please, I'm tired," she murmured.

He slapped her across the face. "Your job is to

produce heirs. Are you pregnant? Because that is the only acceptable reason for saying no."

She shrank from his touch, holding her cheek where he had struck her, her eyes vast dark pools in the dim light. She shook her head no, one tear cascading down her cheek.

"Why do you insist on being frigid?" he asked angrily, his blood coursing hotly through his veins as he yanked at the remaining buttons, tearing the fabric in the process. One large hand reached out and grasped a round breast. She moaned and tried to pull out of his grasp, but he held on, seeking answers.

"You know I only want to love you."

She turned her face aside. His anger reached its zenith as he sought to break through to her only to be met by stiff indifference. *What does Mamá know about the lust of a man? A man must take what he wants.*

———

JACKSON PEERED up at the night sky where a billion stars shone through the black canvas. He sighed. They'd be shining just as brightly when he was long gone.

He slumped on the wicker chair he'd tilted backward, his feet braced by the balcony railing. *Why am I torturing myself?*

He took a deep breath. He should pack up and go home. Pick up the pieces of his life. Get on with things. There was nothing he could do here. Guards everywhere. No way to disable this number of men. Even collecting intelligence for Rand felt stymied in the dense darkness. Hell, he wasn't even certain of his exact coordinates. He hadn't even been allowed to bring a cell phone onto the property, making his whereabouts untraceable.

Horses whinnied to each other in the stables where he

could see dim lights glowing through the crisscross window frames. The horses reminded him how much Elena loved to ride, her speaking of being free. *If only I could free her. Maybe that would make up for everything?*

A vehicle's motor raced in the distance piercing the darkness. He sat up straighter. Listened. It was getting closer and closer. His boots thudded nosily on the balcony floor as he scrambled to his feet. Someone was headed straight for the house.

He made the top of the stairs and took them two at a time in his rush. In seconds, he was out the front door. The truck loomed in the darkness, the headlights blinding him as he descended the steps. He put his hand up to shield against the brightness until they were turned off. Two men got out of the front seat on each side of the truck, one opened the rear passenger door and pulled out a limp body.

Hector rushed out of the front door with Elena hard on his heels.

"Bring him inside," Hector said tersely, pushing his way past Jackson.

Jackson waited as the men struggled up the steps, the unconscious man dangling between them. He followed them into the foyer and into the first room on the right, watched them place the man on an examining table.

Elena pulled on a white lab coat that hung from a coat rack over her jeans and shirt. Washed her hands in the sink and donned a pair of white latex gloves.

"Please, give me some room," she said as she pushed the men away and inspected the man in the bright overhead light. Mesmerized, he watched her examine the young man's wounds. He'd been shot, once in the shoulder and once in the leg. She deftly cut the fabric away from the bleeding areas.

If Jackson didn't know better, he'd think she had an

identical twin. This didn't add up. If she had medical training, why was she here and not working in a hospital somewhere?

All her actions were confident. Gone was the reserved woman of earlier. He lingered by the doorway as she gave the young man a needle. Hector and the other man hovered about the room, closely watching her work. She disinfected the bullet holes in her patient's flesh. Then she dug out one slug still lodged in his shoulder, closed the wounds with a few tidy stitches, and dressed them with white gauze and bandages.

"There," she said with satisfaction, swiping at her forehead with the back of her hand. "He'll need antibiotics for a few days, but he'll recover. I wouldn't recommend moving him again tonight. He's lost some blood, but not enough to warrant a blood transfusion. He'll be weak for a few days."

"Thank you, Señora Torres," one of the men said with reverence, his lined face illuminated with a smile of relief. "For helping my son."

Elena gave him a warm smile in return. "I'm pleased I could be of some help. That my training has allowed me to assist your son." She didn't look at her husband but instead turned away and began to tidy up, throwing the bloody used gauze in a covered metal container and sterilizing her equipment before placing them back on the steel tray. She covered them with a clean white cloth, ready for next time.

Why wasn't this woman treasured? It boggled his mind.

The men solemnly walked out into the foyer.

"We'll come back in the morning to check on Manny if that's okay with you, *padrino*?" the father asked Hector, his face haggard from exhaustion now that the worst of it was over and he knew his son was out of danger.

"Of course, my dear friend. You may come and visit all you need. Stay the night if you like. We have plenty of room. What's ours is yours," Hector said with simple sincerity. A light bulb moment for Jackson realizing the level of loyalty the community had for the Torres family.

"I thank you, but I must get home. My wife and children are alone and need me. I'll be back tomorrow to check on my son. Please call if anything changes."

"Of course. Do you need someone to go with you for protection?"

The man shook his head.

Jesús and Hector walked the two men out of the house. Jackson drifted back to the infirmary.

"Why do you put up with this family?" Jackson asked bluntly, standing in the doorway as he watched Elena finishing up.

She looked up. Startled.

"It's what I have to do," she said with quiet conviction, her eyes going from confident to sad in a split-second as she made a grimace with her mouth. He was angry for upsetting her, angry at her predicament, angry at the world.

"Nobody has to do what you're doing. Why don't you leave?" he demanded.

"I can't."

"I don't believe you."

She pressed her lips together. Hector joined them, making further conversation impossible.

"Any problem?" he asked, looking at both of them in turn.

"No, I was just going back to bed," Jackson retorted, turning on his heel.

CHAPTER 11

Righteous anger followed him all the way back to his room. Kept him twisting and turning during what was left of the night. Annoyed him during his early morning shower. Why was Elena putting up with it? For the money and prestige? Common enough goals, but dear God, he prayed he was wrong in his crass assumptions. He needed to get her alone, find out her side of things.

"Ah, Jackson. Good. I'm heading into breakfast as well. Most important meal of the day," Hector said as if last night hadn't happened. Maybe having a wounded man rushed to his house was a normal occurrence? A side effect of his occupation?

"How's Manny doing this morning?" he asked, remembering the name of the patient as he sat down at the dining room table. Hector took the larger, more ornate chair at the head of the table.

"Fine, fine. Elena's a good nurse," Hector said with a rare smile of pleasure.

"Yes, a fine woman who deserves respect," Jackson retorted, not bothering to check himself.

"You think I don't respect my Elena? I love my wife, but

with two women in a man's life, mamá and wife, sometimes it is difficult to keep both equally happy. Elena is fine, and truly, she is none of your concern, Jackson." The last statement contained a sabre-rattling of warning. Rand was right, he shouldn't be here. It was one huge, tangled web.

"Good morning." Mrs. Torres swept into the room followed by her daughter Teresa, a stack of steaming pancakes a gift in her outstretched hands. She plunked them down beside Hector. "Your favorite blueberry pancakes," she said with a beaming smile at her son.

"Thank you, Mamá," he said. She leaned down, claiming a kiss for her efforts.

Teresa scooted around the long table to slink into a chair beside Jackson.

"Good morning, Jackson," she purred, her ample cleavage in full evidence above her tight pink tee shirt. She must have sprayed the skin-tight jeans on her lower body.

"Morning," he murmured, dying for coffee laced with bourbon.

As if the coffee gods had heard his pleas the housekeeper hustled into the room through a pair of swinging doors, pouring everyone a steaming cup.

Life took on a new brightness after a couple of gulps of good strong coffee.

He felt something on his leg and looked down to find Teresa's hand edging up his thigh. *Great. Just fucking great.*

He discretely pulled his leg away, earning a quick pout from the girl.

"You don't like women, Jackson?" she whispered in his ear, her eyebrows arching upward, her abundant perfume assaulting his nose.

He pressed his lips together to avoid answering

though it pained him to have his manhood questioned. Maybe it was best if she thought him gay. *She'd leave me the hell alone.*

"I'm going riding today," Teresa announced. "Joe says the devil horse is almost—"

"Stay away from him," Hector growled, giving his younger sister a stern look.

A mutinous stare in return, but she said nothing.

Elena came into the room and Jackson's ire grew stronger as she murmured a demure good morning and took her place next to Hector's mother. She was dressed simply in a blue linen shift that left her arms and legs bare, her hair pulled into a high ponytail with soft tendrils of hair framing her face. Beautiful. He remembered her diligent care of her patient during the night, the efficient use of medical implements, and her carefulness in going about the work.

"How's Manny this morning?" he asked, searching her face for clues.

Her soft brown eyes locked with his for a stolen moment. His anger died a quick death.

"Better," she said in her soft melodic voice. "He'll be able to go home in a couple of days. No signs of infection this morning which is good."

"You're a very good doctor," he said with quick approval.

"Nurse. And I didn't quite finish my training before—"

"Elena has a habit of never finishing, or coming in second," her mother-in-law said, her mouth downturned making her even less attractive. Wicked bitch. Hackles fired down his spine.

"She's a *very* capable nurse," he said to the room at large, then turned toward Elena, "I was impressed last night as I watched you work on your patient. Perhaps you should consider going back to school?"

"Elena's married," Hector said flatly as if that settled it.

"What? Married women don't work in Mexico? Most would disagree with you on that." Jackson knew he was stepping on toes, but he didn't care. He's had enough of this charade.

"I'm fine," Elena murmured. "I'm needed here."

"See, it's all settled," Hector said. Jackson caught a rare glimpse of what looked like relief in the man's eyes.

The others trailed in and conversation shifted. How much more could he take of this bullshit? He picked at his breakfast. He had to get Elena alone, even if just for a few precious minutes. He needed to know more. He tuned in as he realized Hector was speaking.

"Jackson, we're hosting a party in your honor tonight. A chance for you to meet our friends and neighbors. But first, I thought you might like to take a ride with me and see the land."

Perfect. The kind of intel he was hoping for.

"Sure." Then doubt flashed its ugly head. Was Hector planning on murdering him? Living on this razor's edge was proving exhausting. A part of him wanted to pack up and go home. But he couldn't look the coward. Not in front of Elena.

IN THE BACK of the all-terrain vehicle being driven by one of Hector's henchmen, Jackson bounced along the goat's trail of a road, his mind on edge. The driver had even taken care to pat Jackson done. It was obvious that both men were armed and the vehicle armored to the hilt, covered with external steel plates slightly rusting. They had become the norm in Mexico's drug war.

"A little *Mad Max* don't you think," Jackson dead-panned, pointing out the futuristic-looking armor.

"Safest way to travel in Mexico. I want to show you something," Hector said. Jackson worried about the man's bulletproof vest visible under his flak jacket. How dangerous was driving around the man's own property, for heaven's sake?

The trail began to ascend, the vehicle easily up to the challenge of climbing. The day was cloudless, the hot sun masked by the dark slits of tinted glass. The path steepened, then smoothing out on top of a rise.

The vehicle came to a stop and the driver turned off the motor. He remained seated like a silent sentinel.

"Come," Hector said. The hot sun bore down on Jackson's head, and he was grateful for the wraparound sunglasses he wore. The dry desert smell assaulted his nostrils while he took in the vastness of the semi-arid land. A river snaked its way through the valley and out of view in the distance, green on both sides then quickly fading away to brown.

"I own as far as the eye can see," Hector said. "I own politicians, I own law enforcement, I own law makers and legislators. And now I want to own you, Jackson Banks."

"I'm not for sale," Jackson said.

"Family's most important, don't you agree. I wouldn't have done all this, worked this hard, if not for family. It's my way of keeping them safe."

"Are you threatening my family?"

"I make a better friend than enemy," Hector said, his lips thinning.

"I've said I'll help."

"Ah, but can you be trusted? I've built up a life here. *Never* will I do anything to jeopardize that life."

"I can help you move a vast amount of product through Los Angeles." Jackson launched into the plan that had come to him during the long, restless night. "I've come up with a plan—a good plan. I have a friend who runs a brokerage house, a legitimate business, but he's able to get things through the system. Hundreds of container ships pass through his hands every week. Guy's name is Mike Ramsay. You can come to LA and meet him. He'll see you any time. He needs money. He gambles and loses far more than he wins. Typical gambler. But the point is—he's bribable."

"Good. I'll check him out. But, if that plan fails, you must know the cost. I would go to the ends of the earth to kill an enemy and wipe out his entire family."

Jackson's bile rose, making him swallow. The man lived by a set of rules that disgusted him beyond measure. How could Ben have taken such risks? Of course, he hadn't known things were going to unfold like they had—become so extreme.

"We differ in our basic philosophy of life."

"You're an American." Hector shrugged as if that explained it all.

"Some Americans think as you do—most don't."

"If your plan's as good as you say, you've nothing to worry about, my friend. Your debt will be paid. I can even forgive your choosing not to aid me with your unusual gift." He slapped him on the back. Jackson suddenly realized he didn't believe him for a second. His gut twisted.

The trip back was even faster. They bounced along the back road, the heavy vehicle hitting the potholes with great force, making the springs squeak in protest. Hector appeared unperturbed, lost in thought as he stared at the countryside.

Jackson's head reeled with the implications of his plan. What had to be set in motion soon as he got back to LA.

They parted ways at the mansion. Jackson went to his room for a shower and Hector left to take care of other business.

Fresh from the shower, he heard a knock on his door so soft he thought he might have imagined it. He dropped his hairbrush on the dresser, and opened the door to check. *Elena.* His heart lurched uncomfortably in his chest.

"May I come in?" she asked, her glance locking with his. Bambi eyes.

He held the door open wider, and closed it soon as she ventured inside. She turned around to face him, her expression grim with determination.

"We need to talk."

He gestured.

"You being here—it's dangerous. You don't know my husband—"

Jackson crossed his arms over his chest. "I think I know enough."

"No! You don't."

"Tell me."

"You think I've sold out—but it wasn't like that."

"Then tell me what it is."

"I come from a large family. There's history between the Torres and the Cortez families that goes back generations. Bad blood; it had to be put to rest."

"So you're the sacrificial lamb?" he asked scathingly.

"Yes, better me than my sisters."

"I can help you, Elena," Jackson moved forward to grab her upper arms.

"Go home, Jackson. You'll only get hurt here—become another victim."

He kissed her. A sweet, searching kiss on her soft, pink lips. A quickening of breath, his senses reeling as she responded in kind.

The kiss deepened. He drank her in. His brain tilted, lights firing off in rapid succession.

"*Oh my god, Elena,*" he murmured against her warm, responsive lips. She turned her head aside and he breathed into her fragrant hair, its silkiness tantalizing all his senses. *What was happening?* He had never been this attracted to a woman.

"Meet me outside in the loft above the stables in an hour," she whispered in a shaky voice.

A second later, she jerked out of his arms and rushed from the room.

Jackson paced up and down the floor, his every nerve on edge as he waited it out.

The stables appeared deserted as Jackson opened the side door, all the workers having gone for their afternoon siesta. He entered the tack room first, and took a moment to view the display of medals and ribbons from glory days lining the particleboard walls. Walked back outside into the main barn and spied a ladder to the second story. His heart in his throat, he climbed the steep ladder, one rung at a time. The iron metal bit into his insteps but he barely noticed, focused on finding Elena.

The loft was warm, warmer than the main floor and a light sheen of perspiration broke out on his skin. Made him acutely aware of his situation. Precarious hardly summed it up. He must be mad. But something beyond the keen was pushing him forward. Dangerously forward.

Elena was waiting for him. Tucked in a back corner sitting on a blanket, so pretty his breath squeezed tight in his lungs. She beckoned him with one curled forefinger, her eyes alight with excitement.

He went to her.

He lay down beside her, and tenderly tucked a strand of shining hair behind her pearly shell of an earlobe. Everything about her was exquisite. Perfectly formed. He lifted a now visibly trembling hand to her pink cheek as he gazed deep into her mesmerizing golden eyes.

Lost.

A man could get lost for days looking at her.

She nipped at his fingers, slid a finger into her mouth, and sucked at it playfully. She ran her tongue over her lips. He swallowed hard, feeling his groin tighten and thicken. Then his mind shut down entirely as he leaned forward and captured her lips with his. He pressed against her mouth, seeking entrance. She melted against him, fit perfectly into his arms. Made for him.

She tugged at the buttons on his shirt and he grabbed her hands to still them. Remembered. He came back to himself in a rush.

"Elena, I'm scarred. Quite badly, I'm afraid," he said, admitting the harsh truth.

"I don't care," she insisted, keeping to the task of trying to get his shirt off. He hesitated. Relented. An invisible chord tied him to Elena, brought him all the way to this moment in Mexico.

She peeled the sweaty shirt back from his chest. Ran her fingers tenderly over the knotted and roped flesh.

"It must have hurt so much," she whispered with fierce compassion.

She leaned forward and gently kissed the scars, one by one. His heart opened at her gesture, binding him to her.

"It's who you are that I care about, Jackson. The way

you care about people. The way you take care of your sister. You're a good man."

"A good man would not be here, kissing another man's wife." His voice sounded hoarse.

"I would rather have one moment with you than a lifetime with him." She pulled away and undid her blouse, jerking it off her arms and throwing it down on the black and red plaid horse blanket, exposing her lacy white bra barely concealing her erect nipples.

Then he forgot the right or wrong of it as she slid down the straps of her bra and her naked breasts spilled into view. He bent forward and captured one in his mouth, sucked hard and she bent her body backward, giving him full access. He thumbed the other nipple into a tight bud, heaven under his fingertips.

She moaned.

His hand drifted lower and up under her full cotton skirt. His hand stilled, she was naked underneath. His heart racing he placed his hand between her legs and found her ready. Wet. For him.

His turn to moan. She pushed down her skirt, tossing it away to join her discarded blouse.

She was every man's fantasy. A beautiful hot gorgeous woman in a hay loft, sunlight streaming in the paned windows, golden skin naked and glowing, flushed with arousal. Wild shiny hair flowed about her shoulders, her breath coming in harsh gasps making her body's curves and valleys shimmer. Surreal. Beautiful.

Dangerous.

He undid his belt, slid down his zipper, and pushed his pants and boxers down his thighs and off his body letting his shoes go within the tangle of fabric. Naked, he pulled her to him, her warm body hugging his flesh all along the full length of his own.

"You're so beautiful, Elena," he murmured. "God, I

can't believe you're here—with me." He crushed her body to his, overcome with emotion. No words could describe it.

"I'm with you, Jackson. Believe it. Take me. Please—take me now. I want you so badly. Since I first saw you, I've thought of nothing else. No one else."

Her unexpected confession sent excitement pulsing through every inch of his body. He slid his hands over her sweet curves, devouring her mouth, her flesh. His rock-hard erection stabbed her belly, he had to be inside her. Right now.

His found her core. Her wetness.

He gripped her hips centering his groin between her soft thighs, thrust inside her incredible heat. Alive. Sweet Jesus, he was alive again. Every cell vibrated with the knowledge.

The air electrified. The fragrant odor of the clean straw drilled its memory into his feverish brain, forever associated with this moment, this one perfect moment of his life.

CHAPTER 12

Narcocorrido Ballad

Ode to Hector Torres
Padrino Torres our man of the people,
Risen from ashes his papa so dear,
That day on the river eons ago,
Passed into infamy by seer songs near.

Champion of children and patron of many,
He brings us wealth and fights to the finish,
His legendary generosity a help to all,
Though the war for drugs will never diminish.

Married to Elena,
Her beauty so rare,
His life now complete with children to come,
We wish him much happiness to live and to share.

THE SWIRLING DANCERS FLANKED BY THE MARIACHI BAND singing his praises created a kaleidoscope of patterns on the dance floor as Hector watched from the balcony of the second floor, his eyes darting among his guests, seeking answers. He spied Jackson talking with Teresa and Elena. His paranoia surfaced. Grew stronger. His gut never steered him wrong. It was all he had between him and failure and he always relied on instinct. No. Jackson had to go. Gift or no gift. Tonight, after the party.

———

"LET ME SHOW YOU THE STABLES," Teresa demanded, dragging on his arm and spraying spittle on Jackson's face. The wild, uncontrollable force of an inebriated young woman used to getting her own way surfaced.

"I think we should stay right here. Your brother wouldn't like it," Jackson said lightly, keeping his voice calm and slow like he was taught to when speaking to demanding drunks.

"*Fuck* Hector."

"Come outside with me. Fresh air will help," Elena suggested. She looked amazing. A long shimmering gold dress hugged her curves in all the right places, the gleaming hair piled high on her head an elegant crown. The steamy memory of earlier lodged in his mind and he couldn't let it go. He wanted her. Again. It was all he could think of. The soft velvet skin, the wondrous curves, her willingness. Her acceptance of his scars that had made him feel like himself for the first time since it had happened. He brought his mind back to the present with great difficulty. Insanity to think he could go there again. A one-time gift. Let it go. *No way in hell can I do that*.

"Fuck that! I want Jackson to take me outside."

"I can't do that."

"Fine!" she said. She grabbed a flute of champagne off a hovering waiter's tray before lurching out a sliding glass doorway. Her quick movements caused the curtains to billow behind her as she vanished.

"I think I'd better follow her. She could hurt herself," Jackson said with resignation.

"I'm not certain that's a good idea," Elena said.

"Probably not, but what other choice is there? Don't worry, I got broad shoulders, beautiful." *And not much to lose. Except the here and now.* Then his sister's face came to mind and he swallowed hard. Leia had a lot to lose.

He made his way into the backyard, scanning the dimly lit area, worry edging the corners of his mind.

"Teresa," he called. *Where had she gotten to so quickly?*

"Fuck!" Her voice echoed in the darkness near the staples. He heard a heavy door slam shut.

He strode toward the sound, hoping she'd not put up a fuss about going back inside the house. Yeah, and swallows like to walk all the way to Capistrano in the springtime.

He opened the side door of the barn and stepped inside. Teresa's high heels made a clicking sound on the stone floor making it easy to track her down the aisle. She was opening the wooden door of a stall at the far end of the barn when Jackson spotted her.

"Hector swears the devil's horse is too strong for me —but you and I know who's the boss—right?" she said, obviously talking to the horse in the stall, slurring the words slightly. Jackson heard the animals' increasing disturbance as he hurried to catch up, the whinnying and knocks against the stall walls a dead giveaway. The agitation increased as Teresa vanished from view. His heart squeezed. He realized which horse Teresa was visiting. He ran full out.

Loud punches of hooves striking wood.

A scream.

A thud.

Then complete silence for one agonizing suspended moment.

Jackson reached the doorway of the stall, his heart racing with adrenaline. *What was he going to find?* The horse partially blocked his view, but he could see the young girl's body crumpled on the floor under the window.

Without thinking he went inside, pushed past the horse that nipped at his arm with sharp teeth, kneeled beside Teresa. He picked her up and turned to find Hector in the doorway, breathing hard.

Jackson strode forward holding her tightly in his arms. Past the horse that Hector had now grabbed hold of and out the doorway. A cot was pushed up against the wall and he laid her down carefully. Checked for a pulse in her neck.

"She's not breathing," he said. Shocked, he barely noticed Hector joining him.

"My god, Teresa!" Hector's voice sounded strangled, anguish contorting his face. He dropped to his knees. Began to pray out loud.

He had to do something.

Fast.

He laid his hands on her head to check under her hair, felt the egg-sized contusion and sticky blood seeping from the cut. He didn't think he could do anything about her concussion, but maybe he could restart her heart.

He went down, far, to the dark place, and drew on the strength that constantly flowed in a strange well deep, deep inside him like an uneasy beast. Channeled it, tugged it to the surface in a conquest of wills. Forced it out, pulling it through the vast network of veins to surge through his hot fingertips into the body of the prone girl.

Flashes of a similar experience flew through his mind saving his buddy Rand. God, let him do this, he prayed. Just one more time.

He didn't let up. Let the energy flow from him to the girl in one long endless stream. The universe hushed, as if all energy of the world was focused on them. He helped her back from the light. Pulled her soul from the vastness of eternity and into the land of the living, like he had done once before. White light shadowed and played across his hands as he held them against her poor damaged head. Prayed for her recovery. Gave her all the help possible. Hoped it was enough.

Hector stirred. Quit praying out loud. He reached out a hand to touch Jackson's arm, his eyes filling with hope. "Please, *please* save her."

Jackson knew the exact second her heart began to beat again. He understood the miracle of birth a doctor must experience as a newborn draws in its first vital breath. Her chest rose as air rushed into her lungs. Then she took another, her body naturally trying to fill her lungs with life-giving air.

Her eyelids fluttered.

She opened her eyes.

"Hec...tor?" she said, her childish voice sounding tired and confused.

Jackson stepped back. Let her brother take over.

He was exhausted.

All the excess energy and flowing adrenaline vanished. Left him bereft. Drained. He stumbled. Slumped on a bench. Leaned against the cool stone wall in an effort to catch his breath. Watched Hector tuck a lock of hair back from his sister's face while murmuring soothing words. He was a drug kingpin, a misfit, and likely a psychopath, but the man loved his family.

"Jackson! Hector! What happened? Is Teresa all

right?" Elena was running down the wide aisle of the barn, her dress billowing out around her slim legs, sections of her loosened hair streaming out behind her. She stopped a few feet away, frantically looking from Jackson to Hector kneeling and cradling his sister's head.

"Elena," Hector commanded and she took the last few steps. Joined him on her knees by his side to take a look at the prone girl, her golden dress pooling around her.

"With her heart condition and what looks likely to be a concussion, we need to airlift her to the hospital in Ojinaga," Elena said after a quick check.

Hector picked Teresa up in his arms and carried her past Jackson, who was still trying to gather himself. Harsh breathing resounded in the quiet and Jackson realized it was coming from him. He knew he was too light-headed to stand and just sat with his limp arms at his side, grateful he had done something to atone for past sins. *Why did it take more energy to heal than to tear down?* At the thought, flames once more seared his mind and he shook his head as if he could dislodge them. Was he going to be tortured all his life? Was this it?

Elena looked back toward him as she accompanied Hector, doubtful of leaving him alone, but he nodded her away.

Time alone was best, much as he wanted to be with her.

He listened to the horses breathing and snorting in their stalls for a time. A few crickets began to sing a chorus in the dimness and he breathed in the scent of fresh sweet hay as he slumped there knowing he was an easy target. He slowly recovered some strength. It had not been like this the last time he'd restarted a heart as he remembered Rand's accident. Helping Teresa had drained him, taken up all the energy he had to give. Before he knew it he was fast asleep.

A door creaked open sometime later waking him instantly before banging shut. Heavy footsteps. Hector came back into view. Alone.

"I was uncertain if I could trust you, much as I wanted to," he said as he stood directly in front of him.

Jackson nodded.

"But you saved my Teresa's life and for that I will be forever thankful," he said in a grave tone of voice. "And so I will let you go."

Jackson's body instantly chilled at the knowledge. He'd been that close to death. That was more than he'd bargained for, though it did not surprise him now hearing the words. Perhaps he was just that tired.

"You know the stakes—I won't disrespect you with them again."

He paused, rubbed at his jaw. "Go back to the United States. Set up the deal. I'll join you in a couple of days."

Jackson nodded. An uneasy thought pressed into his mind. He wished he could give this man a heart attack for real, and set Elena free. The idea pressed at him, but in his weakened state he doubted he'd be successful. And what about all the other men surrounding and protecting Hector? Hector would have him killed and Elena would never be free.

CHAPTER 13

"ANYTHING ELSE?" RAND ASKED TERSELY AS HE LEANED forward in his chair, iPad in his lap keying in the highlights of their conversation.

Jackson scoured his brain. "No, that's it." They sat in Rand's living room, the gathering twilight softening the edges of the room. It had been a tense few hours as they went round and round with the specifics of what had happened in Mexico and the newly hatched operation *Get Hector*. Jackson was getting antsy, tired, but mostly worried. The hardest thing he'd ever done was walk away. And now he was helping the DEA bring Hector down. Hell, they'd even implanted a secret GPS tracking microchip in his arm with the hope it would keep working. Unlikely, but what the hell, it was worth trying. Going after the drug kingpin, hell, might as well poke the devil with a stick. And how to rescue Elena from his claws? The worry nagged at him every single minute of every hour of the day and night.

"I'm not sure about all this, Rand," he said tentatively, not meeting his friend's eyes.

"What's not to be sure of? Leia and Ben will be safe

up in Oregon, the agency will see to that. You have the means and our support to set up a believable sting, and Hector Torres and his minions go to jail. Hopefully, not too far into the future." Rand set the iPad off to the side and took a swallow of his drink.

"Hector has a longer reach then you think."

"This is the great U S of A. What can he do here?" Rand scoffed.

"I hope you're right."

"Don't worry, buddy. It's all going to work out."

There was that *don't worry* again.

"Okay, I'm going home to break the news to Leia. At least getting her and Ben squirreled away will take some of the pressure off." Jackson stood up. The room darkened for a split-second before it righted. He was still weak, only able to hide how much Mexico had cost him if he stayed focused.

"Good luck with Leia. By the way, the guy who will be escorting them north is Kyle Smith. Has a good rep with the agency—bad taste in women. Been seen with Catherine lately," Rand said dryly, saluting him with the dregs of his drink.

"Yeah, sucker for punishment, all right. But if he can commit, who knows? Catherine might turn into a real sweetheart."

Rand tossed a sofa pillow at him. It bounced harmlessly off Jackson's shoulder though he instinctively ducked.

"You know, my therapist says I got a preoccupation with vengeance. So I said, we'll see about that!" Rand quipped.

Jackson snorted. "Catch you later."

He drove home through the congested streets of LA wondering what Elena was doing. He hadn't gotten to speak with her alone again before he'd come home. Had to leave her in the rear-view mirror of the vehicle as he was driven away from the mansion. The image haunted him. And it would forever. Only a reunion had a chance of scouring it away.

A few minutes later he pulled into his back lane. He saw a slight movement behind the kitchen curtains as he turned the motor off. Good. Somebody was home.

"No! I don't want to! Absolutely not!" Leia shouted, banging her small fist on the kitchen tabletop making the utensils clatter and the sugar spill from the bowl. He'd found her making a sandwich she had abandoned soon as he began telling her what was up.

"I'm afraid you've got no other choice," he said, pressing his lips firmly together. His body was hurting again, filled with a strange sensation of pins and needles. He took a deep breath to steady himself. "The DEA wants the big guy in charge—the man behind everything. Taking him down will only help Ben."

She shook her head, stubborn as a mule. Sisters.

"A DEA agent will come to take you there. Best to go peacefully, sis. Hector Torres has threatened to harm my family and they're promising to keep you safe. Witness Protection." He banged the gavel down. It was time she started growing up.

"Then why help them? You can keep the bad guys at bay like you've been doing."

"You don't mean that, Leia. You believe in justice, right? Here's a chance to help the system. Put the bad guys away."

"What if Ben won't come?"

He shook his head. "He's got no other choice. The pair of you will be taken there tomorrow—early. You'll have a DEA escort and he'll take you both to the Portland, Oregon treatment facility. You and Ben—this is your chance to straighten your lives out. Maybe your last chance. Then when you come back, I'll help you go to school. Study writing if that's what you want. What do you say, sis, this could be the fresh start you've been waiting for, right?"

"Like I have a freakin' choice," she grumbled and got up from the table, tossing the remains of her sandwich in the garbage, the tin lid thudding back into place as she released the lever with her foot.

"Where's Ben?" he asked.

"I don't know," she said with a shrug. "He didn't share."

"Let me deal with him. Don't tell him what we just talked about. It'll spook him and he might run. Might cause trouble," he warned.

"No way I'm telling him. He'd going to be so angry," she said and flounced from the room.

Yeah, well, the moron had it coming. And it was for his own good though he doubted Ben would see it that way.

————

"No fucking way!" Ben was as amenable to going to Oregon as Jackson had expected.

"You really have no other choice," Jackson explained patiently. "Might as well man up and do the right thing for Leia. Make it easier on her."

Kyle Smith, as promised by Rand, had arrived only moments before and waited in the living room. Jackson had decided to postpone to the last possible minute telling Ben where he was headed to stop him from bolting. Last thing he needed was Ben getting himself killed. Leia would never forgive him.

"Keep some dignity, pack a bag, and go with the guy. Things have gotten rocky again with your connections."

"What the fuck did you do?" Ben accused his normally pale face flushing red with anger.

"These people you deal with—they don't play fair. They have threatened your life and Leia's life."

"Why? Are you a snitch?" he sneered.

"For heaven's sake, go to Oregon!" Jackson was exhausted. A night of twisting and turning worrying about the situation had taken a further toll on his resources. He instantly regretted his outburst, but the damage was done.

Ben got up without another word, the chair slamming against the floor as his body jerked upward, his expression murderous. Jackson hoped the time Ben spent cooling his heels in Oregon would repair what little relationship existed between them. But right now, that was the least of his problems.

"Okay, Ben's packing. Shouldn't take more than a few minutes. You want coffee?" Jackson asked the man waiting patiently in the living room. The man had an average face, average build, of indeterminable age and could easily fade into a crowd. Probably an asset in his work. Mr. Average Joe with a passive personality to match.

"No, but thank you. Long drive to Oregon. Can they escape out a window?" he asked with a nod toward the back of the house.

"No, been bars on them since Leia—began to have problems a few years back." He didn't feel a need to explain further.

"Once they get a taste of it, they chase that first high forever," the man said solemnly. "And never recapture it."

"Yeah, addiction's a bitch. You got any family members affected?"

"With the flood of cheap heroin invading the US from

Mexico growing, seems every family's affected. People get hooked on prescription drugs and then move over to opiates. Easier to get their hands on and a whole lot cheaper. Costing our great nation *billions* in lost productivity. But give the people what they want—right?" he said with a fatalist shrug of his shoulders. Jackson wasn't certain if he was being sarcastic or not.

"Even if they want to throw their lives away?"

"Well, I'm here in the hope your sister's life can be saved. Insurance against future events."

Jackson frowned. He found the agent's words somehow disquieting. "That's my hope as well."

Leia came into the living room carrying her backpack, a sullen Ben on her tail.

"Okay, now you're rid of us," she said.

Jackson rubbed at his forehead, feeling pins and needles prickling his skin, his inner compass strangely off.

He stepped forward in front of his sister. "It's not like that. Have I ever *not* been there for you?"

She kept her eyes downcast, the picture of a young person put upon.

"I'll come and visit when I can. You'll be fine in Oregon. I promise." He leaned down and kissed her cheek. "I want you safe. I love you so much, baby sister," he whispered in her ear. She had an instant change of heart and threw her arms around him. Hugged him back like the clingy child she still very much was.

"I love you too," she said, tears flooding her eyes as she pulled away from him, swiping at her reddened nose with the back of her sleeve.

"Okay, let's hit the road *Jack*," Kyle Smith a.k.a. Mr. Average Joe said, making a small joke while giving Jackson a last nod before exiting the house. Hard to believe the guy would be interested in Catherine. No accounting for taste. Maybe he should have warned him? But then most men didn't take kindly to being told the woman they were dating was a nut job. He didn't want a foul mood by the driver making Leia's trip any harder than it had to be.

Ben didn't bother to say goodbye and dragged his feet as he followed the agent out to the waiting black SUV like a character in a zombie apocalypse movie. Leia trailed behind them, her wistful face sweetly endearing. Jackson prayed they could help her in Oregon. He had a bad feeling it truly was their last hope.

With difficulty, he switched gears, picking up the untraceable burner phone Hector has supplied him with. Jackson was to call him when everything was in place. No time like the present.

"Hector." His rough voice spoke the one word with such force it sounded like it was being shot out of a cannon.

"Bad day?" Jackson deadpanned without thinking and got a moment of complete silence. Shit. He needed to be more careful and not rile the beast. Exhaustion was making him punchy.

A gruff chuckle broke the tension.

"Jackson. Yeah, you could say that. Fuckin' supply problems. Business can be a real bitch."

Hector was a businessman first. Jackson got that after he had explained how he had modeled his enterprise after high profile American companies that had fared enormously well. And some of his businesses were legitimate, though most were fronts for laundering the enormous amounts of drug money that must be flowing into his hands. He refused to think of those dirty hands on Elena.

"How's Teresa?" Jackson asked.

"Improving. The doctors say her concussion doesn't

appear to have done any permanent damage. We got off lucky, thank God. But the downside is she'll need a new heart."

"Did I cause that?" Jackson's breath stilled.

"No, we've always known this was coming, since she was a child. Too bad your *vudú* doesn't mend hearts as well. It must only work on new damage. I'm truly grateful you were able to restart her heart. It saved her life." The gruff voice softened for a brief moment.

Jackson had a flashback. *Yes, thank you, God.* Knowing he had helped someone eased some of the massive guilt he would carry forever.

"I'll call with a time," Hector said. The line went dead as he hung up.

Jackson was under no illusions. Hector's goodwill only extended so far and he needed a fallback position if things went south. He rubbed his aching head with a grimace of annoyance. What was causing this continued lethargy? No time to see a doctor. That would have to wait until the deal was done.

———

"Dig up anything?" Hector asked George as the pair watched the horses put through their paces by the trainers. He had one foot braced on the bottom rail of the corral, a favorite spot for a noon hour break. They both had a cold beer in their hands.

"Yeah, been arrested once for drug possession. Paid his dues and did his full time so doesn't look like a guy who snitches to save his own hide or has ever been an informant. Has a seedy past with some bikers that may or may not still be ongoing. Was given a second chance by the look of it by his current employers. Though with the family connections to the business they may be felt obligated to help him. Talk on the street is he's shady, a gambler with mounting loses." He shrugged. "Is there any other kind? That's it. Going to see him in LA?"

"Maybe." Hector was noncommittal. Though he trusted George, no one was allowed to know all his moves.

"Taking Elena again?"

Hector grunted. "Possibly."

"Glad to hear Teresa's stable. She's on the donor list, right?"

"A willing donor is as rare as hen's teeth in Mexico."

"Maybe going abroad will bring better results, *padrino*?"

"We'll see. Or I may need to take more drastic measures. Soon. She's getting weaker. I can see it in her."

George nodded his head sagely. "Not impossible, the timing would matter most. Hearts only last so long, even on ice."

"A donor, willing or not has to be found soon. Doctors say we got six months at most. When I get back from LA, we move on this. I have an idea."

"Sure. Whatever you need, *padrino*."

"Even if I asked for your son's heart?"

The air electrified between them. George's eyes grew large with panic.

"No. Family's first—that's the thing. I would never ask such a thing of you, my friend."

George swallowed the rest of his beer and swiped his mouth with the back of his shaking hand. His skin had paled. Sweat broke out on his forehead. Had to keep the men on their toes. Remind them of who he was and what he was capable of. He'd have the heart stolen from someone he didn't know. Someone unimportant. A nobody.

CHAPTER 14

Jackson spotted Hector through the sparse crowd at the hotel bar. His mind froze as he saw who was at his side. Elena. Unexpected. He unconsciously pressed the palm of his hand to his chest, the taunt abraded skin reminding him who he was, his throat tight. He didn't know if he could take it having to watch her leave with Hector all over again.

"Jackson," Hector said, his keen eyes missing nothing.

Keep it together. You can take this bastard down. His determination to carry out the plan intensified. It was his only hope for a life for him and Elena.

"Hector—Elena," he said, forcing all the emotion out of his voice. "Nice to see you again."

"How are you, Jackson?" Elena asked. Her words slid down his body like a cool drink of water consumed after a hot day in the desert. Brightened his very soul.

"Fine. And you?" He dared a brief glimpse into her eyes and wished he hadn't. His quick look also registered that she had no visible bruises. *Thank Christ.* He couldn't be held responsible if that was the case.

"Good. Teresa's better. Thank you for helping her. We

can never repay your kindness. I wish I had your gift." Her sincere tone was heartbreaking.

"No. You don't," he said the words with such harshness he hardly recognized his own voice. He was more on edge than he realized as he told himself to calm down.

Everyone looked shocked in his immediate vicinity.

"Sorry, I didn't mean that. Please accept my apology," he said backpedaling.

"All gifts come with a price," Hector acknowledged.

"Mine has been too steep," he said with bitterness.

"Surely saving someone's life more than atones for any problems your gift has incurred in the past?" Elena asked.

Jackson shook his head, surprised that he would like to come clean with her. Tell her the whole sordid story. Never happen. It stayed locked up. His burden to carry.

"Come. Have a drink," Hector invited and flicked a finger toward the bartender.

"Bourbon. Neat. And I'll have the same. Elena?" Hector gave Elena a glance.

"Nothing. I'm fine."

"Thanks," Jackson said to the waiter as he placed his bourbon on a printed coaster advertising the hotel chain.

"To the success of our venture," Hector toasted.

Jackson took a swallow of his drink. "It's all set for tomorrow morning."

"Good. Tonight, we celebrate. Anything you want my beauty. Anything," he said to Elena, who gave a slight smile.

"I'd love to go dancing," she suggested.

Jackson had an instant sensation about how it would feel to take her in his arms again, even if just for the length of one song. His blood heated. He knew better. *But oh my god, it was so hard to sit there and have her so close and not be able to reach out and touch her.*

"Sorry, I can't stay." Jackson polished off his bourbon.

"But I insist. You can't desert us now. I have a woman who wants to meet you. An old family friend. She'll be here any minute. Please, stay."

The last word was a command. Jackson hesitated. He didn't want to jeopardize the mission, but all his instincts said it was a bad idea.

"Ah, here she is now. Such a gorgeous tall redhead. But of course, not as beautiful as you, my dear." Hector gave a nod toward his wife, raising her hand to his thick lips.

Jackson caught Elena's almost hidden grimace before he swiveled his head toward the bar's entrance where a very beautiful woman strolled with supreme confidence toward their booth. Model tall, she had on a short skirt that showed off long shapely legs and a trim figure to advantage. Her long auburn hair flowed around her shoulders and she tossed it for full effect, making her runway debut.

"Ah, Josie Jones, meet Jackson Banks," Hector introduced them. Jackson got up and shook her hand.

"Nice to meet you, Josie." He waited until she sat down before sitting.

"A gentleman. I like that. Jackson Banks—good name," she complimented him with a smile and an admiring look, her voice smooth as she scooted into the booth alongside Jackson. Her perfume drifted his way reminding him of the more enticing tones of Elena's intoxicating fragrance. Was she a hooker? He wouldn't put it past Hector.

"Still drinking bourbon?" Hector asked Josie as the waiter hovered near their table.

She nodded. "Sure. Finest available."

Hector indicated a round and the waiter hurried away to get the drinks.

"My Elena wants to go dancing. Any suggestions for a good place?"

"Well, at it happens, I do know a place and it's right here in this hotel," she purred. "We can enjoy ourselves and not even have to venture outside."

Of course you do, Hector hired you. Jackson pursed his lips, resigned to an evening of watching Elena and being unable to touch her. *So close and yet so far.* The words of the song were so damn apt.

"Now tell me, Jackson, what is it that you do?" Josie asked, leaning forward to offer a calculated view of her lavish cleavage pressed upward in her tight dress. He idly wondered what Hector was paying her.

"I work for US Customs as an SI—special investigator."

Her smooth Botox forehead moved ever so slightly as she tried to frown. She was in her late twenties or early thirties and should have earned at least one or two wrinkles. Elena was obviously too young for wrinkles. "What does an SI do all day?"

"I don't want to bore you," he said hoping she'd get the hint.

"Let me be the judge of that," she said, giving him a seasoned look.

"If you'll excuse me, I need to visit the men's room," he said. Josie made a production of sliding out of the booth, brushing up against him in the process.

Hector gave him a self-satisfied smirk.

"When you get back, we'll all have dinner and then go dancing next door in the ballroom," he said like the supreme patriarch Jackson knew he viewed himself to be.

Just one night. I can handle it.

He threw cold water on his face at the bathroom sink, scooping it up with his hands. He dried off with a paper towel and checked his appearance in the mirror.

Took out a pocket comb and hastily ran it through his thick dark hair, pushing it back from his face. Well past time for a haircut. A memory of Leia with her newly returned hair color, a thousand percent improvement made him smile in the mirror. She was safe in Oregon. He watched his eyes brighten with thoughts of his sister. Then there was Elena. The blue in his eyes deepened and he had to look away from the troublesome honesty laid bare.

Bracing himself, he rejoined them.

"You two have something else in common," Hector announced as he sat down.

"Yeah, what's that?" Jackson asked.

"You share the same birthdate. August seventeenth."
Bullshit.

"That makes you a Leo as well," Josie said. "Prone to being vain and proud and yet very protective of family and generous to a fault. Sound like you at all, Jackson?"

He didn't ask how Hector knew his birthday. Meant that Mike had likely checked out as well and things could be set in motion.

"Maybe. But my clothes—don't think they shout 'vain' exactly." He looked down at his simple white cotton buttoned-down shirt, tan chinos, and simple navy blazer. Very different from Hector's dark suit, blue silk shirt and expensive tie. With the prerequisite heavy gold jewelry of course. He was loaded up even more than usual. Enough to pay the GNP of a small country.

"Maybe not, but you're protective of family, a quality I most admire," Hector said.

Elena has been sitting quietly, twirling her half empty wine glass between her long elegant fingers.

"How's Leia, Jackson?" she asked, her golden eyes locking with his.

Why when she looked at him did he feel like the

entire world dropped away? Why was the universe taunting him? With a woman he could never have?

"Fine. Getting help."

"Where?" Hector asked.

Jackson's blood ran cold.

He froze. Didn't know what to say or do. If he lied Hector would find out, sure as shit.

"Oops!" Elena's wine glass somehow toppled over onto the tabletop garnering everyone's attention. "I'm sorry, I'm such a klutz," she lamented, pulling back from the running mess, and trying desperately to mop it up with a bundle of Kleenex she yanked from her purse. She spilled the contents of her purse on the black leather seat in her agitation.

"We'll get you another," Hector said as he nodded at the waiter, his expression tight.

The waiter solved the situation quickly, wiping up the remains of the spilled drink with a cloth, taking away the sodden tissues, and bringing a fresh glass of white wine.

"To family," Hector gave a toast as the commotion died down.

"To family," Jackson said, thanking Elena silently over his glass.

———

"We all want someone to cry over us when we're dead," Hector stated with profound solemnness. He stressed every word, deep into the bourbon. The two women were in the ladies room.

Jackson had been wondering when he could leave, but no opportunity had presented itself. He'd been careful to nurse his drinks. Since he'd met Elena, his drinking consumption had plummeted. It was probably for the best.

"I'm counting on having lots of children to mourn my passing," Hector continued in the same morose tone.

Jackson rubbed his aching temples. Too personal. He couldn't stomach the idea of Elena having Hector's children. The very idea disgusted him through and through. He had to lesson his hold on the glass he held or it would have broken in his hand.

"Most American families try to keep it to two kids or less," Jackson said. The thought of all the danger Hector put his wife and family into with his involvement with the drug cartels chilled his mood further.

Hector made a sound of disgust blowing air between his lips. His dark, pockmarked complexion was shiny with sweat and red from dancing. He'd blown Jackson away with his energy on the dance floor, spinning Elena around like a pro. Explained he'd had lessons as a child. "A real man has a large family and provides for them."

"Don't you worry about the possible fallout of your work on your family?"

Hector's eyes squinted half-closed, his lips turning down as if he'd eaten something sour.

"My family is well provided for and well protected. No concern of yours. My job's to make sure of that. My community loves me because I take care of them. You Americans, you don't understand."

"I envy you, Hector. You have it all," Jackson said. It was true. How had that happened? His envying the man? But his compliment appeared to smooth the waters, that is, until Hector's next words.

"Quit your job. Come work for me. We'd make an unstoppable pair." He clapped Jackson on the back to make his point. "I'll set you up in a nice house. With lots of women at your beck and call. You'd like that, my friend, right! We'd find you a good woman to be mother to your children and your sister can be part of an extended family. And here's a bonus for you. Less drug use in our part of the world. We sell it all over the border!" He laughed out loud at his own private joke, his chest puffed up with pride.

The invitation boggled his mind. So unexpected. He shook his head to clear it. But Hector was right. Historically, there had been more drug use in North America than in Mexico, but that was changing rapidly according to Rand. Middlemen were being paid off in product and dumping it back on the streets of their home country to make their money. A dismal situation all the way around. And with the profits rising over six thousand percent, "from the narco to the nose" as his friend liked to call the supply line; he knew that would not be changing anytime soon. He could only imagine what the profits were from the coca farmer to the *nose* of the crowd in New York City.

"Leia's in LA. She needs me." Then he could have kicked himself when he realized he had brought up her name. He breathed a silent prayer of thanks when Hector didn't ask her whereabouts again.

"She can come with you. Get her away from that bastard who started all the trouble. See, every cloud has a silver lining." The two women rejoined them at the table at that moment. Josie slid into the chair next to Jackson, nudging his thigh with hers. He moved his leg away.

"Elena, we must talk Jackson into joining us permanently in Mexico. He can move his family into one of the new prefab homes that Torres Construction is building. We can move it onto that parcel of land near the north quarter. Nice view from there."

"Jackson knows his own mind," she said earning a frown from Hector.

"Bah, women. Never know a good idea if it hit them on the backside," he said dismissing her disclaimer.

Jackson clamped his lips together. Oh yeah, it would be a brilliant idea for him to join the Torres family in Mexico. Fate was taunting him yet again.

"Hey handsome, how's about we go up to my room? I have a suite for the entire weekend," Josie said, her lips nuzzling on his earlobe. He eased away.

"Sorry, I've got an appointment."

"What! This late?" she said with disbelief. She frowned. Her downturned lips made her look much older.

He caught the slight quirk upward of Elena's lips. She approved.

"Yeah, this late," he confirmed pulling away and getting to his feet. Fatigue shadowed him and he vowed to make that doctor's appointment.

"I'll call you in the morning," Jackson said, pulling his sports jacket off the back of the chair and shrugging into it. He nodded respectfully at the women and strode away, but not before earning a big pout from Josie.

"What a dud," she said, loud enough for him to hear.

The taunt followed him outside and he took a welcomed breath of the cooler night air. He needed a clear head for tomorrow. So much was riding on it.

CHAPTER 15

HECTOR SAT UPFRONT WITH THOMAS IN THE NONDESCRIPT black SUV, drinking coffee and surveying the busy parking lot of *Custom Enterprises* from a vantage point on the street. They were waiting for Jackson to arrive. A couple of sleek black motorcycles were parked near the entrance to the office. An unmarked van backed into the open doorway of one of the dozen loading docks that led to the vast warehouse, two men jumped out, one holding a clipboard.

Parcels and boxes were being steadily unloaded while a few cargo containers lined the area, a couple already hooked up to a cab just requiring a driver to be driven away. A UPS vehicle pulled into the parking lot to join a FedEx truck as they watched. It was a busy hub of a clearing warehouse and perfect for his needs. If the manager was amenable, and George's intel suggested he was, he was poised to increase security for his supply chain. Grow his business.

Jackson's truck turned into the parking lot right at the scheduled time and Thomas started the motor, placed the car in gear, driving into the entrance way right behind him.

"Morning," Jackson greeted them.

"You look tense, Jackson, you should have taken Josie up on her generous offer last night," Hector joked.

"I like to choose my own women, thanks," Jackson said, taking a large swallow of coffee from the cup he was carrying.

"Your loss," Hector shrugged. He'd hired Josie once. She was good, but she lacked the one thing he most enjoyed in a hooker, vulnerability, a slight unwillingness to perform that he was good at overcoming. He thought about the new girl he'd broke in a few nights ago. Now, she had been perfect. His blood heated as he remembered her delicious innocence and how he had methodically stripped her of it. If only Elena would give him what a wife should provide, he would have no need to stray. Other women found him more than enough man for them, why was she different?

"Okay, let's go and have a little talk with this Mike Ramsay guy," Jackson said, tossing his coffee cup into a green garbage can near the entrance.

One of the young women working the front counter gave them a quick glance from behind her computer screen, smiled at Jackson. "What can I do for you today?"

"Tell Mike we're here to see him," he said.

The manager's office was down the long narrow hallway from reception.

"Yeah, sure, tell him he'll have it today. I will personally see to it," said a disembodied voice as Hector followed Jackson into the office. It belonged to a man standing behind his cluttered desk, searching frantically through the stack of paper threatening to topple over.

"Hey, Jackson, good to see you, buddy," he said as he caught sight of them.

"Sit, sit," he said after introductions were made pointing at the posse of chairs positioned in front of his desk. He appeared to find what he was looking for and shoved a thin sheaf of printed paper into another folder.

"I thought computers were going to cut down on the paperwork. Save a few trees," he said with disgust as his hand indicated how swamped he was. "So, what can I do for you gentlemen?" he asked as he sat down across from them, not bothering to hide he was checking them out as carefully as they were returning the favor.

"Jackson has told us you are a good guy to know," Hector said, pulling out a leather cigar holder from an inner pocket of his suit jacket with a raised eyebrow at the manager.

Mike shoved an ashtray across the desk already half-filled with cigarette butts. Hector bit off one end of his cigar and lit it with an engraved silver lighter he pulled from his jacket pocket. In his fatalistic mood he knew smoking wouldn't be the silent killer to take him out. The one who did—he wouldn't see coming. That was why he'd had the grim reaper carrying a black scythe tattooed on his left bicep and an angel on his right. His back, of course, was dedicated to the Los Knights symbol of a dragon and a knight in a deadly scenario, the dragon breathing fire and the knight with his sword raised for the kill. The rocker etched beneath labeled him a member of the Los Knights.

"Well, I'm the guy who can get things done," Mike said amiably, leaning forward on his office chair. It squawked loudly in protest.

"What do you put through here?" Hector blew a smoke ring and watched it break up quickly in the air being disturbed by the air conditioning forced into the room through an overhead air duct.

"Anything and everything."

"What if I want to ship a container? Any problem?"

"Sail right through the port with the right paperwork."

Mike gave a nod at Jackson who had been sitting quietly, observing. "You can send someone to pick it up, long as this guy hands in legitimate reports. We've been clean and secure in his capable hands."

Hector puffed on the cigar, watching Mike. He knew the man checked out from the research meticulously acquired by George. He knew the man could be bribed, had gone to jail and did his time until his brother-in-law gave him a second change, and he knew he was safe considering how he was planning to exploit the situation. Mike was capable, and Jackson was committed. Just a little more insurance, and that wasn't going to be had at this little meeting.

Hector stabbed out his cigar and stood up. Offered his hand. Mike gave it a firm shake. Hector held onto his hand for an extra moment, looked Mike straight in the eyes and made himself clear, reciting a few famous lines from the movie script, Scarface. Hector let Mike's hand go. "Know who said that?" he asked.

"Ah, that guy in that gangster movie. What was his name—Sosa something or other?"

"Alejandro *Sosa*."

"You're a movie buff," Mike said with a grin. "Do you know who said these ones?" He quoted a few lines of his own, obviously one of his favorites.

"Sure. Our friend Tony Montana."

Hector nodded at Thomas who reached into his dark suit jacket and pulled out a sealed envelope from the inner pocket. Placed it on the desk in front of Mike. Mike picked it up, opened it, and thumbed through it. It contained a thick swath of new hundred-dollar American bills.

"There's plenty more where that came from. We'll be in touch."

"Anytime," Mike said with a wide smile. "Pleasure doing business with you."

Hector preceded Jackson down the hallway and out the front door into the harsh sunlight.

"Thomas will pick you up at ten tonight."

"I hadn't planned—"

"Wear a suit."

———

JACKSON GLANCED at the flashy neon club façade from the back seat of the black SUV as Thomas parked at the curb. *Sweet Valentine's*. A new club he wasn't familiar with. Valets were busy parking cars and in moments their party was ushered into the inner sanctuary. A driving beat, meant to get under human skin and make a person think they were missing something, throbbed, seductive as hell. Jackson knew better. Clubs had nothing to offer him. Only being with Elena called to him every minute of every day. The woman he should not be thinking about, the one woman he should not want with every fiber of his being. The one woman he could never have.

He followed Hector and Thomas through the door, past the gyrating dancers packing the dance floor, past the throngs of voyageurs and the exhibitionists, past the band playing on the backstage, down a staircase to a man who demanded a password before he opened a solid metal door and into a space he had only imagined existing. A scene right out of history greeted and stunned him. Pillars surrounded a vast pool. Naked, mostly female bodies sprawled everywhere. Like he could only imagine a Roman bath to be during Caligula's time, history's iconic bad guy. Men in togas were busily administering to the women on their knees, tongues lapping at the spread bodies of compliant females, other men busy fucking women on chalice lounges, still others watching two women enjoy each other with dildos and tongues. Hedonistic and shocking as hell to Jackson. What the hell was Hector doing bringing him here? He was a one woman man, not a fucking pervert.

A dark suited man noticed them and rushed over.

"Welcome, please, may I see your ID?" he asked and was handed a plastic card about the size of a credit card by Thomas.

"Ah, you're a *Platinum* member, Mr. Torres. Then you have the run of our establishment. Anything you wish, ask. What can I offer you and your party this evening?"

Jackson turned away in disgust while the men brokered some kind of deal. Hector gave Jackson a wink before he left on the arm of a slender naked woman, one of the few with the original assets nature gave her. She led him through the writhing crowd and into the back. Then Thomas was led away, his wolfish grin saying it all.

"And you sir, what is your heart's desire?" The man turned to him next, his question left hanging in the air as Jackson pressed his lips together, his anger growing. A married *family* man coming to such a place sickened him.

"Nothing. I'm here by mistake," he retorted. He turned on his heel and left. Out on the sidewalk he breathed a lungful of fresh air, thankful to have escaped the vile pleasure den where a man's or woman's body was thought so little of it could be shared with a complete stranger.

His phone buzzed as he gestured for a taxi, intent on getting home and having a shower to wash away his disgust.

An unknown number.

"Hello,"

"Jackson, it's Elena. I need to see you."

"Where are you?" he asked, his heart thudding.

"The Fairmont, room 215."

"I'll be right there."

Jackson hung up and raced to get in the open door of the taxi cab, Elena's sweet voice echoing in his mind, not allowing himself any time to think about the lurking danger.

"The Fairmont Hotel. There's an extra hundred in it if you get me there as fast as possible," he instructed the driver.

The man nodded and pulled away from the curb so quickly Jackson barely had time to close the back door of the cab before they barreled into traffic.

Twenty-seven minutes later they pulled up in front of the hotel. He handed the cash plus the generous tip to the driver and dashed from the taxi, up the front steps and into the foyer. He ran up the wide staircase, too impatient to wait for an elevator.

Elena opened the hotel room door on his first knock.

She stood there looking at him with her liquid Bambi eyes, so beautiful she made his heart sing and lurch in his chest at the same time. They fell into each other's arms without a word spoken between them, her warm body clinging to his. Breathe. Just breathe.

He rained kisses on her face, her hair, her neck. She tasted salty and sweet, the fragrance of her arousal clear in the heady musk rising in waves from her heated skin. The silk robe she wore fell away, her nakedness increasing his desperation. Her breasts jutted out and he kissed them, his hands all over her, as if trying to memorize every curve, every sweet spot for the drought coming.

She pulled at his suit jacket and he helped her tear it off, followed by the rest of his clothing until they faced each other naked, her robe pooled on the floor. He picked her up and carried her to the bed. They fell onto the king-sized bed, kissing each other as if their very lives depended on it.

"*Oh, my god. Elena,*" he murmured before desperation shut off his voice entirely, finding no other words to describe the passion he was being driven by. He crushed her to him, her long legs encircling his waist. He made love to her, thrusting himself in and out until the room blurred, and only the two of them existed. The last man and woman, more than imagined. More than enough. Something so powerful than the sense of self fell away, tossing him into the sublime. At the height of pleasure, he died a little, before falling back exhausted.

Sometime later he came back to himself with Elena pressed tightly against his side, their breathing still harsh and ragged.

"Thank you," he whispered into her ear, kissing and tracing the delicate lobe and tucking her hair back from her lovely face.

She looked at him, her eyes filled with wonder, a single tear escaping and running down the soft curve of her cheek.

He swept it away with a tender touch and drew her to him, wanting to draw all her pain, all her sorrow into him. To let her be free.

They lay in silence. The alarm clock ticked its steady heartbeat on the bedside table, as if the entire world reminded them time was running out.

"I can keep you safe here in the states. You can enter the Witness Protection program—"

"And leave my family exposed. No." She shook her head emphatically. "This—us—we can never be."

He heard the utter heartbreak in her resolute tone. He swallowed hard, his throat aching with unshed tears.

"Family is important, but you can't throw your entire life away, Elena, that's just wrong!"

"No!" She pulled away. "I need to shower and get back before…"

Her voice trailed off. He placed his hand on her back, felt her trembling. His heart breaking he urged, "Elena, please, if you care about me at all, you must listen to reason."

Her spine stiffened under his touch. "You must go. Now!"

His hands shaking, Jackson got dressed, fumbling with the simple task as if he had never done it before.

"Please, Elena," he said, putting his arms around her to get her attention.

"Just go." Her face was a tight rigid mask; her eyes brimming over with emotion.

"Fine, if this was just sex to you, I'll go." He wanted to take the words back immediately, but pride stopped him. She pressed her lips tightly together, not answering. He wanted to shake some sense into her, but dropped his hands away, defeated. He was acting no better than Hector.

"If you need me, call. No matter when, I'll be there," he said. Then did the unthinkable. He turned and walked away, softly closing the door.

CHAPTER 16

"Hmm, yes, that could work quite nicely," George said, rubbing at his bristly chin.

Hector hadn't wasted any time in LA. He had bustled Elena onto his private plane at first light, leaving before contacting Jackson again. Jackson had disappointed him deeply by rejecting his generous gift and was undeserving of his attention. Keeping him out of the loop might bring him around. If not, he had his connection with Mike, all he needed from him—for now.

His own out-of-control night at Sweet Valentine's had left him hungry to acquire more. Always, always, he needed more. Now he had an idea of how to acquire much more. He scratched absently at the itchy palm of his left hand as he watched Jesús directing the loading of coffins into the cargo hold of the trailer container. A perfectly respectable order, it was headed across the border and into LA for a local mortuary. His first test.

"Has the new wood arrived?"

"Yeah, stacked behind the barn as you asked. What do you want me to do with it?"

"Assemble the men. I've got a job for them. Oh, and

get a truckload of cold beer. We're going to need it for this job."

George raised his eyebrows with interest. "Okay, I'll bite. What's up?"

"Meet me behind the barn with the men and the beer this afternoon."

———

JACKSON WAS GOING CRAZY. He'd heard absolutely nothing from Hector in ten days. He and Elena had vanished like smoke in the wind. He was haunted by the memory of their parting. Torn up inside. Desperate to talk with her. He wanted to apologize for ever doubting her. She loved her family as much as he did Leia. He was the one who had to change, to make this thing right. But he didn't know how to do that. The DEA was squeezing him, expecting results. They'd done their part in keeping Leia safe. What was he doing? Even Rand was acting strangely. Jackson rubbed his head. He'd gone back to work but was having a hard time concentrating, finding it meaningless for the first time.

The problem was his heart was in Mexico. For the first time he thought the unthinkable. No, not possible, *or was it?*

Not giving himself any more time to think about it, he headed for his supervisor's office.

———

LEIA SQUEEZED the poker chip sized sobriety coin in her pocket. A gift from an outgoing patient who said she saw something special in her, it never left her person. Two weeks sober. A week since her body had come around from the extreme withdrawal all addicts had to go through. Her first token. Lucky. It encouraged therapy, helped her embrace meditation, practice yoga, and take long walks. Even take her medication faithfully. Ben. Well, he was less enthusiastic and getting worse by the day. It was like he was only going through the motions, paying lip service until something better came along. She sighed. She loved him so much and wanted him to love her enough to give up drugs. Forever.

"You think a couple of weeks not using is going to help much in the real world?" he sneered, catching her action. They were eating breakfast together in the cafeteria.

Even the food tasted better.

"It's a start." Leia glanced around the room, hoping no one was listening. She was becoming nervous about Ben's comments. He sounded disloyal. Disparaging the staff and all they did to try to help them.

Adam, one of their counselors, walked over. He was barely older than they were. Young and smart. And, she knew, a little attracted to her. She'd seen it in his eyes. Admiration.

"How are you doing this fine morning?" he asked, favoring Leia with a warm smile.

"Good," she said returning his smile. He looked nice. Handsome with bright blue eyes and a deep tan, he was dressed in a white shirt and tan pants. So unlike Ben with his pallor, black clothes, and lank hair.

Ben frowned.

"This food is for shit," he said, throwing his half-eaten bagel down in disgust.

"You can order whatever you like, Ben, you know that. Is something else bothering you? Would you like to come to my office and discuss it?" Adam's face showed nothing but an earnest need to help.

"No, I would not! And I'll tell you what's bothering

me. This fucking place with all its optimism dripping over onto everyone like it's going to sink in with no problem. This is *not* the real world. This is some fantasy you guys dreamed up to make money. You're no better than us. At least drug dealers offer something. Relief. Not this endless dragging out of the inevitable." Ben knocked hard on the table with his fists, got up and stalked away, his anger radiating off him in waves.

"I'm sorry," Leia mumbled.

"It's not your fault, Leia. Look at me," he reached out and tucked a lock of hair behind her ear. "You are not alone in this. We'll help you through this. If Ben cannot—"

"No." She shook her head. "Stop right there. Ben and me—we're together. Forever." She looked away and watched Ben through the large picture windows that lined the dining room. His figure got smaller and smaller as he made his way across the yard to the tree line and the network of trails that crisscrossed the fifty acres of the retreat. He was headed to the lake to feed the geese. She'd seen him shove the remains of the bagel into his pocket.

"If you need to talk—"

"I need to go."

"Leia, please, I only want what's best for you."

"Ben is what's best for me." *Or was he?* Doubts were creeping in, upsetting the smooth rhythm of the day. She couldn't even fully admit them to herself, how could she admit them to someone else?

"Okay," Adam sighed. "There's a yoga class starting in ten."

"No, I'm going for a walk," she announced and got up to hurry after Ben. Maybe she could catch him and help feed the geese. She grabbed an extra bagel from the self-serve counter on the way out the door.

Her pace slowed once she was out of view of the dining room window. What was going to happen? Ben was changing. Or maybe it was her that was changing. She felt him slipping away from her, hour by hour. She turned the final corner before the lake where the shoreline came into view, but instead of only Ben someone stood with him. Who? She tried to catch a glimpse of the face of the female with the bright red hair that glinted wickedly in the sunlight. The woman turned her face to the right angle and her heartrate increased. Catherine. Rand's old girlfriend. She was handing something to Ben that he just stuffed in his pocket. *Oh god No!* Her heart dropped. She'd bet her life on it that she had given her boyfriend drugs. The last fucking thing he needed.

"Ben!"

The pair turned toward her as she called out, Ben looking uncomfortable at her approach, Catherine far too smug. "What are you doing here? I thought you were going to take that yoga class."

"I changed my mind," she said. "Thought I'd help feed the geese."

"Leia, good to see you," Catherine said. Her eyes wary, she offered up a fake smile, red lipstick circling her fake plumped-up lips. "Just visiting an old friend of mine and I ran into Ben."

Yeah, sure you were. "Who's your friend?"

"Jimmy Bond, you know him? He's been here a month or so. I came at the request of his foster mom. We work together and I owed her for covering for me. She sent a care package."

"Nice of her," Leia said. Catherine's explanation was plausible.

"Yeah, well, I should be going. Got a plane to catch. Say hi to Jackson for me."

Leia didn't say anything as she watched her turn and

leave. Catherine was a pill. And she was looking a bit more ragged than normal. Her brother had told her what had happened with Rand, all the shit that went down. But what was she doing giving drugs to Ben?

"Leia, before you go off half-cocked, it was totally innocent. She was already here at the lake when I came by," Ben said, planting himself right in front of her.

"What did she give you? And don't lie 'cause I can always tell, Ben Carson," she demanded.

He reached in his pocket and pulled out a bit of tinfoil.

"There's enough for both of us," he suggested, his eyes smoldering. He unfolded the tinfoil to reveal the cocaine. Leia swallowed hard, her eyes riveted on his hand holding the innocent white powder—the stuff of happy dreams. Of being free.

———————

"OKAY, drink up. When you need to piss—piss on the wood," Hector instructed.

The dozen men looked at him with surprised.

"Piss on the wood?" one asked in disbelief, taking off his ball cap to scratch at his tanned bare scalp.

"Yes! Just do it," he growled.

Obediently, the men took the cans of beer offered by George from the large open cardboard box resting on the ground near the Jeep, popped the caps, and began to drink. More boxes of beer were piled high inside the vehicle waiting to be unloaded.

"Very refreshing, *padrino*, thank you," one of the men said, wiping his mouth with the back of his hand.

"Why urinate on the wood?" George asked. He was also drinking a cold brew and watching the men enjoy the beer, an unaccustomed break in their busy day.

"Confuses drug dogs. We're about to find out if it's an urban legend or not," Hector said.

One of the men stepped up to the first section of wood, pulled down his zipper, took out his cock, and let a yellow stream of urine fly directly onto the heavily scented plywood. The wood gave off the distinctive odor of camphor fumes in the extreme heat.

"Ah, good job. But I can do more. I'm better equipped," one of the men joked, taking his turn next with a wide grin. With a flourish he peed all over the man's first swath.

It became a free for all. Pee splashing everywhere, beer consumed at an alarming rate, until finally most of the men rested their backs against the barn wall, some falling asleep.

"Best day ever," one mumbled as he pulled his baseball cap over his eyes proudly declaring his allegiance for the New York Yankees on its brim.

"And I want round the clock surveillance in LA. I don't trust those bastards for one second," Hector said.

George nodded. "I'll take care of it."

———————

"OKAY, THIS IS IT," George said, setting the powerful binoculars down on the dash and poking Thomas in the ribs. He was dozing on the bucket seat beside him in the van and giving the odd annoying snore. They'd been waiting all night for their shipment of coffins to clear customs. The cargo container and truck cab they were waiting for was nondescript except for the identifying company on the door of the cab, *Custom Coffins*. It was now being driven through the open gates of the vast labyrinth network that housed the endless stream of merchandise flowing both ways across the border.

They followed at a discreet distance the mile to the brokerage house where the shipment was to be cleared and sent on to the mortuary.

"If this works, we'll be back here in a couple of days doing exactly the same thing. A real test this time with a small amount of drugs. You up for it?"

"Sure. Keep the coffee coming," Thomas said, punctuating his remarks by pouring another cup from the thermos. George hit a pothole and the coffee sloshed over onto his suit pants.

"Shit!" he exclaimed grabbing a roll of paper towels from the floor and dabbing at the spreading stain on his crotch.

George grinned. "Should have seen that coming, *pendejo.*"

Thomas glared at him. "Fuck you," he said.

George ignored him and pulled into the parking lot of the customs brokerage house. Picked up his phone and hit redial, "Yeah, looks good so far. Sure, we can do that. Be back tomorrow."

"What's up?" Thomas asked.

"Usual," George shrugged, his eyes following the tableau unfolding before them. A man folded up the paper\work and thrust it in his pocket and waved the driver on. George waited and then followed the vehicle at a discrete distance.

"Good. Hector wants us to follow the truck to the Green Acres Mortuary. Then we're free to enjoy our night in LA."

Thomas gave a wolfish grin. "Nice. First dibs on that hooker he's always talking about. What's her name? Yeah, Josie Jones. What happens in LA stays in LA, *baby.*"

"That's Vegas, *pendejo.*"

"Fuck you," Thomas said mildly before drinking more coffee.

"You keep that up and you'll be pissing your pants for real."

"Think the trick will work with the wood?" Thomas asked.

"Don't know." he shrugged. "But we get to come back to LA and have another night away from the nagging with easy women begging us for it. Good enough for me."

George once more parked the van on the street and they watched the tractor trailer pull into the curved driveway of the mortuary. The vehicle continued around back to the unloading area where they wouldn't be able to see the actual unloading, but getting any closer was risky.

Twenty minutes later the vehicle pulling away from Green Acres was empty. George was certain. The trailer was riding higher now that the heavy load of coffins was removed.

He hit redial again. "Yeah, looks good," he said into the pre-paid one-time-use cell phone.

"Okay, now we play," George said with satisfaction and pulled into traffic.

———

"LET me know when it's done." Hector spoke into his cell phone as he watched Jesús directing the loading of a shipment of coffins, five hundred kilos of uncut cocaine sealed in one kilo bags under their fancy white linings ready for the big load. He just had to do one final test before shipping it. *And* get his insurance. No other way to operate effectively and efficiently guaranteeing loyalty in business as human insurance. Which reminded him. Time to push for a donor. He had more than enough funds, and with so much more promised by this new enterprise, he could buy many new hearts for his Teresa.

He was already overseeing the building of the on-site private hospital nearby, under the guise of doing more good for his community. Such modern facilities for his fallen soldiers would allow his Elena to give up her last tie to the modern life and become only the mother of his children. He kissed the Saint Christopher medal that hung round his neck, glancing at the depiction of the big man carrying his staff with the small Christ child riding high on his shoulder. *Keep my family safe from all harm.*

CHAPTER 17

THE MONSTER OF A STEPFATHER WHO HAD MURDERED HIS mother in cold blood with a claw hammer and left him and Leia to burn alive, had died, short of his actual execution date. Once more he'd won, got off easy. Jackson held the final letter that the man had written in his clenched hands, his mind racing. It had been delivered this morning. *Should I open it or burn it?* But he had to know what it contained, even it if was all vitriol. But why had he written to him, now of all times? There had been no contact between them in many years, long as the man had sat on death row. Too bad they didn't fry them anymore.

Finally, after a drink to brace himself, he tore the white envelope open and yanked out the missel. It would haunt him more not to know. He just had to hope that the knowledge it contained wasn't worse than being left in the dark.

JACKSON,
I WANT YOU TO KNOW THAT YOU ARE THE

ONE TO BLAME FOR WHAT HAPPENED TO YOUR MOTHER. IF YOU HADN'T PULLED THAT SHIT ON ME, GAVE ME A FUCKING HEART ATTACK, I WOULDN'T HAVE GONE LOCO AND KILLED HER. HER DEATH IS ON YOUR HEAD. NOT THAT THE BITCH DIDN'T HAVE IT COMING. SHE PLAYED ME THE FOOL.

YOU KNOW YOU GOT MEXICAN BLOOD, BOY? YOU COME BY YOUR BASTARD LOOKS HONESTLY. YOUR SAINTLY BITCH OF A MOTHER CHEATED ON YOUR DADDY WHEN SHE WAS IN OJINAGA THE SUMMER BEFORE YOU WERE BORN. YOUR SISTER LEIA'S YOUR HALF SISTER. I SUSPECT YOU GOT LOTS OF RELATIVES IN MEXICO. HOW DO YOU LIKE THEM ROAD APPLES? NOW WE'RE EVEN.

JACKSON SAT stunned and struggled to keep himself together. He and Leia didn't look much alike. Sure, she had the same black hair, but she was fair like the one photograph he'd seen of his father. Could there be some truth to it? But even as he asked himself the question, he knew. The man was telling the truth about this one thing. Trying to lash out before he died—do more harm. A part of him had always suspected that his mother had been hiding something from him. In particular her rants against the validity of DNA testing had made him wonder once or twice.

He felt he was also burying some part of himself along with the old man as he struck a match to the letter and burned it in an ashtray. But he was also more determined than ever to get what he wanted. Like a phoenix rising, he said goodbye to his old life and began arrangements to head back to Mexico.

———

TWENTY HOURS later Jackson stood on the side of a dirt runway waiting for someone to pick him up. The plane had come and gone, dropping him off at the location. The spot was deserted expect for insects and bees hovering above wildflowers, the air alive with their insistent droning. A puff of dust growing in the hazy distance finally announced his overdo ride. A few minutes later the Jeep pulled up alongside him.

"You Jackson Banks?" the new driver asked, his teeth flashing white against his sun darkened skin. Jackson knew Thomas was busy in Los Angeles. Rand had been excited that their guy on the Mexican side had caught a shipment from Hector and managed to add a tracker to the container. Thomas was in in LA overseeing its delivery. Perfect.

"Yeah," he said. He threw his kit bag in the back seat, hurried around the back of the vehicle, and climbed in the passenger seat, holding onto the top rail in anticipation of another wild ride through rough territory. He wasn't disappointed. The Jeep was soon bumping and grinding down the back roads toward Grand Torres at an alarming rate, the reckless driver grinning at the wheel.

This time they didn't pull up to the main house but drove on by. There was massive construction going on and he wondered what was being built. He was taken to a private dwelling at the back of the vast property, feeling like a clandestine relative everyone wants kept hidden away.

"Señor Torres says to wait here," the driver said curtly before speeding off.

The isolation did not bode well, and Jackson wondered if he had just made the worse mistake of his life. He opened the front door of the hacienda and stepped inside. The air was cooler being sheltered by the thick adobe walls. He wandered from room to room of the three-bedroom house, finding it had been outfitted with modern facilities run by a large generator and didn't have any bars on the windows. Not that Hector needed them. How could he get away unless he walked all the way to the nearest airport a hundred miles away?

His cell phone rang as he tossed his bag down on the bed.

"Hector," he said recognizing the number.

"Ah, Jackson, how do you like your new home? Soon you will have many new neighbors as we expand our operation."

"It's good. Fine," he said, relieved to discover this was about his being courted by the man. He looked out the back window. A dark plume of smoke was rising into the air in the distance.

"I can see smoke. Anything wrong?"

"Nah, just the dump burning refuse. Settle in. There's food and refreshment in the refrigerator and good bourbon in the liquor cabinet. I will be by in a couple of hours. Business calls at the moment, I'm afraid."

"No problem." He hung up. Time for a shower.

He was checking out the refrigerator's offerings when he heard a vehicle pull up. Hector was early. He strode to the front door and looked through the peephole. Elena was stepping out of a vehicle. She walked toward him, her hair flowing softly behind her in the slight breeze like a goddamned TV ad. She wore a bright yellow sundress that made her look surreal against the landscape. Innocent and luscious. His heart in his throat, he opened the door.

"Jackson," she said simply, the goodness shining in her eyes.

He moved forward on limbs tingling with nervous anticipation. Swept her into his arms. Crushed her to him, breathed in her intoxicating fragrance.

She pulled back, her small hands pressed to his chest. "I can't stay, but I wanted to welcome you back. Will Leia be joining you soon?"

"I haven't talked to her about it. She's still in rehab. And I don't know how long I'll be staying anyway."

She nodded. "Rehabilitation takes a lot of time and a great deal of patience. We hope to include such a place in our new hospital being built right here on the ranch. Your assisting Hector is going to help pay for it."

Shock chilled the very marrow in his bones. It reverberated inside, finding no easy release. For the first time he became fully aware of what drug money could do. He tried rejecting the knowledge, but looking in Elena's sweet face with her happy-sad eyes made him pause. A lot to digest.

"Will you be nursing there?" he asked and watched her eyes turn sadder still breaking his heart.

"No. It will be staffed with qualified doctors and nurses."

"You should be one of them," he said. "I watched you help a man, take out a bullet with infinitesimal care. You're good, Elena, very good at nursing. Don't sell yourself short."

"Hector doesn't want his wife working there or anywhere," she said with a small fateful shrug of her graceful shoulders.

"What do *you* want?"

"Doesn't matter what I want."

"I recently learned—again—how quickly life can change or end for any one of us."

"That's very fatalistic thinking, Jackson. What brought this on? Does it have something to do with you coming to Mexico so unexpectedly?" she asked softly, her golden eyes warm and interested.

"It's complicated—my life." He raked his hair back from his face with his fingers.

"I'm a good listener."

"No, I won't burden you with any of it. It wouldn't be fair."

"Since when has life ever been fair," she said. The bitterness was obvious even in her angel voice.

"You know what I want. The sun rises and sets with me thinking about you every moment of the day. You fill up all the empty spaces inside me. Make me whole. Hell, I even dream about you at night. I can't say it better than that." His confession was more a plea.

"I'm sorry. I can't help that."

"Then you can't help me at all."

They stared at each other across the chasm of their lives.

"I shouldn't have come."

"Why did you then?" Elena demanded, her expression turning pensive with a tinge of anger. She leaned forward and took his hand. Her expression changed again like quicksilver as she pleaded, "Please, tell me. Something happened, right? I can tell by the shadows in your eyes. Something bad has happened."

"Yeah, something happened all right. Something that made me question things. I'm sorry. I needed to see you to make sense of it all."

"I want to share the burden with you. Tell me. I need you to tell me. At least I can do that—let me do that at least…" Her voice trailed off leaving sadness and heartache in its wake.

He hesitated.

Never, other than the few facts he shared with his best friend Rand, had he been tempted to talk about his life. He didn't want to burden others.

But something broke free inside him. The memories of that past that the letter and the missed execution date blaring so loudly in his mind was too much, held back by a dike crumbling under its own crushing weight. And the beautiful woman standing so enticingly before him helped it to finish tumbling down like the walls of Jericho.

And so he told her.

They sat side by side on the sofa, holding hands, as he shared the story of his and Leia's life. All the stark facts. Even the worst of it, the night his mother had died in the fire deliberately set by his stepfather after Jackson had used his strange ability to stop his blows earlier in the day. How it had been revenge for using it on him and why it was so difficult for him to use it now. How the flames had pushed at him, the fire too strong for him to break through and how the searing heat had kept him from rescuing her. How he had just heard the man had died in the prison without paying the full price for his crimes. And finally, even of his heritage that was now in dispute and he'd asked Rand to investigate. When he was finished, he was drained, his burdens fallen away like dry leaves being shed by a mighty oak tree in the late fall after a violent windstorm. He felt cleansed of emotion. Newborn. Stronger.

"Oh, I'm so sorry. I had no idea." Her beautiful eyes swimming in tears. Over and over during his tale of woe her eyes had brimmed with moisture and she swiped them away with the back of her hand. She hugged him then. Held him tightly as the tears began to fall. The tears the first he had shed in many, many years.

The sound of the door opening broke them apart a moment too late as Hector walked through it.

"What's going on here?" he demanded.

Elena spoke first. "Jackson's stepfather, who was to be executed for murdering his mother and attempting to murder him and his sister has died. He also sent a letter questioning his parentage, saying his mother was fooling around on his father. He doesn't know who his real father is."

"Is this true, Jackson?" Hector's suspicious eyes were bouncing back and forth between the pair of them.

"Yeah, it's true all right." He pulled himself together with great difficulty. Discombobulated by events, swimming in doubts and emotion, he dug his fingers into the back of his neck, the sharp pain working to keep him focused.

"I'm sorry," Hector said and walked over and sat down across from them. Elena got up quickly and joined him. Elena's eyes were still red and Hector's were still suspicious.

"Well, then, all the more reason for you to stay in Mexico with us. No more ties to your country." Hector's voice was a bit too hearty.

"Maybe."

"Come, let's all go back to Grand Torres and have dinner together. Teresa has been asking about you. You're her new hero since you saved her life."

"I don't think—"

"Nonsense, I won't hear any objections. You're coming to dinner." He turned to Elena. "Are you ready, my dear?" he asked.

She immediately stood up, her face pale. She nodded. "Of course."

"Fine."

"Give me a minute," Jackson said.

"We'll wait outside."

Jackson rushed to the bathroom. He immediately opened the toilet lid and began throwing up, emptying the contents of his stomach. Finally, only dry heaves remained. It was if all the bitterness of his life was leaving his system. He quickly brushed his teeth, washed his face, and tidied his hair. His mind felt clear for the first time in days. He knew what he had to do. More pieces were falling into place in his mind. The risks were enormous, of course. But there was no going back. Not now. Not ever.

"Yeah, the dogs walked right on by. No takers. Exactly what you figured, *padrino*." George's voice came over the cell phone clearly as Hector listened. He knew Thomas was also listening to their conversation in the front seat of the van the pair had been living in most of the week. And both sets of eyes were most likely watching the drug-sniffing dogs pulling at their leashes as their handlers wound their way up and down the rows of cargo containers. He appreciated their loyalty and devotion even though expected.

"You enjoy another night out. You've more than earned it," Hector said, wishing it was him headed out for a night out in LA, but he'd have to cool his heels. For now.

"Sure, thanks." He could hear the rush of pleasure in the man's voice. "You want us to hang around for the next shipment?"

"No, it's not until next week. And I want to be there." And be rewarded with spending time at Sweet Valentine's.

"Fine. We'll head back tomorrow."

Hector hit end on his phone, slipped it into his pocket, and sat back with satisfaction. It was all coming together. Just a few more pieces of the puzzle in place and he'd be guaranteed to have things work smoothly. Only surprise was Jackson turning up unexpectedly. What was that about? It could be chalked up to recent events. Jackson had changed since he'd come back to Mexico. Their evening talks had shifted. He was beginning to like the new Jackson even more. He sensed a more determined man. Good. He needed strong men on his team. And tonight he was going to find out how strong.

CHAPTER 18

"Okay. Good. I'll be in LA on Thursday. Yeah, book that same place. Elena liked it."

Jackson sat in the front of the armored Jeep in the darkness beside Hector while the man spoke on the phone. His borrowed bulletproof vest felt too tight against his chest and made his breathing constricted. He took a couple of deep breaths. Only a few more hours.

"Going to get bloody tonight—real bloody. Fuckin' guys screwed this one up. Sure you're ready for this?" Hector asked.

"Yeah, I'm sure."

"Good. *Pendejo* thinks he can move in on my operation. First lesson of business—kill the competition. And my guys let him get away. I'll take him down if I have to take him down myself."

Hector started the Jeep. A half ton loaded with several of his men fully armed followed. Hector had been livid since his men had reported that the raid hadn't been entirely successful, it was rumored the main culprit had escaped.

"Their camp is up in the hills. Mendez is still hiding

there—you can take that to the bank. Bastard has nowhere else to go and nothing left to lose. A piece-of-shit-small-time hustler hoping to get a leg up on Los Knights. Fucking loco."

They bumped along the dirt road in the dark, headlights turned off. Jackson was thankful the moon had not risen yet, and the operation would be under cover. He released the safety on his borrowed pistol as the two men exited the Jeep. He'd practiced with it earlier in the day, shooting a target positioned on a hay bale out behind the barn. It tracked slightly to the left, but it would do.

"We walk from here."

His mouth dry, Jackson crept toward the area he'd been studying on his iPad. He'd smuggled the electronics inside the country hidden in his luggage's lining. The map showing the camp in detailed relief had been sent to him by Rand earlier in the day helping him navigate. The job was so chancy. Too many things could go wrong. It was a long hike to the camp, through rough underbrush that ripped and tore at his jeans. He was sweating profusely by the time they neared the outskirts, but he had a fair grasp of the terrain and was as ready as he was going to be.

Hector pointed with his gun in the direction he was to take and Jackson moved forward alone as the men split up to encircle the camp.

Gunfire erupted. A burst of staccato sounds hammering the night. Hector's soldiers were well armed with AK-47s converted to machine guns. Jackson ran toward it, his heart thudding in his chest.

Another burst of semi-automatic bullets pierced the darkness. Jackson nearly tripped over the body half hidden under a thorny bush near the large overhand of rock he was using as a landmark. Stopped in his tracks. This was it. He had to do it. He pointed his handgun at the body that only he, using spy-sat-quality photos, Rand, and his crew knew the location of. Squeezed the trigger. He shot the recently dead Mendez. Twice.

Rattled, he stood and waited. The sacrilegious act brought bitter bile up from his stomach. He swallowed it back down. No time to show weakness, the hyenas were circling.

"The gringo, he got him!" One of Hector's men was at his side, excited, peering down at the body.

Hector rushed up. Ripped off a thick gold chain that was circling the man's neck.

"Here," he said to Jackson as he handed it to him. "Take it. Trophy for you of this night, you proved your loyalty to Los Knights."

Jackson automatically took it and slid it into his pants pocket. Thank God it wasn't an ear or worse. He tore open the front of his vest, finding it nearly impossible to catch his breath.

"Come, we celebrate this victory!" Hector said with enthusiasm, clapping him hard on the back. "You are now officially one of us, Jackson Banks. Though I have to admit you've always looked like it. We could be blood-brothers, my friend."

An hour later, bodies left where they had fallen as carrion for the wildlife, they arrived at Big Rosy's. Jackson had overheard one of the men talking about it.

"Food, booze, and pussy, my amigos, all you want or can handle. And I'm paying tonight," Hector said with a self-satisfied smile. The men had entered the main salon with a long hallway of smaller rooms leading off in two different directions making the estab-lishment L-shaped. They milled around checking out the lineup of women, making rude macho jokes with each another. Some of the young women stared shyly at the floor, but most stood with out-and-out invitations in their body language, seductive well-practiced smiles at the ready.

"Hector, welcome." A huge Mexican women broke away from the pack and came right over, her red silk gown rustling from stiffness. The other men gave her a wide berth. She must have weighed close to three hundred pounds, though she looked comfortable in her own skin.

"This is Jackson Banks, the one I was telling you about. Is everything prepared?" he asked. His words were a red flag to Jackson. *What the hell have I got myself in for?*

"Jackson Banks." She gave him a brief nod her eyes glittering with satisfaction as she looked him up and down. "Yes, we are ready for him. Banks. That's not a Mexican name, but I think you have some of our rich blood flowing in your veins."

"Yeah, well, I just found out that I am probably half-Mexican." It felt strange to admit it. But a relief as well. He wanted to spend the rest of his life being as honest as possible. He was sick to death of the lies people tell themselves and others, and the harm they did. "Apparently my mother had an affair—oddly enough—right here in Ojinaga before I was born. Only found out myself. Truth is stranger than fiction, eh." He didn't want to discuss it. "So, what's this surprise you have in store?"

"Come with me. The tattooist is waiting."

Jackson stopped abruptly, bumping against Hector who was following.

"Tattoo?" he asked turning around and facing Hector.

"Yeah, you earned one tonight. You're one of us now. Wear it with pride, mi amigo."

Jackson didn't know what to say to that. He didn't want to piss Hector off, but he had never planned on this. He ended up silently following the mountain of a woman into one of the smaller cubbyholes off the long hallway. If he hated it, he could always get it taken off by laser he rationalized as he took his place on the reclining black chair.

Hector came right into the small space and removed his shirt, exposing his multitude of tattoos. He proudly showed them off, flexing his muscles.

A slender woman with many tattoos including a tear drop at the corner of her left eye checked them out from where she sat on a stool. She was wearing latex gloves and had equipment arrayed on a tray near Jackson's chair.

"I think you should go for the big one like the one our *padrinos* back. It is magnificent." Big Rosy encouraged him as she ran her fingers lightly across the intricate design.

Jackson, startled by the idea, remained silent.

"That would take all night. No time for pussy then," Hector joked which decided for him in the moment.

He nodded. "Okay," he gave his consent wondering how much it was going to hurt. Probably not nearly as much as his heart had already been.

Hector grinned at him, donned his unbuttoned shirt, and left with Big Rosy. He could hear them laughing and joking all the way down the hallway.

The slender tattoo artist turned to him. "I just have to get the stencil ready first. Then we can begin. Would you like a drink to dull the pain?"

"Sure," he said.

"Could you leave out the name Los Knights?" he asked as she was tracing the template onto the inked stencil that would be applied to his back.

"Sure. I could leave the rocker blank or put some other name there."

He was tempted. But it was far too dangerous.

"Leave it blank." He took a swallow of the decent bourbon. It was going to be a long night.

And it was.

A long night of listening to the strange, muffled cacophony of a whorehouse and the whirl of the tattoo gun as it traced over his skin. The pain was sharp at first, but the sense of being stuck by a thousand needles abated as he adjusted. He lay on his stomach, occasionally stopping for a quick gulp of an always filled tumbler of bourbon by the artist. The woman drank as well, water, from a large plastic bottle. She was relentless in her detailed work, explaining it was a big job and would take many hours.

As she worked, his mind drifted. At one point he fell asleep, surprising even the tattoo artist when she gently woke him up.

"Sorry, Señor Jackson, you must stay awake. I don't want to make a mistake on your tattoo if you move suddenly in your sleep."

As he was beginning to despair it would never be finished, she finally got up and said, "It is done. Some of my best work, I think. Would you like to see?"

He got up awkwardly, his limbs stiff.

"Yeah, sure."

She gave him a hand mirror and pointed to the larger one attached to the back wall. "Turn around and check it out."

He stared at his back. It was much more than he expected. Beautifully crafted, the dragon, knight, and sword all appearing surreal. It was one step away from being a gang tattoo. Something shifted in him as his eyes took in the vast changes. *What in the hell did it all mean?* He felt like he was being pushed onto a path. Life was changing—fast. He struggled to understand the hand of fate. Was he to blame for all the recent changes in his life? He had made love to another man's wife…

"Beautifully done. I thank you for all your efforts. It was a lot of work. What do I owe you?"

"Nothing. Our *padrino* will reimburse me."

"I insist. A tip," he said as he fished out a couple fifties from his pants pocket. "You did a beautiful job." *And how in the hell could all this work be taken off by laser?* It couldn't. Instead, he'd add the names of the women he loved.

"Thank you," she said shyly, her smile widening.

She spread a film of Vaseline and then laid plastic over his tattoo, taping the edges. Gave him oral and written instructions on how to look after it. He gingerly pulled on his shirt, feeling tender spots where more ink had been injected to complete the design.

"It'll heal quickly. You look very healthy," she said with a smile as she began cleaning up her station.

"Thanks. Do you have a business card I could show around? You do really great work."

She shook her head. "No, but maybe I should get some," she mused.

"Definitely. You'd get more clients that way. Charge more."

"Thanks," she said, looking happier than she had all night. Spending time in such an intimate way had created a temporary bond and he was happy to help her. Wasn't her fault he had been pushed into the tat. But had he been? *Really*? He could have refused. But then he'd have to explain not wanting free pussy.

He walked back into the main room, feeling a bit lightheaded. The feeling soon passed. He checked out Hector's soldiers slumped on chairs around the room that stunk of sweat and beer, looking much the worse for wear. Better to have spent time getting the tat. Most of the men were dosing and a couple of loud snores and snorts rattled the air.

"Where's Hector?" he asked one of the men he'd been introduced to yesterday as Joe. The man glanced up with red bleary eyes and noticed him.

"Not sure. I think he went home already. How's your tat? Hurts like a son of a bitch getting it done, eh," he said with a ghost of a grin. "Got mine years ago, but I gotta good memory."

"Not so bad. At least I'm in better shape than the rest of you even after an entire night of being under the needle."

"Yeah, we're a sorry lot this morning. Too much celebrating. Glad I don't have to pick up the tab. I can drive you home soon as I've had coffee if you want?"

"Sure, that works."

Joe got up and ambled over to a coffee bar, took a mug from the tray housing a couple of dozen, and poured a cup of black coffee.

"Want some?" he asked and turned back toward Jackson.

"Oh, yeah."

Jackson joined him and grabbed a white mug for Joe to fill noticing the logo of Big Rosy's printed in fancy black script along with a very dramatic outline of a curvy female figure. Joe filled the cup to the brim with the steaming liquid.

Two hot cups later and both men walked outside. The early morning air was cool but held promise of another scorcher. Jackson climbed in the passenger seat of the half ton while Joe took the wheel. Soon he would be back at the bungalow and be free to contact Rand. Tell him of the success.

———

HECTOR WAS DRINKING coffee in the kitchen nook, looking out at the stables as he did every morning when his *mamá* came into the kitchen. He was tired. Bone tired.

"Morning, my son," she said.

"Morning, *Mamá*," he said dutifully. She was looking tired as well, her shoulders stooped as she gave him a wan smile. His *mamá* was normally filled with vitality. A vitality that had kept her sharp for decades.

"Are you feeling okay?"

"I didn't sleep well," she said and poured herself a cup of coffee, added thick dairy cream that was delivered fresh daily to the mansion. She sat down across from him.

"This is my favorite time of day," she murmured before taking a sip.

"*Papá* liked this time of day as well. Remember how he would take us on his knee and tell us a story before going to work. I loved best the tall tale about the side-hill horses. The special breed of horses with one set of legs shorter so they could navigate our mountainous terrain. I believed him for many years."

They shared a smile at the comforting memory.

"Your *papá* was a good man. That's why what I have to tell you is so hard." She swiped away a tear. Hector sat his cup down and took her wrinkled hands in his. She still wore the simple gold band she had been given nearly forty years ago on her wedding day. He'd seen photographs. She had been a beautiful bride and his father had been proud and handsome as the pair posed for the photographer.

"What is it, *Mamá*? I can handle whatever it is you have to tell me."

She patted his hand before pulling hers away. "I know. You've been a good son, a very good son." She sighed softly, the sound slowly escaping from between her lips.

Her reluctance added to his concern.

"Are you well? Has the cancer returned?" he asked, allowing his biggest fear out in the open.

"No, no, nothing like that, my son. It concerns our family history." She bit her lips. He noticed she was less than well-groomed this morning. Her hair had been hastily pinned up and she wasn't dressed, but still in her robe.

"Please, tell me. You're worrying me," he urged.

"Your *papá* was a born rebel much like you. The first years of our marriage were difficult. I was very spoiled, like your Elena. Perhaps I am a bit jealous of her. I see how you care for her."

Hector was surprised by her admission but remained silent.

"We fought a lot at first. Fighting and making up and learning how to get along. Not uncommon for couples who marry so young. I was only sixteen. Then we had many years of peace after the babies started coming and I thought life would be fine. That we had outgrown our problems."

Hector nodded. He felt the same would happen for him and Elena. He wished she would prove to be pregnant this first month of their marriage, raking his brain as to her monthly schedule. It was possible. The next couple of days would tell the tale for certain.

"You've heard of the seven year itch?"

"Yes, but what has that to do with anything?"

"Your papá experienced it one summer though a couple of years late."

"Are you saying he had an affair?"

"Yes, with an outsider. A young woman from LA who came to visit some school friends one summer." His mother's lips became downturned with bitterness and sadness.

"*Mamá*, that was many years ago. Why bring it up now and torture yourself?" An affair wasn't that worrisome to Hector. His father was a macho man and it was not uncommon for a man to have a woman on the side. Sometimes many women.

"Jackson Banks has come back."

"I know. I put him up in one of our newly built homes." He frowned. "What has that to do with anything?"

"Have you noticed that Jackson looks a bit like you?" she asked bluntly, straightening up and looking him in the eyes.

"He just discovered he's half-Mexican. Are you saying that we're related in some way?"

"*Si*, I had investigators check it out. I'm fairly certain he's your half brother. Born of that affair. I'm sorry, my son. He even carries your father's name. Jackson *Antonio* Banks."

Hector pulled his hand away. Stunned.

Could it be true? His *mamá* was not impulsive. She had to be certain before she would share such a thing. Was this why he felt a certain affinity for Jackson? And allowing his strange code of ethics on not wanting to use a power that he coveted? It was not such a bad thing, he realized. It would bring the man closer. Of course, that meant Teresa could not be with him, something she wasn't going to want to hear. Should he tell him now of his heritage? Would it bring more loyalty? Perhaps better to hold the information back a bit longer. Things were running smoothly at the moment, Jackson appeared even more onboard now that he was here again, and the operation was going well in LA. The man has just been through the death of his murderous stepfather, discovering he's half-Mexican in the process, perhaps the timing was off. Wait a bit. He loved to hold cards close to his chest. Gave him satisfaction to play them at the right time —for him. The thoughts raced through his mind a million miles a second, as always.

"Why wasn't this discovered when I first investigated him?" Righteous anger fueled him.

"Perhaps no one was looking for this kind of information."

"Who else knows about this?"

"Only George, who I asked to help me discover the truth. His loyalty is beyond question."

"I thank you for bringing this to me, *Mamá*. I will think on it and decide when the time is right to tell him. Until then, please don't tell anyone else. Understood?"

"You're a wise man, my son. Your father, he was beguiled by a spoiled *puta*." Her tone had turned to one of disgust as she called Jackson's mother a whore.

"More coffee?" he asked as he got up to get himself another cup.

She nodded.

He sat down, placing the refilled cups on the tabletop, debating. "Jackson is no ordinary man."

"What do you mean? He's flesh and blood like the rest of you." She appeared annoyed and he smiled. Her children would always be the best. Like his would be in the years to come.

"Don't worry, *Mamá*. He's no more special than your children—just different."

"Less than with his mixed blood," she hissed. Then she crossed herself, looking slightly ashamed. "But I am grateful he helped my Teresa. And he does share our blood. It's not his fault who his parents are. Has this something to do with that?"

"Yes." And so he told her the tale, quid pro quo for her vital information. Her eyes widening as she listened.

"He's been touched," she said, awe tinging her tone. "His destiny ordained."

"Perhaps. But he has also been useful to me." He didn't believe in curses or superstition. Only results.

"Be careful, my son." She crossed herself once more. "But still, he shares our blood and I will try to overcome my concerns. If he continues to help his family—our family, he's a good man. Time will tell the tale."

—————

"YEAH, went down fine, Rand. It was exactly where you said the package would be." Jackson swallowed bile remembering what he had done. He winced as he leaned against the hard chair, coming into contact with the freshly inked flesh.

"I took another one for the team," he joked.

"Yeah?"

"Got a tattoo last night that covers my back. Dragon fighting a knight with his sword raised in valor."

"Really? Sounds like a Los Knights tattoo. What the hell!"

"There is no gang name attached. Calm down. It's only a tattoo. She did a great job."

"Did she sterilize? Fuck, Jackson, you could get hepatitis or even worse."

He sighed aloud. "Of course, they're not heathens."

"Yeah, well, remember who you're dealing with."

The unnecessary prejudice riled him. He was half-Mexican now. Then he realized Rand didn't know. What would he think? It was vastly different from being teased for his deep tan to being of a different race than was checked off on his birth certificate. The situation had shifted the very ground under his feet.

"Are you on your iPad?"

"Yeah."

"Check out this latest communique. I'm forwarding it right now."

"Okay." Jackson clicked on his encrypted web mail account, signed in. "The one from Johnson?"

"Yeah, he's not too happy about developments. The last shipment was a few grams of cocaine in a very stinky can. We let customs have the honor of searching it and he was assigned."

He could hear the grin. "Just a test. He's careful."

"Well, something spectacular better happen soon or we all may get pulled off the case. Less than a kilo does not a drug cartel arrest make. Fucking pathetic."

"It'll happen. Tell them to be patient. And you got me at this end watching things."

"I hope we don't have to go through another scenario like last night. That was nip and tuck. The guy had been dead for hours. If they had checked too closely, they would have seen that. We'd be up shit creek."

"You mean *I'd* be up shit creek."

"I haven't forgotten who's taken the most risks. In fact, wasn't I the one who said—*don't do it*?"

"Yeah. It's all on me."

"Besides, before I'd criticize a man, I'd want to walk a mile in his shoes. That way, I'm a mile away and I got his shoes!" As Jackson chuckled, Rand added, "I gotta go. Incoming from Catherine."

"Catherine! What the hell does she want?"

"Been sniffing around again. I can't seem to lose the bitch."

The words were out of character. "Want to tell me about it?"

"No. When you get back. Any idea when that will be?"

"Soon as I know when he's headed back. I want to be

there for the big one. Probably in a few days." *But did he?* He realized he was experiencing some reluctance at watching the bust that would destroy Hector now that he was getting to know him better. But then he thought of Elena.

"Stay in touch, okay?"

"Sure." Jackson hung up and stared at the screen looking at his new screensaver of a photo he'd found of Elena on the internet. She was heartbreakingly beautiful. She and Hector were at a charity fundraiser when it had been taken. He had his arm around her like she was his possession and looked straight ahead at the photographer as if warning him to back off.

He opened Photoshop and began to crop Hector out of the original digital image, working diligently to take out the offending arm and replace it with a cluster of flowers on the shoulder of her dress. He then uploaded the new one of just Elena standing by herself on his desktop. Much better. He could almost smell her exotic perfume. All female.

His cell phone rang. Hector.

"How's the back?"

"Healing."

"Wait till it starts to peel off in sheets in about a week's time," he warned with a smile in his tone.

It was a rare lighthearted moment. Jackson waited for the other shoe to drop.

"Want to take a road trip with me? I need to speak to a guy with important connections."

"Sure." This was *exactly* the kind of information the DEA most wanted.

"Good. We'll pick you up. Pack an overnight bag and bring your gun."

Thirty minutes later, Jackson watched the mountainous terrain ebb and flow with its ragged ravines and a spattering of lakes, a yellow-green blanket far as the eye could see from the aircraft as they made their way deeper into the heart of Mexico. He spotted the giveaway pink color of opium crops dotting the landscape. The double engine plane, piloted by Joe, the guy who'd driven him home from Big Rosy's. He seemed competent enough behind the controls as the plane efficiently sliced through the air, the steady hum of the engines soothing to the soul.

Joe was a cautious man, patted him down before he was allowed to embark, giving a *nothing personal* comment as he did so. Five other men had clamored into the back with Jackson while Hector sat up front with the pilot. All were heavily armed. Jackson had brought the handgun he'd fired the night before, a solemn reminder.

They flew for an hour, landing on a dirt field with lush green crops standing proudly in every direction as far as the eye could see.

"Welcome to the *Golden Triangle* where fortunes are ripe for the picking," Hector joked. Jackson racked his brain to remember all he could. He was somewhere bordered by the states of Sinaloa, Durango, and Chihuahua. Run by the Sinaloa cartel since 1989 far as he knew. Their last leader had been arrested in January of this year and it was suspected that a guy named Ismael would be taking over. What were they doing here? In a rival cartel's territory? On the land of the largest cartel?

Everyone disembarked, hoisted their guns attached to thick straps onto their shoulders, and picked up their duffel bags. The followed their leader into the jungle, trained and alert for any movement like a scene right out of the movie *Platoon*. Jackson felt apprehension building with each stride. He was surrounded by ready to harvest onion plants, their pungent odor filling his nostrils.

"Why are we in another cartel's territory?" Jackson

asked finally, the tension building as sweat dripped into his eyes from the heat and humidity. The stench was overpowering. *Fuckin' onions.* The other men seemed fine with the heat. He wished his Mexican side would kick in and give him a break.

"You think we don't work together when it's in our best interests?" Hector said. They walked side by side, the other soldiers behind them in single file as they navigated the partially cleared path that the onion crops were encroaching on.

"I thought competition was fierce," Jackson said.

"It is. But I have some information to sell. And you're going to help me. This is the day you must step up and earn my complete trust. Have my back if it's required. You can't suck and blow at the same time, bro. Time to decide."

"Thought I had already done that. I have the sore back to prove it," he said lightly. *Bro?* Hector appeared smug this morning, giving him a quick smile. His gut roiled. How deep was he going to be pulled in now?

"I may need far more from you today. I may need your power demonstrated. Are you up for it?" he asked.

Jackson stopped in his tracks and another man bumped into him from behind. *Cursed.*

"That's never been the deal."

"Deals change in Mexico all the time. Just be ready. These men are powerful and have far less scruples than my soldiers."

"Then why are we here?" Jackson felt trapped, unable to take a full breath.

"Power and money. What else is there?" Hector glanced at him, his dark eyes gleaming.

They came to a clearing. A larger group of armed men awaited them, standing around the only man seated on a chair. He got up as they approached. A hard man, lean of body with slicked black hair above a round face, graying mustache and goatee, with a deadly serious look. He stepped forward and shook Hector's hand. He was dressed in similar clothes to his men, camouflage patterned cotton pants and shirts. Nothing fancy. Nothing to suggest his money or his power. "Come, we can talk as we walk."

"Jackson, join us," Hector instructed. "The rest of you —wait here."

The man looked at Hector but did not intervene.

The two groups faced off.

The trio walked a few hundred feet back to the edge of the onion field.

"You wanted to talk, Hector. Go ahead. We are not being taped. You have my personal guarantee."

"Jackson, I want you to meet El León. A very old and dear friend of mine."

The two men nodded at each other.

"You must be special for this man to make you part of this."

Jackson had no idea of how to answer that and stood silent.

"Jackson has my trust. And he's a big part of my plans for the future. He has close ties to the United States with his American citizenship."

"That's an advantage," the man acknowledged.

"And he works for US Customs as a special investigator. He's able to help me move much more product."

"What's your family name?" he asked, peering closely at Jackson.

"Banks, but I recently learned my real father is Mexican. Comes from Ojinaga, same as Hector here. I don't know his name yet." It was at that moment he realized he could still be alive and living in the town. His heart rate increased. He had some digging of his own to do.

"You know where the name *gringo* comes from, Jackson?"

He shook his head.

"Green—go. The caps of the men from *el Norte* who stole our land were a bastard shade of green." He spit on the ground in disgust. Then turned to Hector and addressed him directly.

"We have the geographical advantage in our beautiful Golden Triangle. Blood ties to our farmers, fertile land that grows the best poppy and marijuana plants, over four hundred miles of Pacific coastline, the Sierra's as a vast natural barrier, the port of Mazatlán and big cities to launder our proceeds. What more is there? What can you offer me? Another customs agent? Not nearly enough to make me interested. I need something new, something more. I want power, like you, Hector. You say you want more product. You can have more product. Move more product. Make us both more money. But more than that —" He shrugged.

"Jackson can offer far more than just his help in the states. He's not like us. He can do things that give him the advantage. He saved my Teresa's life."

"I am sorry to hear of her troubles. What could he do for her that the doctors could not?"

Jackson's throat constricted as he recognized the corner he was being shoved into. Help Hector. Or they would likely die right here in the onion field.

"He restarted her heart."

"Everyone can do that with a defibrillator these days." El León gave them both a scathing look.

"Not with an electric device, but with only his own mind."

"What do you mean?" he frowned. Suspicion narrowed his eyes.

"He has a power. A special power that brought him to

my attention." He went on to briefly sketch out events that led to their meeting. Jackson's dread grew.

"I don't believe it." El León became angry. "You're fucking with me and no one fucks with me!" His voice rose. The men caught his tone downwind. *Danger*.

"You must show him, Jackson. Demonstrate it," Hector urged.

Jackson shook his head.

"You promised me your full support. It's now or never. Show this fine man or it's all over between us. The deal will be off on my not involving Leia. Show him by doing it to me."

"What? No! You don't want to experience it, Hector. That would be wrong. It could harm you. Harm your heart—maybe permanently. I don't know exactly how it works or what it does. It's never been tested by doctors." Though he knew Leia was safely hidden away, still, hearing her name was painful.

And the idea of using his ability yet once again, beyond loathsome. But then, underneath his protests he became aware that something darker lurked. He had carte blanche to hurt the man who had hurt Elena. Tempting.

"What bullshit is this?" El León was getting livid, his face flushed. Something had to be done or the Mexican standoff would be over in moments with lethal consequences for both sides.

"It's not bullshit," Jackson said calmly. "I can do as Hector says. I just don't want to harm anyone."

"For fuck's sake, Jackson, do it or we're all dead!" Hector ordered. "You want that on your conscience?"

Trapped.

The very thing he did not want to do.

You'd be saving lives. The voice of reason came out of the worry, pain, and anguish. What else was there to do?

He glanced at Hector, unbelieving at how easily he had been tricked, made a fool of.

He closed his eyes.

Focused.

"No. *Stop!*" El León shouted at the last second. "Such a demonstration is best on a soldier. Not on a king." The gleam in his eyes suggested he thought what was going to happen was a sham anyway and he wanted to prove it. Jackson did not like being doubted. Bad enough to have to do such a thing, worse to have it thrown back in his face like he was a fucking shyster, a trickster. A Loki from legend as his sister would say.

"Are you fine with a soldier of my choosing?" he asked.

Jackson warred with himself. Shit happens and he was up to his neck in it anyway. He reluctantly nodded.

"Juan, come over here!" El León shouted at his troops.

A man immediately broke away from the ranks and trotted over.

"Do it to him," El León said while pointing at him.

"Prepare yourself," Jackson said with an apologetic expression. "I'm afraid this is going to hurt."

Juan's eyes widened. Uncertain of what was being asked of him.

Jackson began to focus again, searching for the beast inside.

He released it and sent a smaller charge into the man, praying it wasn't too much.

The soldier looked bewildered and grabbed at his chest, before dropping like a stone, the look of agony on his face only adding to Jackson's guilt.

He glanced at the pair of kingpins. While Hector looked smug, the Lion looked contemplative.

"How long does the effect last?"

"I'm not sure. I've seldom done it."

"Why not?"

"It's just fucking wrong."

El León's eyebrows rose. "An ethical man. Don't see many of them in our business," he murmured.

The soldiers waiting were getting unnerved. A few stragglers began to move closer, obviously wondering what they were supposed to be doing about the strange events unfolding right before their eyes.

El León left his man on the ground and strode back to his troops. Jackson crouched down beside the stricken soldier. "Are you all right?" he asked.

Juan gritted his teeth but allowed Jackson to give him a hand up from the ground, beads of sweat standing out starkly on his pale, clammy skin. They trickled down his cheeks and dripped off his chin. "What the fuck was that? What did you do to me?" He bristled with a tired anger as he lurched to his feet.

"I'm not exactly sure, but I can somehow interrupt the electrical impulses to the heart. Sorry, man. I had to do it."

Juan shook his head, still pissed off. He slowly made his way back to his group, trying to hide his pain as he limped across the grass, occasionally stumbling.

"Excellent, Jackson," Hector said with satisfaction, rubbing his hands together.

Jackson was not prepared to talk about it. He had just done something he never wanted to do, but damn if he'd die in an onion field in Mexico like he was planted in a Joseph Wambaugh novel.

El León came striding back, all smiles after settling with his men.

"Come!" he said with an expansive welcome. "We go back to my home and have refreshments."

Jackson silently followed the line of men down a winding path that led past more pungent onion fields.

Where were the distinctive red and purple blossoms of the poppy flowers with their fat opium-filled bulb? So far this guy just appeared an onion farmer. Not a drug kingpin.

Over cold beers, sitting around a vast living room with Hector and their host while the soldiers made off to some other area of the hacienda, he asked the question nagging at him, "Where do you grow the poppy?"

"Ah, you needn't worry about that. We have many connections to small farmers willing to take the risk of growing fine crops of the poppy to support their families hidden deep in the gorges and valleys of these fine mountains. Then, other men, smaller traffickers, they take the risk of turning the opium paste into powder. Everyone has a job, a share in the supply chain, and everyone prospers. It's an ancient tradition in Mexico. One hand washes the other," El León said, sitting back with supreme satisfaction on his couch. "But, until today, I never thought to see such a thing. It is a rare gift you have, Jackson Banks."

"More like a curse," Jackson muttered and took a swig of his beer. The heat had left him parched and tired. Off his game.

Hector took a few puffs on his freshly lit cigar. "Know who said, *See, ya are what ya are in this world. That's either one of two things: Either ya somebody or ya ain't nobody.*" He went on without waiting for an answer, "You got to make up your mind what you want to be, Jackson. Sometimes a man has to step up and do the hard thing. The right thing for his family. Be a somebody. No mileage in being a nobody."

"True, Hector. Well said." The Lion nodded his head sagely as he puffed on his cigar. The room was beginning to stink like a den of iniquity. He continued, "*American*

Gangster's Frank Lucas to answer your question. Unfortunately, life's not a movie."

"No. It's a fucking war," Jackson said. Exhaustion and being used made him cranky as hell.

"Doesn't have to be," El León said as he contemplated the lit end of his cigar that burned red in the dim of the room. Somewhere a radio or television set was playing, the artificially animated voice droning on. "We pull together, cache our resources"—he gave a pointed look at Jackson—"and take over the rest of the lion's share in Mexico. Hell, no limit to what we can do. Just like there's no limit for the appetite for our product in *el Norte*, eh." He gave himself a congratulatory pat on the back.

Jackson wasn't surprised. The man knew he was a valuable commodity. Was making a play for him.

"I need to speak with you alone, El León," Hector said.

"Sure, sure. Be right back. Make yourself at home, Jackson. Anything you need—just ask." The predator smile was not helping.

The men were gone for a good ten minutes. Jackson finished his beer and contemplated having another from the dozen lined up on the coffee table, frosty dew running down the sides of the deep-brown bottles over their colorful labels to pool on the glass tabletop below.

The two men finally walked back in, both looking at him with speculation. *What now?* They had shared something he would dearly love to know, he felt it right down to his bones. *Fuck.* It was a long way from LA to the middle of fucking nowhere Mexico. Soon as the meet went down next week, he was done with all this. Time to get his life back on track. Get away from all the craziness.

CHAPTER 19

"I WANT TO TALK WITH JACKSON—ALONE," HECTOR SAID, giving the nod to his family in the library. They had gathered there after a late dinner and were enjoying coffee and sweet liqueurs. The trip back from the onion fields had been uneventful.

"Of course," his mother murmured, got up, and led the exodus. Jackson watched Elena glide from the room as if she were the lead in a ballet troupe, her grace quickening his breath. He understood for the first time how it felt to be addicted. Unfortunately, it was to another man's wife.

"Life is a strange game of roulette, I think," Hector said as he swirled the golden brandy around in the sniffer. He took a swallow.

"Long as it's not *Russian*," he said with an edge to his tone. Every moment he spent in Mexico could be his last. He had to keep his guard up, not be lulled into a sense of normalcy. Nothing normal about this situation.

Hector gave a harsh laugh. "You're much more use to me alive, Jackson. Settle your mind on that score."

"I want to look for my father," he said, not realizing he was going to say it beforehand. But it was the closeness of his host's family that called to him. Even with the illicit activity of the family, still, it was obvious they would defend its members against the outside world. To the death. He wanted a part of that. Always had desired to be in a large family. It had all been stolen from him and Elena when they were so very young.

"I understand," Hector said, nodding his head wisely.

"Ojinaga is not a large place. Surely it couldn't be that hard to track down someone who would know something." He knew he needed some help, and Hector was the key to speeding things up.

"I'll see what I can do. In the meantime, I want you to talk to your sister. Get her to arrange to join you in your new home. We must have a party. To celebrate the two newest members of the Torres clan joining us."

"Adopted members," Jackson reminded him. Leia was staying put.

"You are becoming like a blood brother to me, Jackson. More than simply 'adopted.' Now, I must share a story with you, to help you realize the history of this place. I warn you it's not a pleasant story, but it is important that you know it and understand where we come from."

Jackson sat up straighter in his easy chair and swallowed the last of his drink. Hector reached out and poured him another, ignoring the negative shake of his head.

"You will need this. Trust me." He added a full measure of brandy to his own snifter and sat back in his chair, contemplating the sparkling amber liquid before beginning his tale.

"The Torres family has deep roots in Ojinaga that go

back more than a hundred and fifty years. My forefathers were peasant farmers, lived in dirt floor shacks, grew the poppy, and sold it to buy a life for themselves and their families. It worked for the most part eking out a poor living. They were never going to get rich, but it was better than going down into the dark dusty coal mines as you work the land that nature provides and breathe in the fresh air and feel the sun on your face. An honest living, one my grandfather inherited. But he wanted more for his sons—wanted them to prosper and have a better life. Slowly, he got all the local farmers to sell to him. Persuaded them that he would be the one to obtain the best prices for everyone. A co-operative of sorts. And to deal with paying off the people that would ensure their protection. But one other family, Perez, had the same idea and conflict between the two families broke out. Retribution for buying from the wrong farmer was swift and deadly."

Hector took a drink, his expression far away.

"Something had to be done. Blood was being spilled and crops destroyed. No money to be made that way. Boundaries had to be worked out. There was a sit-down in neutral territory. Rules agreed upon. But the black sheep of the Perez family was not satisfied. Wanted it all. Greedy *fucker*. To drive his point home in the dead of night he had his thugs kill all the sons of one of our families. Hung them in front of their shack for all the world to see. Raped the daughters and left them alive to tell the tale. One poor girl had a child from this devastation and her father drowned it in the river. Madness. Then we come to my father's generation."

Hector once more stopped, his expression as grim as one carved from the coldest granite. Flint sparked behind his eyes.

"My father believed in fair play. A good man, he

talked truce. Talked about laying the bloodshed aside and beginning anew. But he also knew the culprit—the man behind the killing had to be avenged. There was a raid and a Perez son was captured and killed. Retribution for his sins. But it turns out the intel was wrong. They killed the wrong son. That left the black sheep still alive. Of course, he plotted revenge. Tricked my father into going down to the river and murdered him in cold blood on the banks of the Rio Grande."

"I am very sorry for your loss," Jackson murmured, horrified at the tale. "How old were you?"

"A young boy of twelve. I vowed upon hearing of the death to make all the bastards pay. But I ended up following the more peaceful way of my father and married a Perez family member, one of his daughters, to guarantee their continued allegiance."

Shocked, Jackson could only stare at Hector for a long moment. "Elena is a Perez," he finally said as if in a dream.

"Yes," Hector bit off his one-word answer. He abruptly changed the subject. "You have little time to get Leia here before I must go to LA on business. See that it is done, Jackson, no more delays. She can obtain treatment at our new hospital and live with her brother. You will both be better for it."

Back in his new house, Jackson sat in the dark by the open window and looked out across the land. The lights of the Torres mansion gleamed in the distance. He wondered which light led to Elena. Like the Great Gatsby watching Daisy's house from the dock, it haunted him. He worried for her—now more than ever. Hector had reason to hate her. Her father had killed his.

———

A SOFT KNOCK on his front door. He was wrapped in a towel, shaving at the bathroom sink. He put his razor down and hurried to the bedroom, pulled on a pair of pants and grabbed his pistol from the nightstand. All senses alert, he padded to the door. Hector always told him when he was arriving and this did not fit that pattern.

He peered through the peephole.

Elena.

He took a deep breath and opened the door, aware of his scarred bare chest. Nothing she had not seen before.

"I had to see you," she said as she came inside, her hands filled with a large vase filled with an array of flowers, her excuse for the visit.

He closed the door behind her, tucked the gun in the small of his back, and took the flowers from her trembling hands before they could fall on the floor.

"What's wrong?"

"Nothing—everything! You must go back to the states. It's dangerous for you here in Mexico."

"Why? What's changed?"

"I'm pregnant."

"Does Hector know?"

"It's not his. His sperm—they're not viable. I am ashamed, but I had it checked at the hospital where I worked by a trusted friend. I refuse to have his children. It did make marrying him easier and I guess I hoped he might throw me out if I produced no sons." She blushed pink while a defiant expression entered her eyes as she shared the subterfuge. "He was kicked by a horse in the groin many years ago—I think that's when it happened. If he *ever* finds out we're both dead. I can't chance it. I love you so much I will let you go. You *must* leave Mexico immediately and not come back. Promise me!"

Stunned, Jackson stood perfectly still for a moment

and felt the ground drop away from his feet. He teetered on the edge looking into the abyss for a split second before he gathered the remnants of his thoughts and before the abyss claimed him.

"No! I won't let you go this alone. We'll find a way. I promise you. There's a way to get you away from him."

"You know it can't be done." She shook her head violently, her long hair swaying side to side.

He grabbed her by both arms to calm her, looked into her eyes. "I love you. I will not leave you." He realized the truth as he spoke it.

She began to cry; big tears ran down her cheeks unchecked. "No! You must go home. He will kill you—us —if he ever finds out."

"Then he won't find out. I didn't tell you this before, but we're in the middle of a sting operation to bring Hector down. Once that happens, you'll be safe. Your whole family will be safe from him when he's in prison. They'll never let him out. You can come live with me in LA. We can make a home together. A life together. Take in some of your family."

"A sting operation?" She pulled away, her expression a mix of overwrought emotions that tugged sharply at his heart.

"Yes. The DEA's involved. It's all going to all work out just fine. Trust me, Elena."

She shook her head. "No, it won't. Hector's too smart. He'll suspect and do the unexpected. No, *please, please* drop this thing and go home. Live your life. Forget about me."

"Never."

"What about Leia? Doing this thing could endanger her."

"She's safe. At a facility in another state."

"Hector has a long reach." She shook her head with

despair, biting her lips nervously. "No, fate has been kind; I have a part of you inside me now. Please, don't take chances. I'll be fine—"

"I hate to interrupt this touching scene, but time is ticking by."

Startled, Jackson turned on a dime, instantly placing his body between Elena and the intruder to act as a shield.

"What the fuck are you doing here, Joe?" Jackson demanded.

"More to the point, what are you two doing?" Joe had a gun pointed at them. A semi-automatic AK-47 rifle. It struck a deep chord of fear into him. If timing was everything, this moment sucked.

Just one man? But his finger was on the trigger and he couldn't take the chance with Elena.

"What do you want?" Jackson asked.

"All will be clear in a couple of minutes. Looks like we got two for the price of one." He grinned, exposing crooked front teeth. "Shut up and don't move."

The sounds of a helicopter landing and other boots stomping on the floor dashed any hope of getting away easily. A half dozen of El León's men faced them, heavily armed.

"Okay, get moving!" Joe commanded. He backed it up with a gesture of his rifle toward the back of the house.

"Could I at least put a shirt and shoes on first?" Jackson asked.

"No time," Joe said, glanced down at the thick scars on his chest and then relented. "Okay, grab something and let's go."

Jackson took Elena's hand, tugging her down the hallway to his bedroom. They would only have a moment before the others would be there. "When I say 'run,' you run like hell back to the house," he whispered in her ear. Her eyes wide, she nodded. He grabbed a shirt and thrust his feet into a pair of boots as two of the men watched from the doorway.

Never allow yourself to be taken to a second location.

The words burned into him. He kept his expression guarded as he walked toward the two men in the doorway, Elena on his heels. Soon as they were all in a group and headed into whatever transportation was supplied, he would strike. He turned the corner out of the bedroom. Down the hallway they went, found the others waiting in the kitchen that led out the back door to their transportation—a sleek black helicopter, about a hundred yards away.

Fifty yards away.

Thirty yards away. A pilot waited in the cockpit. *How close did he need to be?*

Ten yards—nine—eight.

He gathered his resources waiting for the right moment.

Just as he was set to unleash hell a sharp jab in his neck. *What the fuck?* The bastards had injected him with something. Overcome with wooziness, he was half carried and half thrown into the belly of the beast. Elena! In a few moments everyone was onboard, crowding him in. He felt the lurch of the helicopter rising into the air, then his vision darkened and he knew no more.

———————

HE DRIFTED SLOWLY up through the choppy levels of consciousness, his head throbbing, ready to split wide open and spill its contents. He coughed. It made his head hurt more if that was even possible, his mouth parched and his limbs lethargic. Near useless. He tried to sit up but fell back on the bed. *Elena.* Worry charged his blood stream. He forced his burning eyes open. He was alone in the room. Where was she?

He forced himself to sit up. The room was about ten by twelve feet with a door ajar that led to a bathroom, menacing bars on the windows. A couple of bottles of water stood on a wooden crate near the bed and he reached over, grabbed one. Downed it in a few thick gulps, wincing at the pain in his raw throat and aching head. What the hell had been in that cocktail they'd injected him with?

The door burst open and Joe stood grinning at him.

"Cinderella's finally awake."

"What the fuck are you doing this for? Hector will have your head," he predicted, anger edging his tone.

"No fucking chance of that. El León runs the biggest empire in all of Mexico. Hector's a small fish, gringo."

"Hector's a cunning man with a long memory. A bad man to cross."

"Yeah, well he doesn't pay what El León does. Hector's gotten soft, it's all about the family—*his* family and helping the community. Wasting money on hospitals and funeral parlors and free help instead of paying us— his soldiers more. I will be a rich man now," he crowed.

"Is it worth it, always having to look over your shoulder for the rest of your life?"

Joe looked abashed for a second then shrugged it off. "With what I know about you and Elena—that she's carrying your kid, I think it's more *you* who should be worried for his life. He's not going to take too kindly to being made a goat of."

"Where is she? Is she all right?" Instant dread filled him. *If they had harmed her in any way.*

"She's fine. Don't worry, she won't be hurt. Not if you do what El León says."

"I want to talk with her. Make sure she's all right."

Joe shook his head. "Not my call. Clean yourself up." He abruptly left and Jackson heard the door being locked behind him.

He stood up and the room swam for a few seconds. With pure strength of will power he forced himself to walk the short distance to the bathroom. It was rudimentary, a shower stall, sink and toilet. It would do. He stripped his clothes off, lamented the loss of his gun, and got under the tepid water flow, letting it try to wash away his sins.

Clean, he stepped out and dried himself off with a towel from the rack. Rubbed his upper arm where they had implanted the GPS. Was it working? Or had his fucking ability shorted it out? It could mean the difference between life and death. In the small tin mirror he saw the reflection of a man on the edge. He turned away and finished up before dressing in the same clothes. They felt clammy, made his skin itch, but they were all he had.

He went and fetched another bottle of water from the stash. Downed it. Feeling more human, he went to one of the small windows and looked out between the thick metal bars. Green fields as far as the eye could see. His spirits sank. Back in the onion fields.

Jackson slumped on the one wooden chair the room possessed, bracing his feet on a small table. A ceiling fan whirled overhead valiantly trying to make up for the lack of air conditioning. Nothing to do but wait. The room possessed not one extra amenity to keep his mind distracted.

He drifted.

His mind went back over the last weeks, days, and moments of his life. More had happened than in all the thirty-five years previous. With the good, had come the bad. Karma could be a bitch wasn't just a saying. But there had to be a way out of this mess. And damn, he was going to find it. If he could survive a demented and twisted stepfather, cheat death, surely, he could find a way clear for him and Elena. And their baby. A child. He shook his head in wonder. He couldn't dwell on how precious that was now. He had to be ready. Be prepared.

CHAPTER 20

THE SOUND OF HEAVY FOOTFALLS AND THE DOOR BEING unlocked. It sprung wide open.

"Get up. Time to see the boss," Joe said, motioning with his rifle to precede him out the door.

Jackson walked along a path obviously well-worn from hundreds of footsteps having packed the earth flat, taking in his surroundings. A different view from his last visit. He was at the back of the Lion's mansion, housed in one of many whitewashed concrete units that littered the property. Apparently, they sprung up haphazardly when needed. *What disgusting deeds had gone on behind the bars of these rundown buildings?*

He was marched into the same living room as his first visit, El León already seated comfortably on the sofa, every slicked black hair perfectly in place, his round face with the graying mustache and goatee expressionless. He gestured for Jackson to take a seat. Joe stood standing, gun at the ready.

"Jackson Banks," he said.

Jackson nodded a curt greeting. He sat across from the drug kingpin, a coffee table all that lay between them.

"I'm certain you know why you're here," he said.

"Not rocket science," Jackson said with a grimace.

The Lion gave a snort of laughter. "No, it is not. Joe, you may leave."

Joe frowned, but obeyed, stomping from the room.

"Of course, you know what I can do to your Elena if you don't cooperate. Turn her into a drug addict and have her sold off to a brothel. She'd bring a pretty penny. But that would be a shameful thing to do to such a beautiful woman. She's a precious commodity in Mexico—a former beauty queen." His mild tone made the words all that more chilling.

Jackson's guts began churning with a fiery seething anger, a volcano about to explode. It was all he could do not to get up and choke the last shred of life out of the disgusting worm. If it was just him, he would strike. Now. But he had no idea where Elena was and couldn't take the chance. And now that their secret was out, she needed his protection more than ever.

"And how long does this indenture period last? At least those working of the cost of their passages to the Americas only lasted seven years."

"A well-read man, I like that." The Lion leaned forward, tented his fingers. "We have much to offer each other. A man with your gifts—a rare commodity. I am a man of immense power and wealth. I run a business ten times as big as Hector Torres or any other drug lord." He said Hector's name with dismissal, his hubris obvious, and went on in a more persuasive tone of voice. "Join forces with me and I can offer you a very good life. A life of luxury that can far exceed any expectations you may have had."

"Yeah, and a life of constantly looking over my shoulder."

"True, but with your ability to stop men in their

tracks, you should have little difficulty in staying safer than most."

"How do you do this?" Jackson asked, spreading his arms wide.

"What do you mean?" the man was genuinely flummoxed by the question.

"Live with all the pain and suffering your choices have caused others?"

His black eyes narrowed with steely intent. "A man does what he can with what he has. I make no apologies. I was born here, and I will die here. I have clawed my way through the muck for everything that I have now. Nothing was ever handed to me. Nothing. You take or you lose. What are you, Jackson? A taker or a loser?"

Silence. What was there to say to such a thing?

The man got up and went to the bar. Poured a drink and drank it down.

"Drink?" he asked.

Jackson shook his head. He needed to stay sharp.

"Okay, here's the deal. You work for me and your woman stays safe. We will set you up in a nice home nearby. What do you American's call it? Yes, a 'starter home.' If things go well, you will be well paid and your bank account will grow each week, regardless of how many times I have called upon your services. Say, in six months' time, if you still want to leave us, you and Elena are free to go. Do we have a deal?"

Jackson's turn to be flummoxed.

How could he agree to such a thing? But then he thought of the time he would have with Elena. Days and nights in each other's arms. *No.* He shook his head. They would be in prison no matter how much luxury it held. But the idea crept into his mind, planted a seed. Of course, he could appear to agree, await his chance.

Everyone slipped up. They wouldn't be at this juncture otherwise.

"I suppose you're surprised. You know I don't have to offer you this. I could, of course, just keep you here and keep the pair of you apart. Make you work for nothing for all the years you have left. But you're an American, a man I want on my payroll that's satisfied by his treatment. Your gift—your power is invaluable. I think it best we work together on terms we can both live with. See— I'm not an unreasonable man. Not a monster like you think."

Jackson could not deny his last statement. No point. It was true. "Okay. Let's give it a try—take it one day at a time." At least he could verify that Elena was okay.

"Excellent. I will have someone show you to your new home. She's waiting for you there. You'll start working for me tomorrow. A short honeymoon, si. Enjoy." His wolfish grin said it all.

Joe ended up being the one to escort him. The men strode silently down the path, the sturdy foliage that lined it thick and working to reclaim the land. They came to a clearing and a house came into view. An elegant one-story structure, surreal, a hidden oasis discovered in the rainforest.

"This is it." Joe grunted and turned to leave, his gun dangling from a strap over his shoulder. He really did look like an average Joe though one thing set him apart. A thin scar seamed one cheek, narrowing missing his right eye.

Jackson said nothing but continued up the path that had now changed to cobblestone under his feet. The front door was painted red. The color of passion. He turned the doorknob, and his breath stilled.

"Jackson!" Elena sprang from the sofa, a tissue

clutched in her hand, her eyes teary and red-rimmed as she ran toward him.

A few months of this guaranteed. If such a thing existed. But a gilded cage is still a cage. He couldn't face it, but that quandary waited for another day.

He took her into his arms feeling her warm, precious body against his. Held on for dear life.

"Are you all right?" he asked, finally using his thumb to swipe away the tears on her soft cheeks.

She nodded. "Fine. I wasn't drugged or anything. I was so worried. What's going on? Why have they taken us? Do they want money from Hector? Are we being ransomed?"

"No, unfortunately, it's not about money. It's about my ability, he wants to exploit it. He says he'll pay me for six months and then we can leave together."

"And you believe him?" Hope stirred in the depths of her eyes.

"I don't know him well enough yet to say for certain." He couldn't say how much he distrusted the man and worry her even more.

"What are we going to do?"

Suspecting the room was bugged, he leaned down and whispered a warning in her ear pretending it was a kiss. He straightened back up to answer her question.

"We do as he asks. We have this nice home, time together. Things will unfold as they will. No point in stressing it, beautiful. It's not good for you."

She nodded her head with understanding of the need to be careful of who was listening.

"Are you hungry?" he asked. His stomach was rumbling a warning.

"A little," she admitted.

"I'll make you something to eat if the kitchen is stocked," he promised.

"A man that cooks," she mocked. "I need to see this."

It was so good to see her eyes brighten and lose some of their sadness. He wanted to spend his life eradicating every last bit of it.

He found a carton of eggs in the refrigerator along with an onion—figures—a couple of peppers, butter, and a brick of cheese. The freezer compartment held a loaf of bread. Perfect.

"What can I do?" she asked.

"Sit. Watch the show."

He smiled at her as she perched on one of the kitchen stools lined up alongside the island. The kitchen was just the right size and he soon had the sweet onions and red peppers simmering in butter, figuring that they both could use extra fuel. Did women still eat for two? The smells enticed his taste buds and his mouth watered while he scrambled up the eggs, added a dash of cream, then poured them over the onions. Hash was quicker than an omelet. He grated the cheese and put the toast into the toaster soon as the cheese was added to the pan. It was all in the timing.

He pulled two dinner plates from the cupboard, then rinsed and dried them with a tea towel before divvying up the colorful mixture between them. The toast popped, added its warm and inviting aroma to the room. He quickly buttered it, adding it to the pile of food. He sashayed to the table and set it down. He'd do anything to make her smile and not worry about the danger they were in. He'd become the best actor in the world if that was what it took.

"Milady, may I present Jackson's famous cheesy eggs."

"Thank you," she whispered. Her eyes brimmed with tears.

"Are you okay?" He was at her side immediately, pulling her against him.

"I'm fine. It's just so nice to be treated this way," she confessed, laying her head against his chest.

He sucked up his instant sadness and hugged her before instructing, "Eat! You're skin and bone, woman."

He got a small smile for his silliness.

"With what, my fingers?" she asked playfully.

He had forgotten the cutlery. But before he could get up, she flew out of her chair and began yanking drawers open in the race to find some.

"Yes!" she said as she discovered her quarry. She brought forks and knives back to the table and plunked them down.

"I also forgot something to drink. Water okay?"

"Sure."

He fetched two bottles of water from the refrigerator.

"Okay, I think we're finally set."

"Thank you, Jackson. Is it all right if I say grace?" she asked.

Surprised, he nodded. "Sure."

She reached for his hand, bowed her head, and murmured a few words of thanks.

"And thank you God for this precious time with the love of my life."

She turned to him. "One moment with you is worth a lifetime with him."

Her words touched him deeply. How had he gotten so lucky as to meet such an incredible woman? *God, please help me to keep her safe.* He whispered his first real prayer in years. It felt good and he was able to relax enough to enjoy the food. He needed his strength, though it seemed this time with Elena, too good to be true. The specter of death and being torn away from the woman he loved hung over him. *Hell, he would walk across hot coals to be with her.* Each moment was more than precious.

———

BEN LEANED against the doorjamb leading into Leia's room. High. She could see it in his overly bright eyes though he tried to hide it under the brim of his baseball hat. The craving to use made her skin crawl. She sat up on the edge of the bed and pulled on her sneakers, tying the laces tightly. Her fingers trembled uncontrollably, making the task all the harder.

He came in, kneeled down at her feet, and took over the job.

"You can join me if you like. It will help with the shakes."

She pursed her lips, torn and indecisive.

"Are you carrying now?" she whispered. The very walls seemed to have ears in this place. It was suffocating, squeezing the life out of her since Ben had begun using again.

He shook her head, and she didn't know whether to be relieved or disappointed. "All out. But I'm headed down to the lake to feed the geese. Want to come with?"

"Sure." Exercise always helped get her mind off the pain. *Why was life so fucking painful?* It was still a mystery to her after weeks of therapy. Sometimes, like a swimmer raising their head about the pool to breathe, she saw a shimmer of hope in the distance, a fleeting vision of how it was supposed to be before she slipped under the water and it closed over her head, sending her right back to the murky bottom.

She followed him, finding it difficult to keep up once they made the path that led through the trees. "What's the rush? The geese aren't going anywhere."

He turned, looking impatient with her lagging behind. "Just want to get there sometime today."

What was the matter with him anyway? One minute he could be so sweet and the next a complete dork. She wondered if she should turn back and take a yoga class instead. Would serve him right. She hesitated, earning an impatient frown from Ben.

"Come on, Leia. I have a surprise waiting for you. Something I want to give you."

"A present?" she asked, perking up. She loved presents.

"Yeah, sure. Come on. We're almost there."

She increased her speed, feeling the ache in her calves. But the sprint had also released endorphins into her system and she felt better as they neared the lake. That was until she saw who waited for them as they left the protection of the trees and bushes.

CHAPTER 21

HECTOR STORMED INTO JACKSON'S HOUSE WITH GEORGE AND Thomas riding his heels. The door slammed shut behind them. He looked around the room, sweeping it for clues. A vase of flowers drew his eyes. Elena.

"Anyone seen Joe?" he barked, his anger causing his heart rate to soar and his guts to churn.

"No, no one, but Garcia spilled he was bragging about finding a new job that would make him a rich man."

"*Fuck*, with no ransom note and no phone call, I have to assume the worst. The target was Jackson. Why did I take him to see El León? Now Elena has been drawn into this thing." Hector clawed at his scalp with his fingernails, the pain temporarily numbing his remorse. It ate him alive. His ambition had steered him wrong. His pride had blinded him. He could see that now. Too clearly. His beautiful Elena. His life would be empty without her. He knew the hope of ever seeing her alive again was dismal—she was no use to them, unlike Jackson, who they had a whole host of reasons to keep alive. The Sinaloa cartel was the most brutal, the most powerful. And what had he done? Eagerly walked right into the lion's mouth, thinking he was safe from reprisals. But fuck if he wouldn't go down without a fight remembering what his mamá had found in the trash this morning. No self-respecting man could live with himself otherwise.

"Get the men together."

"You have a plan, *padrino*?" George inquired respectfully; his face carefully unreadable. The man knew better than to suggest how insane it was to go after the culprits.

"I will soon," he swore and stomped out of the room.

———

RAND CLOSED his eyes and took a deep breath. What was he going to tell Jackson? That they had somehow misplaced his sister? "Okay, so you're telling me they just walked away. No one was paying them any attention? They're supposed to be on a close watch, damn it!" The last was hissed through a clenched jaw.

"Apparently their excuse is lack of funding. A woman was seen by another patient walking down the path to the lake. He said it was her bright auburn hair that drew his attention, but we haven't been able to locate her. No one else saw a thing. The staff said the pair often went to the lake to feed the geese right after breakfast." The fellow DEA agent's voice was neutral, relaying the facts without blame.

"Any drugs found?"

"They're searching their rooms as we speak."

"Let me know what they find out." Rand broke off the call. He decided to put off telling Jackson until he knew more. He prayed it was just a drug relapse, that the pair was out scoring a hit and not something far more sinister. But the sooner the pair were found the better. The sting he was fairly certain right to the depths of his bones was going to be effective, and he wanted nothing to get in the way of his taking the Torres bastard down. And getting his friend back. Mexico was no place for Jackson.

WALKING BACK down the path the next evening, Jackson felt he'd fallen into a parallel world. It could crash at any second, of course. Rand or Hector storming the gates and lives would instantly be placed in danger. That is if his implant still worked and if Hector was foolhardy enough to attempt a rescue. He preferred the third option. Finding a way out of this.

"Evening," Joe came ambling up from the opposite direction.

"Evening," Jackson said.

Joe's greeting was disingenuous; he looked far too pleased with himself this morning.

"I'm to tell you to come with me. Got an assignment for you."

Red flag on the play. Fucking Hector over, how did Joe expect to live long? He had to be one brick shy of a load.

"Okay."

He followed Joe to a convoy of Jeeps loaded with men and weapons. Shit. Something heavy was going down.

"You ride with me," Joe said. He pointed toward the first vehicle.

"Where's El León?"

"None of your business," Joe said, spitting out a wad of chewing tobacco phlegm on the ground and jumping into the passenger side. Jackson got in the back beside two other men. One grunted a greeting and moved over enough to give him room to park his ass.

Joe used the palm of his hand to hit the side of the

door panel with a loud thud. Twice. The driver started the vehicle and the convoy moved off.

They bounced along a fair distance on the rocky road past green fields of more damn onions and some acres planted with tomato crops that at least smelled better. Was every damn road surface in Mexico a shithole? They finally came to the edge of the plantations and abruptly entered an urban setting. Jackson sat up straighter. This was where things would most likely unfold. The convoy stopped on the side of the road and Joe stood up, addressing the soldiers.

"Okay, listen up," Joe's voice rang out. "We go in strong. I want them so overpowered they just lie down. We get the stuff and we round up the culprits. Got it?"

A few cheers from the men and the convoy started up again. They went another couple of tension filled miles, twisting and turning through a maze of streets before pulling up in front of a large building that advertised *Girls! Girls! Girls!* Everyone jumped out, Jackson was handed a rifle by Joe, and the soldiers stormed through the front door. He had no idea what was going to happen. The fact he was even there at all was insane.

"Everyone! Down on the floor!" Joe ordered, shouting loudly enough to make himself heard above the pounding music. The crowd of men with a few scantily dressed females mingling and dancing in two cages suspended over the bar immediately froze. Bodies dropped to the wooden floor, hands over their heads or out at their sides in a bizarre pantomime to show they were no threat. They must have been through this scenario before.

A heavy-set woman hurried over, looking indignant for their intrusion. "Why are you here? What is wrong? I have paid my dues," she screamed in Joe's face. He pushed her aside.

"Shut it or I'll shut if for you," he warned.

The shouting stopped.

"Okay. Spread out and keep this lot covered. You—" Joe pointed at Jackson and a couple of other men. "Come with me."

They headed to the back of the establishment, their heavy boots thudding on the wooden floor, stopping in front of one of the closed doors.

It was locked. He nodded to one of the men. The soldier used his large foot to kick it a few times until it gave way. It shuddered as it swayed drunkenly on its hinges before Joe slammed it one last time, the door giving up its intended purpose and falling down.

The men rushed inside.

They confronted a group of frightened women naked and packaging white powder in small plastic baggies. Cocaine. As if in slow motion he watched a man stand up and point his gun at them from the back of the room. Before he could shoot, Joe shot him dead, hitting one of the women in the upper thigh in the process with a stray bullet. She slumped to the floor, blood trickling down her leg. One of the women began screaming. She ran toward the fallen woman, pulled her into her arms, crying and screaming.

"Maria, Maria!"

"Shut her up!" Joe said and stalked past the carnage to the back of the room and another locked door. This time he used his gun to shoot the lock with a burst of gunfire and then his boot to knock the door open. Jackson was too stunned to follow him, his eyes unable to leave the sight of the man lying dead on the floor rapidly bleeding out. He was sickened at the sight. It had happened so fast. No more killing or Joe and the others were going to suffer the worst pain of their lives. *Make that a promise I can live with.* No matter the cost to himself.

"Come in here!" Joe demanded from the other room. The soldiers pushed Jackson along, past the dead man and the frightened women. Softly muttered prayers sent shivers down his spine. The next room was empty except for a large round opening on the back wall near the floor large enough for a man to crawl through. A hastily pushed away filing cabinet glared at them from a haphazard angle, exposing the exit.

"We follow him. El León's orders," Joe said. He ducked down beside the hole and peered into it, cradling his rifle. "You first," he said, nodding at Jackson. "If it blows up it's your hide. We'll be along shortly," he joked with a smile that did nothing to hide his meanness or enjoyment at ordering Jackson around.

Should he head down the tunnel or just drop the men in their tracks? Sixty-four-thousand-dollar question.

Reluctantly, Jackson lowered his body down to the floor and climbed into the tunnel. He began to make his way into the unknown, awkwardly crawling through the distance in the semi-darkness. The air was musty, creating the sensation of the walls closing in on him. But he pressed ahead, the tunnel taking a couple of twists and turns making it impossible to know the direction he was heading.

A hundred feet or so later he came to the end of it, sweat dripping in his eyes. It was blocked at the opening. He pushed against the metal plate and it fell away, ringing as it hit the floor. He crawled out, blinded by the light.

A man sat on a chair looking straight at him, rifle splayed across his lap. Behind him stood a half dozen men with automatic rifles pointed straight at him. They were in a small room, perhaps fifteen by twelve with rusting bars on the windows. There was one small door. The walls were a stained a dingy yellow, unpainted in decades, and debris littered the corners. Right beside the hole in the wall stood a large steel safe that looked well used, scuffed, and dented. A small table and one rickety wooden chair sat in a corner. One item sat on the table-top; a shiny silver handled pistol that looked out of place in the dingy room.

"Welcome, *pendejo*."

Could I fall any deeper into shit?

The men coming along behind clamored out of the hole and joined the party one by one, each wearing an identical expression of surprise and dismay as they emerged from the tunnel. They were directed to stand close together, their backs to the wall. A few minutes later, when it was clear no more were coming through, two of the soldiers grunted and strained to place the heavy safe over the entrance.

"I want a clear message sent to El León. There's a new cock in town and I'm not going to allow my operation to be fucked with." The leader of the troop paused for dramatic effect. "Now that we understand each other, we'll have a little competition to discover who takes the message back, and who doesn't get to go back. If we had more time, I'd set you up in the ring with the dogs. You could fight it out there." The man had enjoyed his little speech. His mustached-face gloated as he inspected them as if searching for clues as to who would win.

Out of the corner of his eye, Jackson saw Joe nod in his direction. Jackson knew the deal, what he was after, but some perverse part of him wanted to know more what this wannabe kingpin planned.

"What are you looking at him for?" the leader asked, his eyes narrowing while his glance moved like a tennis ball between two players as he glanced from Joe and back to Jackson.

"Nothin'," Joe mumbled. "Just get on with it."

The man's face darkened.

"Then I'm guessing you're choosing to go first," he said through gritted teeth.

The man nodded at one of his soldiers standing behind him. The soldier gave a wolfish grin as he advanced toward Joe and yanked him out of the lineup. He dragged him by the arm and slammed him down on the chair facing away from the table and toward the room full of silent, watchful men.

With a quiet series of deliberately exaggerated actions, the soldier loaded the gun with one bullet. Spun the chamber before locking it in place. He handed the gun to Joe. "Hold it against your head and shoot," he ordered.

Joe looked from the man's deadly expression right into Jackson's eyes, as if to implore, *are you really going to let this happen?*

ELENA HUMMED, worked at cleaning the already spotless house. For the first time in years her heart was allowing a little happiness to light her way. She was refusing to think ahead. The future loomed large, just out of sight. It lurked, waited for a chance to pounce and perhaps destroy a few precious hours of contentment in an otherwise bleak existence. That way led to worry and pain and she was having none of it today. No. She was going to enjoy what little happiness exited in the here and now. Jackson's presence filled her mind. She stopped dusting the furniture, pressed her hand to her flat stomach, knowing it was but a tiny clump of cells dividing over and over. A miracle growing inside her—becoming a little larger and stronger with each passing breath. She would do her best to see it safe, even if that meant doing the unthinkable.

———

JACKSON CLOSED his eyes as white noise buzzed in his brain. Joe was waiting for him to take action. To save his bacon. Fuck. The man had kidnapped and killed people without mercy, and *now* he wanted mercy? Another idea rose to the surface. Just how grateful would Joe be to avoid the hand of fate? Enough to help Elena escape? Highly unlikely. Joe was all about the money. Something Jackson was in short supply of. But if he did help, would Joe's men then harm the rebels while they lay on the floor in pain? They were men of evil deeds as well. No better or worse than the men he'd come with. The dilemma ate at him. Scorched his soul. Then, the right answer came to him in the next instant.

Every man in the room dropped to the floor in a synchronized parody of a bizarre dance. Jackson's head swam with the extreme effort required to affect so many men at one time, blinking to clear his vision. He raced for the door, twisted the knob praying it was unlocked, and felt a relief so powerful when it turned freely in his hand that he nearly dropped to his knees. He stumbled outside.

Spying the lineup of Jeeps, he hurried along the street, his head swiveling in all directions to watch for intruders. He made it to the first vehicle and checked the ignition. *Keys.* His luck was holding. He got in and started the motor. He jerked it into gear, floored the gas pedal, and drove off into the twilight. He turned off the headlamps to avoid detection making the journey that much harder. His memory served him well and soon he was near where he'd started the evening's odyssey. Jumping out near the mansion, he ran the last quarter mile to the house. And Elena.

He ran up to the front door and burst in on her as she sat on the sofa reading a book.

She looked up in alarm.

"We have to go. Now! I have a Jeep outside."

She didn't question him but got to her feet. She ran toward him. They embraced and hurried back through the open door and onto the patio steps. They ran, holding onto each other down the path. Jackson felt his heart fluttering in his chest straining to keep the pace, but he pressed on. No choice. He had to ignore the warning signs.

They clamored into the vehicle. Jackson turned the key. Thankfully the motor caught and started. He made a sharp U-turn on the road, headed back down. He took the first turnoff. Prayed it led to safety.

The sweat was dripping into his eyes and he used his sleeve to swipe it away. Elena stayed silent, a beacon of light at his side. He was too tired to think. All he could do was drive, desperate to put miles behind them.

The gas tank indicator read full. His third bit of luck, after weeks of falling deeper into the shitter.

They bounced along the rutted goat trail, the full moon rising and helping to light the way. Any direction they took was an ultimate crap shoot, though if memory served him correctly from studying maps, the road they were on held some promise. Problem was how far did El León's grasp reach? Biggest kingpin who ran the largest cartel in Mexico—possibly the world—it did not bode well. But still he pressed on.

He glanced at Elena as she fished around in the narrow glove box and found an old manual fastened with a dark yellow tie. She slipped the elastic off the bedraggled booklet, pulled her hair that had been blowing every which way in the windy Jeep into a bunch to the back of her head, and tied the elastic around the thick mass.

An hour later they came to the edge of a village. Jackson skirted it, continuing to drive west toward the Pacific coast. The mountainous terrain made the journey difficult. The swaybacked road narrowed sharply at times making Jackson slow the speed to a crawl. The perfect view over the edge as it dropped sharply away to the ravine bottom located hundreds of feet below was disconcerting. It sent fear into his tired, ailing heart. With every passing mile he found his strength depleting. Soon he would have to stop and rest. No other choice.

CHAPTER 22

"Okay, we've got intelligence from our man that Hector's on his way to the states in a matter of days—if not hours." Rand addressed the group of assembled men in the briefing room.

"How recent was the intel?" *Of course. That would be the first question out of the asshole's pie-hole and not the more pressing details of the plan.*

Rand knew better than to give an exact time. "Recent enough to matter," he said briskly. "The point is—"

A man with a piece of paper clutched in his hand raced into the room and right up to Rand, his expression dire as he handed the dispatch to him.

"Sorry to interrupt, but this just came in and it contains time sensitive information," he said.

Rand took the paper. Read the few lines it contained. The bile soured in his stomach as full realization hit him.

He looked up at the men's faces, most trying to hide their curiosity behind professional boredom and cynical poses. "Jackson Banks and Elena Torres have been kidnapped by the Sinaloa cartel." As dire as the information was, it did mean more resources would be poured into the case and every man in the room knew it. He could already hear the minds whirling wondering how they could spin it to their advantage.

"Okay," Rand added, more authority to his tone though his heart was racing, "we need to get down there ASAP. I'll head the unit while Agent Johnson continues with our plans to nab Torres right here in LA."

"Do you think he'll really be coming to the states now that his wife has been kidnapped?" a scoffing voice from the front row annoyed him more than he could say.

"Hector Torres is a drug kingpin—a hard and brutal man. Nothing gets in his way of doing business. So, though we can't be one hundred percent certain, do you want to be the one to explain why we didn't apprehend him as planned if he shows his face?"

The opposition remained silent this time. "Okay, I'll be in touch." He stepped away from the podium and strode away, apprehension and tension making his skin crawl. First Leia and now Jackson. His mind raced ahead, planning his next move.

———

"WE NEED TO FIND A PHONE," Jackson said, breaking the mutual silence.

They'd left so quickly they'd brought virtually nothing with them and most likely his implant was not going to be of much help. But he was grateful. They had their lives and were free. For the moment. Maybe they would have been fine at the compound, but most likely not. He'd had to take advantage of the first opportunity to escape that presented itself. His mind flew to more pressing things. Contact Rand. Let him know the state of things and arrange a rescue. He did not allow himself to think beyond that point.

Elena gave him a deliberately woeful smile. "Wish I could conjure one up for you like a witch, but I'm all out of spells I'm afraid. We'll need to stop at a village."

Jackson glanced over at her, barely able to take his eyes off the road for fear of their going over the steep edge. He appreciated her light attempt at humor, meant she was coming back, finding herself. A good strong woman. How had he gotten so lucky?

"I'll try the next one we come to. We're a fair distance away and hopefully no word of our escape has been sent ahead. They don't know which way we're headed."

Even so, he experienced the dreaded sensation of having a target painted on his back as he drove them around the handful of shacks that lined the valley floor. They'd descended into the ravine a few miles back, driving at a snail's speed to avoid disaster. Could he risk stopping? No other choice. Soon they'd be out of gas and all decision would be taken away from them. Surely word of their escape hadn't reached this far?

He finally chose one of the cinderblock houses set a fair distance back from the road with a couple of lights on. He cranked the wheel to the right, driving the Jeep down the narrow trail that led to its door. An old man sat in the dim light, slouched on an old rickety chair, the lit end of a smoke flaring as he drew on it with his lips. He watched as Jackson stopped and turned off the motor.

"Wait here," he said and got out. He had no gun, but he had money in his pocket. Hoped to make a trade. A goat tied in the yard gave him a curious look as if judging if he or his clothing was fit to eat while chickens scattered excitedly clucking at his intrusion. He made his way up to the swat dwelling, trying to avoid stepping in animal droppings in the dim light.

"Qué quieres?" the old man asked. His tone and voice were rough, his face seamed and wrinkled from too much sun, his back bent from hard labor. He wore old, patched clothing that hung off his skinny frame.

"A phone. Do you have a phone—a teléfono?" Jackson asked as he made the universal gesture of speaking on a device held to his ear.

"*Si, por qué?*" the man asked, his face drawn with suspicion.

"I have money to pay—*dinero para pagar—mucho dinero.*" Jackson pulled his wallet from pocket, grateful they hadn't taken it off him back when he had emerged from the tunnel. He pulled out a sheath of bills and presented them to the man. It was almost all he had, but he didn't care. No time to hold back.

The man looked at him, looked over at Elena sitting in the Jeep, back at Jackson. It was all Jackson could do not to scream his need aloud. It would not help, but weaken his position.

"Si," the man finally said and gestured for him to follow him inside the shack. He crushed his smoke out in the cheap ceramic ashtray sitting near the doorway. The odor of ripened tobacco was not unpleasant as it hung in the air. Jackson followed him inside.

The room was cool and smelled of recent cooking, the odor of bacon grease making his stomach rumble. It had been hours since he'd eaten. The man smiled and pointed at his stomach with a finger.

"*Hambre?*" he asked.

A woman entered the room about the same age as the man. Jackson assumed it was his wife. She shuffled as she walked, but her smile of greeting was universal.

"*Llevar comida. Tenemos invitados,*" the man instructed her to bring food.

"No, not necessary," Jackson said. He wanted to make his call and get the hell out of there. Find some gas.

"Si!" the man said, expanding his hands wide. "Usted come—you eat. Nuestros huéspedes—guests."

Jackson nodded reluctantly, not wanting to offend the man before he had a chance to use the phone.

"Obtener—how you say—get your woman," the man said. He pointed in the direction of the front door.

Jackson nodded.

Ten minutes later, they sat down to a decent meal hastily pulled together by the woman. She set plates in front of them on the cheerful vinyl tablecloth decorated with strutting roosters. The food was good and plentiful and went a long way to making him stronger. Elena sat by his side and ate her serving of beans and rice, drinking fresh buttermilk.

He smiled his thanks. "Gracias, very good." He mimicked eating.

"Gracias," Elena murmured.

"Teléfono?" he asked the man making the cell phone gesture again.

"Si," the man said and got up to retrieve it. He plucked it off a charging station on the counter and handed it to Jackson.

"Gracias." Jackson got up and headed into the living room to gain some privacy. He punched in Rand's private number praying he'd pick up. He bit his lip as the phone rang once. Twice. Then Rand's voice came on the line and Jackson could begin to breathe again.

"Rand—it's Jackson!"

"Oh Lord, I hate to tell you this, but Leia and Ben— they're missing from the Oregon facility!" Rand's voice was frantic over the crystal-clear phone connection making his words all the more chilling and surreal.

Jackson's heart lurched. He almost dropped the man's cell phone. He'd been feeling somewhat better the last couple of weeks knowing his sister was safe in Oregon, but that vanished as icy dread swept through his veins. "What happened?"

"We're not sure. They didn't show up for a head check at lunchtime."

"Wasn't anyone watching them?" He spit out the words.

"Apparently not, but the grounds are considered safe. They had a habit of going down to the lake and feeding the geese after breakfast. No one noticed they were missing until lunchtime."

"What's being done about it?" he demanded.

"We're trying to find them," Rand said.

"But I thought the shipment went through customs without a hitch. How could Hector know it was a setup? That the drug dogs were fake? Because why would he take Leia otherwise? Makes no sense."

"I don't think he did. I think he's kidnapped Leia as insurance to make sure you keep helping him. For insurance against the next load—the big payoff."

"You've *got* to find them. You can't make a move until Leia's safe—promise me. Nothing happens until then." Jackson felt powerless in Mexico. He had to get home. Now.

"We've got a lot of manpower out looking for them. We'll leave no stone unturned."

"Yeah, sure," Jackson said, surprised by the bitterness that under laid his words. At least he he'd been spared the "don't worry" speech.

"I'm sorry. I wish things were different. My fault. Never suspected this could happen."

"Hector warned me. I should have listened."

"We need to take him down more than ever now," Rand pressed, his voice filled with fervor.

"Yeah and how's that going to help Leia how?" Jackson said. Taking Hector down now placed her directly in the crosshairs. He had to get home first. See her safe.

Silence for a moment.

"Where are you?" Rand asked.

Jackson explained the situation and what he knew of their whereabouts. Discovered the implanted beeper was working sporadically.

"Okay, here's the plan," Rand said, his voice stronger, more in charge. "You keep heading toward the coast. We've pinpointed your location on the map. Stay on the same road. How much gas have you got?"

"Not much—maybe enough to get about another thirty miles. I'm not certain if I can get more."

"Okay, then drive about twenty miles toward the coast, the flatter terrain will allow for an easier helicopter landing. A place the locals call the Red Hand. Easy to spot, it's a landform that rises about fifty feet into the air nearly straight up and looks like five fingers."

"Red Hand, got it," Jackson repeated.

"You need to get away from where you are now in case you've been compromised by using the phone, then turn off the road, hide and wait. We're on our way. Should be there by morning. And Jackson, I know I don't have to tell you this, but be careful. I'd like to discuss the state of Western Civilization in more depth with you—you're the only one I know who gets it." Rand's voice had gotten husky and a lump came to Jackson's throat.

"I'll see what I can do, buddy, no promises."

"And Jackson, there's something else—" Rand's voice was full of hesitation making him wonder what else was up.

A stifled scream in the kitchen interrupted his thoughts.

"I gotta go, Rand. I'll call you later."

Jackson hurriedly ended the call.

He ran to the kitchen and was dismayed by the sight of an old pistol being pointed directly at his mid-section. The old man stood taller now, a grim look shut down his recent friendly compassion. Jackson froze. *What the hell?* The old man had no idea of who he was and what he could do, but he was so damn old, he hated to have to harm him. He swiped a hand over his head pushing his hair back. The room was hot. Stifling. Elena was still sitting at the table, her face pale, her golden eyes wide and frightened.

"Sit down," the man barked and gestured with his gun to the chair Jackson had occupied earlier.

Jackson sat. The old woman had a length of rope and she advanced toward him with grim intentions.

"Why?" he asked.

"You think I was born yesterday?" Interesting how his English had improved. "A *gringo* comes into my village in the middle of nowhere and needs to use a phone with a fine-looking woman with him. The woman I know as Elena Torres, a former beauty queen, the wife of a drug lord and you don't think I wouldn't wonder why? Someone is going to want her back. A big reward, si."

"I beg you—don't do this," Jackson pleaded. He had to try. "I don't want to hurt you or your wife."

"Hurt us," the man scoffed. "I'm the one holding the gun. Tie him up," he ordered his wife, who scuttled about to do his bidding.

"I warn you. It's not going to be pretty." Could he ratchet it down enough to just give the pair a good jolt?

"Quit stalling. Do it!" he said.

The woman grabbed his right hand and looped the rope around it. He had to act. Now. He carefully located the source. Concentrated on sending a small pulsing stream into the man staring at him with steely intent, and the woman behind him still fumbling with the rope. He could only hope the energy he sent would be enough to stop them, not harm them. The man's eyes opened with surprise a second later, his face going slack while his fingers clenched involuntarily on the trigger. The gun wobbled.

A shot fired, the sound deafening.

Jackson knew the bullet had hit him but all he felt was paralyzed, thrown back against the chair back. If he'd been standing, he would have dropped like a rock. Then the pain hit. Hurt like a bitch. Damn. The old man dropped the weapon and was holding his chest. He slumped against a cupboard.

"Oh my god!" Elena bent over him, checking for the entry wound.

"Get the gun," he said through gritted teeth.

Elena scrambled to retrieve it from the floor. The old woman had dropped the rope and slumped on a chair, taking deep rattling breaths.

She handed the gun over. She laid her hand on his side where a bloom of red was spreading quickly. Elena reached under her dress and tore off her slip, pressing it to the wound. He opened the pistol's chamber and let the five other bullets drop out onto the floor before he would allow her to tear open his shirt and check the damage.

"It went straight through. That's good. And I don't think it hit anything vital. But it's bleeding badly. We need to get you to a hospital."

"You'll have to take care of it."

"Hold this against it," she said and took his hand to hold the wad of silky white material in place. "I'll check the bathroom. Maybe they'll have some supplies."

The old couple were still incapacitated. No threat at the moment.

Elena left his side and came back with some gauze

and rubbing alcohol. "This will help. I'm sorry, it's going to sting," she warned.

He took a deep intake of breath. She removed her bloodied slip and poured the alcohol over the damaged flesh. She quickly pressed pads of sterile gauze to his side and wound more strips around his middle, tying the ends off.

"I could use a glass of water," he croaked.

She poured him a full glass of cool water from the pitcher on the table. He downed it in one huge gulp. Being shot. Thirsty business.

The two old people were recovering. Both looked at him with stunned disbelief on their faces.

"What did you do to us?" the old man asked in a hoarse tone of voice, his eyes wide with fear. "El *vudú*?" The man whispered and crossed himself. His wife did the same.

"Nothing you didn't deserve," Jackson said. "Elena, we need to tie them up, otherwise..." He left it hanging. The answer was so obvious.

The pair were surprisingly docile as Elena carefully but competently accomplished the task.

"Does anyone check on you?" Jackson asked as he got to his feet, fighting a slight wave of dizziness.

The man stayed stubbornly silent.

"Look, if you don't tell me I'll have to take the two of you with us and drop you off far from home."

"Si, my son comes by every morning," the man said.

Jackson grunted. "Good. I'm taking your phone. I think I paid you enough for it."

The man didn't object but watched him warily.

Elena offered Jackson her assistance but he was mobile enough to make his own way to the Jeep. She'd filled a large water jug and threw it, the first aid kit, and a few corn tortillas wrapped in plastic in the back seat while he looked around. The area was still deserted. The gunshot had weakened him, but he no choice but go on for a while yet.

"Bumping down this road is not going to be good for that wound. I should drive," she said as he eased in behind the wheel. She got in beside him, her eyes dark with worry.

"I'll be fine. I just hope no one heard the shot."

She looked around with concern, her expression pensive.

"Looks quiet enough."

"You know you can never go back to him, right?" he said. Being shot had pulled him out of his fantasy world he had been living and made him all too aware of their precarious position. He had to make certain that if anything happened to him, she would be all right.

"What are you talking about?" she asked.

"Hector. Joe will tell him what he overheard at the ranch at some point. Too juicy not to. Promise me, if anything goes wrong, you will make a new life for yourself and our baby in the states. My friend Rand Givens, a good DEA man, will help you. Promise me, Elena."

She pressed her lips together. Anguish and pain passed briefly over her face before her expression cleared. He knew she was thinking of her family. He could also smell her femaleness in the heat of the day. He closed his eyes, breathing her in. If only there was a guarantee that they would make it out of this alive in one piece, he'd promise to go to church every Sunday for the rest of his life. Just when he hadn't been looking for a woman to spend his life with, he had found her, and a moment with her was worth everything. Was it greedy to want those moments to continue indefinitely?

"Okay," she said in a quieter tone.

"Promise me," he pressed.

"I promise."

CHAPTER 23

Leia sat in the back seat and watched the landscape float lazily by the window. Sweet. All her pain and worry had magically dissolved. She looked over at Ben. He was listening to his iPod, eyes closed. Catherine sat up front beside the man who had driven them to Oregon, Kyle Smith. They were an item and he was just helping out on the drive back to LA. Leia vaguely wondered why? Wasn't it a conflict of interest or something like that? Ben didn't seem worried about it so she gave up the fleeting thought and concentrated on the landscape, counting every red barn. She was up to twelve when a cell phone rang in the front seat. She wore earbuds for show to keep from having to converse.

Kyle answered.

"Yeah, we got 'em. On our way back," he said. *What?*

She looked over at Ben. He was oblivious, nodding his head to the beat of the music.

She reached out and touched his leg to gain his attention. Nodded at the front seat. She leaned over, whispering into his ear when he pushed the headphones back out of the way.

"Something's not right," she mouthed.

He raised an eyebrow at her and grinned lopsidedly. "Something's always not right with you," he said. "Relax."

"No, I mean it."

"What are you two yattering about?" Catherine asked, turning around in the passenger seat to confront them.

"Nothing," Leia said.

"Leia thinks you guys are up to something," Ben joked as if she was the one with the problem.

Catherine and Kyle shared a look. "What makes you think that, Leia?" she asked.

Leia shrugged. "I don't know. Where are we going?" she asked.

"Back to LA, of course. We'll drop you off wherever you like," she said, her eyes cold while her lips grimaced upward into a tight-as-hell smile.

Leia pursed her lips. Something smelled wrong.

"We'll go to my crib. I'm not living with your sanctimonious brother anymore," Ben said.

"Fine. But Jackson was just trying to help." She wished she was back in Oregon feeding the geese. Such graceful birds, innocent of the crap people pulled.

"Help? He was a pain in the ass. A bullshit artist."

"Relax, you two, it's a long drive back," Catherine warned and turned back around in her seat.

Leia bit her lip. Thought hard. She had to get away. She racked her brain. Adam's concerned face came to mind, her fave person at the facility. She would call him soon as she was alone. He'd help her.

———

"I'M afraid we're out of time," the doctor explained to Hector, his eyes sad and watchful. The man had a good reputation as a heart surgeon though he appeared too effeminate for Hector's taste, his hair in too perfect curls, and his eyelashes as long as a woman's. "Teresa's heart has weakened so extensively I can no longer guarantee we can keep her alive, even with all the technology you have provided us. I am sorry for this bad news. But if a donor is not found within a few days, I'm afraid that she will most likely suffer final heart failure."

Hector took a deep breath. So much happening out of his control was making him want to scream and break things. But he was not a child. He controlled himself with great difficulty. Then an idea came to him.

"Prepare her for surgery. You'll have your donor within the hour."

"But—" the doctor began to object, his expression confused.

"Just see to it." Hector's chilling tone silenced the man.

"Fine," he said though his skin had paled and turned clammy in the stark light of the hospital corridor. They stood outside Teresa's room. He had given the surgeon an ultimatum—do this operation or have his entire life wiped out. Due to the child pornography discovered on his computer from his last trip to Taiwan recorded in stark digital images that would shock and dismay any normal human being, Hector had enough evidence to destroy his career. But all the heart surgeon had to do was this one operation and he would be free to work else-where, if he wanted. Hector would have the intel buried and let the man resume his life, that was the promise. With a warning, of course. Continue on the same path and he was a dead man. Children were a blessing from God. Then he'd shoot him himself. Sick bastards like him could never be cured.

"I want a moment alone with my sister," he ordered.

Hector waited for the man to get out of earshot. He pulled out his cell.

"I need that new girl," he said. He already knew she was a match, having had everyone tested. "And I need her now. Someone will be there in twenty minutes. See that she is clean and ready to leave."

He made a second call to one of his most loyal soldiers and asked to have the woman picked up and brought to the hospital, then went to see his sister.

She was lying so still his heart lurched in his chest. My god, was it already too late?

Then he saw the white cover rise ever so slightly and he knew she was still with him. He took her cold limp hand as it rested on the coverlet.

"Hector." Teresa opened her eyes and looked at him. Her eyes were clear and shone with a light that unnerved him.

"Don't speak. Save your strength. You're getting your new heart today, sweetheart," he said.

"No...I heard...you," she said, shaking him to the core.

"What do you mean, little one?" he murmured and brushed the dark strands of limp hair back from her beloved face.

"No one... can die...for me. I could not...live... with it."

Stunned, Hector tried to swallow. A huge lump had turned his throat raw.

"You have to live. I won't let you die," he said, tears running freely down his cheeks as he tried to persuade her.

"Let me go. God is...with me. I love...you. And...he loves you. Don't do this."

Hector made the sign of the cross and kissed her forehead. He gently laid her hand down.

"Promise…me."

"I will do what is best for you, Teresa. You have my word."

He strode from the room and out of the front door of the half-built hospital. He'd had work halted yesterday when Teresa's health had suddenly deteriorated. Work could resume later; she needed complete quiet for the foreseeable future. He entered his home and walked into the chapel. He needed to be alone. Fortunately, there was no service planned for today. He slid onto a pew. He looked up at the large wooden cross and the man who had suffered the ultimate test for his beliefs, warring with his nature and his love of family. Was this his test?

He felt a touch on his shoulder and turned to see his mamá sitting down beside him. He patted the back of her hand clumsily.

"Mamá," he murmured.

Her soft smile was bittersweet. He could see the deep well of sadness and worry consuming her. She'd aged ten years in the past few days.

"Teresa is in God's hands, my son. We can do no more."

"I cannot accept that. I won't accept it," Hector spoke harshly.

"You love your family. That's a fine thing—a blessing. You're so like your father. He loved his family so much and would do anything for us. But it got him killed in the end. You must accept this—some things are beyond our control. It's God's will."

Hector shook his head, unable to speak. His cell phone buzzed. It gave him an excuse.

"I must take this." He kissed her forehead and got up to leave.

"Leave it in God's capable hands, my son."

Outside the chapel, he clicked on the phone call recognizing George's number.

"Yes."

"It's arrived and passed inspection. You want us to hang around?"

"Yeah, keep up the surveillance. I'll be there tomorrow. And get a new phone."

"Excuse my mistake, *padrino*."

"Hire more help. Take the night off. You've both earned it."

"Thank you. A good night's sleep would help."

"Sleep? You have access to LA's night scene and you want to sleep," Hector joked.

George had given him the first good news in days.

"Not so young anymore."

"Then hit Sweet Valentine's. It'll take years off."

"Maybe I will." George gave a small chuckle. "You know, I could take care of all this for you. Save you the trip. You have a lot of balls in the air right now."

Hector hesitated for a moment, considering. Perhaps he should let George handle things in the states? "No. I want to meet with our new distributor. Make sure he understands how we operate." He also needed the distraction. And controlling every aspect of his business was second nature. No matter what else was happening.

Hector ended the call. So, the ruse had worked. He smiled with satisfaction knowing his ability to make cash had exploded exponentially.

He spied a grim Jesús drifting through the hallway. He was the most sensitive of the brothers and would be taking Teresa's turn for the worst the hardest.

"Hey, *mi hermano*. Are you all right?" He clapped him on the back as he joined him, swallowing his own pain. His brother's thinness worried him.

Jesús looked torn up as he spoke, his dark eyes pleading. "Surely something can be done for her?"

"Have you spoken with *Mamá* today?"

"No, I just got here."

"She's in the chapel praying for Teresa. You should go see her. She needs us now more than ever."

He nodded absently and murmured, "Of course."

Hector watched him leave, noticing the stooped shoulders. No time for second thoughts.

His cell buzzed again with an incoming text. He read the cryptic words and smiled. Perfect.

LEIA GOT up from the table in the roadside diner. They'd been on the I-5 since leaving the Good Hope facility near Portland and had finally reached the town of Red Bluff. Nearly halfway home and still no opportunity to call Adam. "I need to use the restroom."

"Me too. I'll go with you," Catherine offered, thwarting her attempt at being alone.

Leia didn't let on how much the woman was annoying her, but led the parade into the ladies' room.

She groaned loudly inside the stall.

"Are you okay?" Catherine asked from outside the stall frustration obvious in her tone. Stupid bitch didn't care one iota if she was all right or not. Just needed Leia to carry out some kind of plan that she and Ben weren't party to. What was the real deal?

"My stomach hurts."

"Relax," she advised.

Catherine waited. Groaned again. "It's a sharp pain in my side. What if I have appendicitis?"

"For heaven's sake! You don't have appendicitis."

"How do you know? You're not the one in pain."

"Finish up. We need to leave." The woman was growing angry. Good. Served her right.

When the woman gave a groan of disgust and finally left the bathroom slamming the door behind her, Leia immediately dialed the Good Hope facility. Her heart hammering in her chest, she waited for someone to pick up.

"Good Hope."

"Adam, I need to speak to Adam, it's urgent."

"Leia! Is that you? Are you all right? Just a sec. I'll page him."

The door of the stall burst open knocking against the steel wall. Kyle Smith glared down at her from where she perched on the edge of the toilet seat and grabbed the phone away before she could react. Threw it on the floor and stomped on it, crushing it to pieces.

"What the hell to you think you're playing at little girl? Get up. We're leaving."

She awkwardly moved around the irate man in the tight confines of the stall, cowed by his extreme anger.

"You need to control your woman," he warned Ben as the quartet left the diner. "I caught her calling that shit-hole treatment center to report where she is. Wanted to talk to her friend Adam apparently."

Ben gave her a strange look. She made a face back at him. *What are you going to do about it?*

"What the hell, Leia. Why are you making waves? Don't you know this is our chance to make some real cash?" Ben sounded exasperated.

She shrugged. She could hardly say what she was thinking in from of the evil duo. Why was Ben so blind?

"You want to be with Adam, is that it?" Ben asked as the full impact of what the agent had said sunk in.

"No!" She vigorously shook her head. "I love you. But

something isn't right." She whispered the last part in his ear.

Ben just gave her a disgusted look. "You can't see a break when it's staring you right in the face. Relax. We'll be in LA in a few hours."

"That guy broke my phone."

"Yeah, well maybe you pissed him off suspecting him of doing something wrong."

There was no winning. Ben wanted what he wanted so badly he was acting like an idiot. She could only hope that someone was out looking for them. Maybe Jackson would find out and rescue her? When his face came to mind, she held onto it for dear life. Her brother had never failed her. Even the times she'd cried wolf.

"Get in the car, you two," the agent barked.

Ben got in and motioned for Leia to join him. She wanted to run. But fear and a sense of duty stopped her. Trapped. Ben would need her when the whole thing blew up in his face—like it always did. She got in, sighing unhappily.

———

The miles had become an agony for Jackson. His side throbbed and his body screamed for rest. He tried to hide it from Elena, but the worry in her bright eyes told him he was failing miserably.

"Almost there, sweetheart," he said.

He spotted the Red Hand rising upward, eerily pointing at the heavens. The rest of the land was leveling off on the high elevation and civilization had all but vanished. Clumps of trees dotted the landscape and would offer cover to hide until Rand arrived.

The odometer read exactly twenty miles since they'd left the shack when he pulled off the road. He steered the

Jeep for a strand of trees that stood in the shadow of the hand. The uneven land pockmarked by animal burrows made his wound throb unbearably. He steeled his body as the Jeep bounced in and out of the deep ruts, the headlights offering a panoramic view that shifted from sky to earth with each jarring lurch.

Almost. There.

He positioned the Jeep so that it was fully hidden by thick bush, shaded by a large tree, and turned off the motor.

Leaning back in the seat, he closed his eyes and let his hands drop off the steering wheel.

"I need a minute," he murmured. He woke an hour later with a start, his mouth dry. He looked over at Elena who had curled up on the seat, wide awake and looking at him.

"Hey, handsome, how are you feeling?" she asked, her voice a tonic in the darkness as she stirred and reached into the back for a jug of water.

"Thanks," he said, taking the cup she poured for him, chugging it down. She laid her soft hand on his forehead.

"You're feverish," she said, her tone grave.

"Rand and his men will be here in a few hours. I'll be fine—don't worry. With what I've been through in my life, this is a skate in the park," he said.

"I think we should avoid parks in the future if they have this much cost attached," she said dryly.

He chuckled, making him wince with pain.

"You need to rest—save your strength," she said, laying her head against his undamaged shoulder.

"There's something I need to tell you. Leia's missing. She and her boyfriend Ben have vanished from the facility in Oregon."

"Oh, no! I'm so sorry."

"Yeah, and I think Hector has something to do with it.

He warned me that he would hurt her if I didn't do what he wanted."

She remained silent for a moment. "Yes, he's more than capable of such a thing."

"A lot of people are looking for them. I can only hope she's found soon."

"Me too."

Her womanly fragrance drifted over him making him wish he was less incapacitated. The perfect opportunity was being lost. He cursed the old man with the gun. He was so tired, so drained. He slipped back into unconsciousness.

Loud whirling sounds entered his consciousness, partially waking him up.

"Jackson!" Elena's voice filled his mind, its urgency waking him up further. "Someone's here!"

He swiped at his mouth. His skin felt tight and he knew his fever had worsened. His side throbbed as he sat up straighter.

"Rand's here?" he asked groggily, peering into the swirling cloud of dust particles raised by the helicopter as it hovered over the ground a hundred yards to their left. In the darkness it only served to further obscure his view. He looked to the sky and registered the moon was descending. It was partially hidden by drifting clouds while the air had turned chilly. He'd only slept a couple of hours. Rand was early.

"I don't know. Drink some water, you're burning up," she instructed and held a cup to his lips. He drank deeply. The water was warm but helped to clear his mind.

"Did you sleep?" he asked.

"A little," she admitted. He could see her eyes were weary from lack of rest.

The dust abated. A group of about a dozen men

disembarked and hurried through the darkness, flash-
lights illuminating the ground in harsh circles of light as
the spotlights danced around the area. Jackson placed a
fingertip over Elena's lips. He needed to be certain. When
one of the lights flashed on and discovered their Jeep
tucked at the behind the bushes, excited voices broke out
in the darkness. Jackson's spirits plummeted. The
language they were speaking clearly told him the men
were not American, but Mexican. The coin toss. Lost.

"Elena Torres and Jackson Banks," a hearty voice
called, echoing in the darkness. "Are you unhurt?"
Jackson recognized one of Hector's men. *Fuck.*

"Jackson's been shot," Elena spoke up. "He needs
medical assistance. Be careful with him—he saved my
life."

She was all efficiency as she directed the men. Jackson
swayed on his feet, the blood loss having weakened him,
but he kept upright as he shook off any assistance of help
and walked stiffly to the helicopter. The old man had
called Hector. How had he known where they were?
Then he remembered repeating Rand's instruction. The
Red Hand had betrayed them.

The flight back to Grande Torres gave him too much
time to think. Elena was buckled into a seat ahead of him
and they couldn't communicate, further making him feel
bereft. He was under no illusions. He would be killed
now or very soon. Joe wasn't the type to keep his mouth
shut forever.

By the time they landed near the mansion he was as
ready to face his nemesis as he would ever be. Did he
regret what he had done to get to this juncture? Perhaps
he should. He didn't have to be here. His pride had
brought him here, his thinking he was the only one who
could fix things had brought him here, and his loneliness,
his craving to find the one woman meant for him. Well,

he'd failed at fixing things; he had not managed to rescue Elena. But was he lonely now? No, in all honesty he was not. He'd met the woman of his dreams. And yes, love, love was enough reason to fight in this world. He straightened his shoulders and disembarked, waiting, watching Hector embrace Elena first.

Hector directed her to go into the mansion and turned to greet him, his expression changing from one of relief as he'd hugged his wife to dark and foreboding as he looked toward Jackson. They stared at one another, their eyes locking horns over the short distance. Neither man moved. The soldiers that had rescued them had vanished into the woodwork. Probably wanted to get out of the line of fire. Jackson didn't blame them.

"I'm very disappointed in you, Jackson," Hector began, running a hand over his hair to smooth it. The early dawn cast a wet grayness that blanketed the sky, adding more gloom and doom to his words. The cool helped make his fever bearable.

"I would have expected you to call me first. I thought we were brothers."

Jackson remained silent, waiting.

"I thank you for saving my Elena's life. I did not expect to ever see her alive ever again." For a split-second Jackson could see a deep well of pain open up inside Hector as he talked about almost losing Elena. The man did care about her. A knife twisted in his guts.

"I will overlook your transgressions for the time being. But trusting you, that's off the table."

"Fair enough," Jackson said.

Elena came back into view, Jesús in tow.

"Jackson needs medical care," she said as she hurried past her husband and took his arm. "He was shot trying to help me escape."

Hector's brother grabbed his other arm, after first

looking to Hector who gave him a curt nod. They made their way across the ground to the partially built hospital. Jackson steeled himself against the pain as each step became more and more an agony.

"In here," Elena said.

The pair helped him into a small room and she directed him over to a gurney. He sat on the edge of it while Jesús stood back. She undid his shirt, pulling off her makeshift bandage. The wound was ugly in the stark light of the overhead lamp, red and inflamed, and swollen at the raw edges. He couldn't see the exit wound on his back, but he imagined it looked pretty much the same.

"It's infected. We'll need to clean it out first, make sure there are no bullet fragments, put in some stitches. I think it would be best for you to be knocked out first before all the probing."

"No. I'm staying awake. Just do it." Jackson steeled himself for what was coming.

"I can give you some freezing and a painkiller, but it's still going to hurt."

A man in a white coat came in, interrupting them. He was a short, slender man and clean shaven, almost effeminate with a head of dark curls and long eyelashes. But it was his expression that gave Jackson pause. The man appeared to be struggling with some inner demons, his face stark and haunted with dark circles around his eyes like he hadn't slept in days. He stood and watched them for a moment before speaking up.

"Hector asked me to attend to this man. He wants you both back in the house, Mrs. Torres," the doctor said, his tone flat.

Jackson had to wonder if he was just back from a war zone where he had experienced atrocities or whether he had just lost a family member.

Elena hesitated and Jackson understood. To have been so close to freedom and now be back in the lion's den as his prey was painful beyond belief for him as well. But they had no other recourse. Not for the moment, anyway. It had once more turned into a chess game, and the stakes could not be higher. When was Joe going to spill the beans and allow Hector to strike? He had to plan and plan fast to get them out of his clutches.

"It's all right, Elena, I'll be fine," he said quietly earning a raised eyebrow from the doc.

"Okay." She sighed heavily, her expression resigned.

"Come, I'll walk you back," Jesús said in his quiet unassuming way, his face suggesting he knew more than he was letting on. *Fuck, were we being that obvious now?* He had to get a grip. Figure things out.

"I'll be back to check on you," she promised and left with her brother-in-law.

The doctor washed his hands at the sink, dried them and came closer to inspect his wounds. Jackson winced as the man probed the tender flesh.

"You look worse than me, Doc," Jackson joked and added when the man said nothing in return. "I don't want to be knocked out. Just do what you have to."

"It will hurt—but it's your choice." He shrugged as if it didn't mean that much to him. Not much of a bedside manner.

"How long have you practiced medicine?" Jackson asked. "He was in Mexico after all,"

"Wondering if I'm up to the job? After what I did today, don't worry. I can do anything," he said, the edge to his tone surprisingly sharp. The man was in tough emotional shape.

"You in some kind of battle today?"

"Yeah, a battle for my soul. I lost."

"Sure you're up to this? I could wait for someone else or—better yet—fly me to a hospital in the states."

"Don't worry. You'll be fine. I'm a heart surgeon with a lot of operating experience."

"Not my heart I'm worried about."

"Relax. I'm going to give you some pain medicine first. And don't worry—you'll not be going to sleep anytime soon."

And Jackson did not go to sleep as promised. Not while the doctor rooted around in his wound like he was looking for the lost city of Atlantis, not while he was stitching him up, and certainly not while he gave him more shots for tetanus and a course of antibiotics.

"Good job," Jackson said as the man finished bandaging him.

"Yeah, well you handled yourself well. Had to hurt like a son of a bitch."

"Not so bad. I still look better than you," he joked.

"Yeah, well, if you work for Hector, there will most likely come a time when you'll look as bad as me."

"Why do you work for him then? If it's so odorous to you?"

"No choice," he grunted and turned away to remove his gloves.

"We all got a choice."

"Not if you don't fit societies' mode of 'normal,'" he said with bitterness.

"What's he got on you? Don't worry. I'm not going to spill the beans to anyone. I think he's got my sister."

"Yeah? That sucks. Just the kind of thing he does to get full cooperation. He's an evil bastard."

"You'd better get out of here, Doc, it's eating you alive," Jackson advised as he tested his strength and got to his feet. He swayed a bit, then held steady.

"You're going to need to rest for a few days. And of

course, be careful of the stitches. They should be removed in a week's time."

"Thanks, you did a good job."

"Glad I could help someone."

"You know, if you need to talk, I live just down the road, the first house in that development that they're building on the property."

"Thanks, but I'll pass. No one could bear to hear what I've done to stay alive. Besides, people want their doctors to be physicians first, people second. We might be the only profession with that strange dynamic, but it does offer our patients some immunity in having to listen to us."

"You might be surprised. I've done some pretty weird shit myself. Anyway, the offer stands. And thanks again."

The door burst open and a white coated woman rushed in.

"Come quick, she's in distress!"

Without another word the man ran out, leaving Jackson to wonder about the man's real deal.

CHAPTER 24

"Sit," Hector said, his tone sharp and curt. Elena took a deep breath and sat down, ignoring her wrinkled and blood splattered sundress.

She remained silent, watching her nemesis. Hector wasn't giving much away. He'd always held his cards close to his vest. Fine. She could too. She felt an inner strength she had not experienced before, perhaps born of their time in the desert. She was stronger than she had imagined. She would need all her resources now—for Jackson and for their unborn child.

"Mamá found the positive pregnancy test in the garbage. Why did you not share this with me sooner?"

She felt a burst of irritation bubble up from inside but held her tongue. No point in attacking his beloved mamá —spy of all spies. All hell would break loose and then some. What made Hector such a cruel bastard? She'd often asked herself this even as she reassured her own mother that she was going to be just fine, that the latest bruises were obtained in a fall down the stairs or her legendary clumsiness that had only come to light after her marriage. She knew her mother didn't believe the ruse anymore, but still, it was a charade they played to keep the family unity. Only once the façade had broken and the glimpse of pain and anguish she'd been party to in her mother's eyes had made her decide, never again.

"I didn't get the chance to tell you. Getting kidnapped kind of interfered," she said. Her cool tone made her rather pleased with herself. She would have to tread a fine line, she was all too aware that pregnancy often upped the violence against women. That, and leaving them were the two most vulnerable times.

"Yes, that was an awful thing," he admitted, his stoic demeanor imploding for a moment. "Well, you're home now. Get cleaned up, rest and eat, and become a mother to our child. That's all I ask of you. Your betrayers will be brought to justice. Especially Joe," he warned, his expression darkening.

"Fine." The thought of his capturing and torturing Joe sent fear striking deep into her body. She shuddered knowing it would spell complete disaster. Her mind raced, they had to get away. Soon. She prayed that Jackson would come up with a plan. If anyone could, it would be him.

"Jackson Banks is more than he seems, Elena, it would be best if you stayed away from him in the future."

"The man saved my life!" she protested.

"Yes, but he can be a danger to others. There is a lot you don't know about him. I must insist on this."

She nodded, unable to bring herself to speak. Intolerable. She had a quick mental image of Jackson bringing Hector to his knees with his power. The thought made her want to smile though she carefully kept her expression neutral.

Hector narrowed his eyes at her as if he suspected something. She gave him a calm look in return. Time to strike.

"Where's Leia Banks? Jackson thinks you've had her kidnapped to ensure his cooperation. Did you?"

"None of your concern how I conduct my business," he said, his face flushing in anger.

Jesús burst into the room, his expression harried. "Teresa's taken a bad turn," he said and swallowed hard. "I'm so sorry, my brother. They're working on her now. Come, Mamá's asking for you."

Hector's face went pale.

He left the room without another word, and Elena followed.

The hospital room was in an uproar. A crash cart by the bedside. Teresa was being given CPR by the doctor who had assisted Jackson earlier. Elena was too polluted with dirt and blood to advance further. She stayed near the open doorway. Jackson came up to her as she stood there, looking pale but upright. She gave him a warning look and whispered, "Hector doesn't want us associating."

He nodded and looked into the room. Hector was busy, shouting at the doctor to do something. To save his sister *or else*.

They stood together. Elena found strength in having Jackson within arm's reach. She could have reached out and touched him, but didn't dare. When they were free, she would make up for all of this she promised herself. Her mind began to fill with images of their raising their child together where they would be free to live and love with all the fiber of their being. It was all that kept her going, a belief that it *could* happen.

The idyllic scene vanished in her mind. More loud noises erupted around her, forcing her to stay focused.

Hector had lost all control. The doctor had ceased his attempts at CPR and stood defeated, the proof of what had just happened clear in his anguished eyes. Hector was screaming profanities at the man. His mother and Jesús were holding him back from throttling the man, trying to calm him down. As she watched it dawned on her something else must have happened while she was gone. Teresa's hospital gown had been partially pulled down during the efforts to save her life and evidence of a very recent operation were staring her in the face.

"It is God's will, my son. It was her time. You must not blame this man. He has done all he can." Though terribly distraught, the clan's matriarch was trying to do what was right.

"Yes, brother, you must calm down. Come, let's pray together," Jesús said with simple dignity.

"Yes, we need to pray for Teresa's soul," the mother said.

Somehow their words must be getting through to him. His expression looked less murderous. They slowly released their tight hold on his arms as he recovered himself.

"Let us pray," Jesús said. He took his brother's hand and his mother's. Spoke a simple prayer. Hector looked too stunned now, too shocked to pull away.

"Oh Heavenly Father, we ask you to safely see the soul of our sister, daughter, and beloved friend on her final journey. We humbly thank you in the name of the Lord our God. Amen."

"Amen."

Elena bowed her head and said a silent prayer. She had found Teresa a wild but a fun-loving girl who had tried so hard to live her life as if she were entirely normal. She had admired her spunk. It was hard to believe she was gone. And so young. She sighed. Life was not always fair. Tears obscured her vision. She swallowed hard to try to grab hold of her emotions and clenched her hands together, fingernails cutting into her palms.

It was then she noticed the doctor was becoming agitated, tossing discarded items haphazardly onto the crash cart, mumbling something she was unable to hear. He turned around to face the trio, his complexion dark, flushed with blood and emotion. Even from across the room, she could see he was shaking violently.

Suddenly he made his move. Slammed into Hector. He tackled him from behind, forced Hector into the crash cart which smashed noisily to the floor. Instruments and blood-soaked bandages were strewn over the floor in an instant, a gory sight on the light gray tiles. Somehow both men stayed on their feet, swaying drunkenly. A few feet apart, they confronted each other.

"You fucking bastard! You made me do this, you monster!" the man screamed, his voice high pitched and desperate. Elena stared at the surreal scene in horror. Jackson moved closer and put his arms around her.

"You made me kill an innocent woman! A healthy young woman with decades to live yet! Now I'm going to rot in hell, all because of you! Well, I'm not going to rot alone! I'm taking you with me!"

It was then that she saw the flash of a scalpel clutched in the doctor's hand. It winked wickedly in the harsh overhead light, holding sway over life and death.

The doctor rushed him, the scalpel catching the light as it descended in a wide downward arch, intent on inflicting deadly harm. It slashed across her husband's forearm. Blood spurted. Hector swayed, but somehow managed to stay on his feet.

From somewhere a gun appeared in his hand. But before he could use it, the doctor was on him again, slashing at him in a murderous rage. *Jack the Ripper*. She shuddered in horror, unable to turn away. Jackson held her tightly, her port in the eye of the hurricane. The pair we so close together now she could no longer see the weapons. She looked over at the others. They were paralyzed into virtual human statues, their eyes wide with the terror of what they too were seeing. Everyone was trapped.

A shot rang out.

Time froze.

Then the pair fell apart. Their bodies separated. The doctor's face was a mask of horror as he slid to the floor and curled up in a fetal position. Hector lurched forward, his wounds bleeding profusely.

Who had been shot?

Elena pulled away from Jackson. "I have to help them," she said as he tried to hold her back. Jesús and Mamá stood silently by, unmoving. Elena moved first to Hector's side, her eyes noting the wounds. Two slash wounds, one on his forearm and one on his chest, but she could see no bullet wound. His eyes were closed but he was breathing fine, if harshly. She went to the doctor next. Gently tried to get him to uncurl enough to check him out. He was the one shot, a gut shot that was bleeding profusely. She quickly retrieved a thick bandage from the floor, tore the package open with her teeth, and pressed it to the wound.

"No point in saving him. He's a dead man anyway," Hector growled. "Stabbed me over a *puta*. Fucking bastard! Over a dead whore!"

She pressed her lips together as she mentally made the connection of the cause of the attack by the doctor. Bile rose in her throat. Her suspicions confirmed. She knew she had married a man capable of bad things, but until this exact moment she had never realized how evil.

She got to her feet, rushed to the sink, and threw up. Couldn't seem to stop. She dimly realized that Jackson was at her side, rubbing her back as she kept heaving. She was long lost past having anything left in her stomach, but still she felt unclean. This evil monster had had his hands on her. Put himself into her life, her body. Could she ever be clean again?

"It's okay. Just breathe, Elena," he said. His voice felt soothing in the darkness of her mind. She shuddered as she took a few deep breaths, swiping her mouth with the back of her hand. She had to get a grip. This kind of emotional trauma was bad for the baby. She steeled herself.

"A glass of water," she croaked.

He filled a paper cup from the tap and handed it to her. She took small sips, hoping to keep it down. The last thing she needed was to become dehydrated. She could hear the men groaning on the floor behind her as if they were far away, in a distant land that made no sense to her. She could not assist them. Not after what she had learned. Not after what they had done.

And for what? Two women lay dead. Two young lives lost. Cut short in their prime. Senseless. One a loathsome crime of murder. Hector should be locked up with all the other murderers.

Finally she was able to turn around with Jackson's help and face the devastation. The brother and mother had moved forward to help the man on the floor she no longer felt any human connection to. A doctor had now joined them from somewhere else in the hospital. Jesús was the only one to look up. He gave her a look of shame and despair. And compassion. She pulled on a mantle of resolve from somewhere deep inside and walked away.

Halfway down the hallway, she took another deep breath. She glanced around to make sure they weren't being observed and turned to Jackson.

"We *have* to find a way to get out of this place," she whispered. She looked into his eyes for the first time since the mayhem and saw the same pain and horror she was experiencing. She hugged him carefully, consciously aware of his recent wounds. She could feel his strong heart beating in tandem with her own. She hung onto that knowledge, placed all her faith in it.

"It'll be okay," she promised.

"Yes, it will be. I'm going to find a way out of this." She was reassured by the tone of his voice, filled with steely strength.

They continued their way down the hall. Walked into the morning sunshine that appeared an ordinary morning. Deceiving. Only a few hours had passed since she had gone through these very doors. It felt like an eternity, so much had changed. She turned her face upward to embrace the healing sun, cleansing her stained soul.

Two vehicles pulled up and a group of soldiers got out of both of them. She recognized some of the men and nodded in their direction.

"Are you all right, Señora Torres?" one of the men asked politely.

She frowned. Wondered who he was talking to? She was no longer *that* woman.

"Yes, I'm fine. I'm going into the main house now. I need to shower and rest."

He nodded and went in the front door followed by more of the men while a pair remained stationed outside, their rifles at the ready. Of course, she reasoned. With the attack on their leader everyone would be on heightened alert for the time being. Her spirits fell. It would make escape that much harder.

She glanced at Jackson and could see he had come to the same conclusion.

"I'm going to go to the house out back. I need to clean up as well. I'll join you later."

She nodded. "Good idea. Take one of the Jeeps—you don't want to hurt yourself further. Come as soon as you can. And please, drink lots of fluid. You have a lot of healing to do."

"Of course, ma'am," he said with a look that warmed her heart further. Even after all they had witnessed, he was still being supportive and trying to make the way easier for her. He was going to make a wonderful father. She couldn't kiss him goodbye, not with the men watching. She could only give him a smile and walk away. But she carried his essence in her heart, and in her belly. She rubbed her still flat tummy with reverence, thinking of the times that hopefully lay ahead. But first they had to get through the next few hours and days without mishap. She hurried toward the house, time to step up.

She was towel drying her hair when one of the maid's came in with an armload of fresh laundry. She made an instant decision.

"Juanita, not in here. I want all my things moved to the east wing. Right away. Get someone to help if you need. I want it done quickly."

"Everything, Mrs. Torres?" The young girl's eyebrows rose in surprise.

"Everything, thank you, Juanita."

CHAPTER 25

Leia watched the mirage from the SUV's window shimmer in the dry desert heat and then coalesce into the stepped outlines of high rises. Nearly home. She pressed her forehead against the glass. She had a feeling that this was all going to end soon, one way or the other.

"I need to take a leak," Agent Smith said, slowing down and turning the vehicle onto a side service road where a huddled group of buildings stood waiting.

"I'm hungry," Leia said. Not because she was, but because it would buy them more time.

"We're almost there," Catherine whined. "Can't you wait another couple of hours?"

Leia shook her head. "I need to use the washroom."

"Fine. Let's all make a pit stop," she grumbled, earning a warning look from the driver.

Agent Smith pulled into one of the few parking spots available on the lot. Leia perked up. With this many people about, surely she could find someone to help.

"Okay, let's make this quick. Just grab something to go," the agent said and got out. They all trooped along behind him while Leia watched and waited for her chance. She heard the SUV beep behind them to confirm the doors were locked in the vehicle as they entered the restaurant. She looked around warily. Who to approach?

Catherine grabbed her arm and pulled her along toward the bathroom in the back. She stumbled and caught the eye of a man reading a newspaper. He sat all alone at a corner table. He frowned at them. Then pursed his lips before carefully appearing to turn his back on the situation and go back to his reading. Her spirits spiraled downward. This wasn't going to be so easy.

"Quit dawdling! You wanted to use the restroom, right?" she hissed.

Leia didn't bother to answer her but went along with her to the bathroom. Locked inside the stall she sat down to think. Should she run over to the man and beg for help? Would something bad happen if she did? What did people do in these situations? Was she making a mistake? Maybe Ben was right. No, they had destroyed her phone. That couldn't be good. These people meant them harm. They'd used Ben's greed to lure them here. What did they want? Did it matter? She just wanted to be rid of them.

She got up and straightened her thin shoulders. It was now or never.

"Hurry up, Leia, for Christ's sake," Catherine said from outside the stall door. Leia heard the air dryer go off and then the door squeak open. It banged shut. Was she gone?

She licked her lips and pulled up the latch on the gray painted door. She peered around the edge. The bathroom was empty. She frantically looked around but there was no window. Okay, the newspaper guy it was.

She washed her hands, absently dried them on her jean fronts, and pulled the door open into the main area of the restaurant. Catherine was waiting for her right outside. She frowned at her. Leia bit her bottom lip so hard she tasted blood. The metallic taste filled her mouth and she stumbled forward drawing the attention of the newspaper guy again. Only this time he had company. Another guy sat beside him at the table and the pair was staring right at her.

She forced herself to take a step forward. Catherine had begun to walk down the aisle just ahead of her working her way between the tables. Space was tight and the restaurant was nearly full of patrons. She took another step. The men got up. Were they leaving? Panicked. She moved forward quicker. She had to stop them.

"Please!" someone outside herself seemed to be speaking the words. "I need help!"

It was over in an instant.

The men moved like lightning, one racing to her side and jerking her away from Catherine. He was so close she could smell his woodsy cologne as she stumbled into him. The other went for the redhead, catching her by surprise and spinning her around in a tight embrace, so quickly the other patrons had no time to notice or react. White noise hammered her ears and adrenaline pumped into her veins as she struggled for a breath.

"Don't move," he ordered Catherine, pulling her arms roughly behind her back. Her purse hit the floor with a dull thud. He clicked on handcuffs. She looked too shocked to resist, then it was too late. She hissed at Leia as the other man kept his body positioned between them. "This is all your fault, you fucking little druggie!"

"Nice mouth," the man muttered. "Where's your accomplice at?"

Leia realized these men were likely looking for them.

And more importantly that they were some kind of law enforcement.

Catherine's mouth firmed into a grim line. "I have no fucking idea. Find him yourself, you motherfuckers."

The two men moved them along through the restaurant, eyes alert to any sudden movement.

Leia spied the agent and Ben outside.

"They're over there!" she said, pointing out the bank of windows that ran along the front of the restaurant. "In the parking lot getting into that black SUV!"

"Wait here," the man barked. One of the men, the taller of the pair, hurried out of the restaurant, gun drawn. The other hung back, guarding Catherine. He gestured for the woman to sit down on a chair near the door. Leia remained standing unable to take her eyes off the scene, ignoring Catherine's profane grumbling.

But before the man could reach them, they took off. A cloud of dust rose from the graveled parking lot as the SUV's tires spun out in the mad dash to leave, gravel and stones flying in all directions. The vehicle tipped to the side on two wheels. Leia's breath froze in her chest. It overcorrected the opposite way, the driver fighting to right it. Just when she was certain it would roll the kidnapper grabbed control and made it out of the parking lot. Leia let out a huge sigh of relief. She didn't want Ben hurt. She sank down onto a chair, her legs watery.

The man in the lot put his gun back in his holster and pulled out his cell phone. Leia couldn't hear what the man was saying, but from the look on his angry face, his dark clothing covered in dust, he had a lot to say to somebody.

"I'd like a glass of water," Leia said. Her throat was parched, like she'd been walking a long time in the desert.

The man who had saved her gave her a tight under-standing smile. "You okay?"

"Yeah, I think so."

Catherine gave them both a disgusted look.

"Miss, this young lady would like a glass of water," the man directed one of the waitresses who nodded and scurried off to retrieve it.

"Young lady, my ass," Catherine said with scorn.

"Shut up," he said to her and then turned to Leia. "I'm Agent Cruz. I work for the FBI and we've been busy looking for you. I hate to admit it, but finding you here is a bit of happenstance. Agent Holland and I were just having breakfast and didn't expect to see you. Quite a happy coincidence."

"Yeah, real fucking happy. Spectacular police work by the way. You guys just got fucking lucky—again," Catherine said.

"I thought I told you to shut up." This time he directed a cold steely stare at Catherine that made Leia shudder. She never wanted to be on his bad side.

"Thank you so much, Agent Cruz. I don't care how you came to be here, but I am so glad you were. Other-wise—" She couldn't go there. "Do you think Ben will be okay?"

He shrugged. "I can't promise anything, but we'll try to take them down safely. Agent Holland's working on that right now. Okay, if you're feeling up to it, we need to leave."

"Okay, I'm ready." Leia finished her water in a large gulp and got up so quickly her head spun. But she covered it up. She wanted to get on with things. Make sure Ben was okay.

Cruz pulled Catherine to her feet none too gently and the trio exited the restaurant. They joined the other agent in the lot, headed for the men's vehicle parked nearby.

"I've got roadblocks set up and a helicopter is on its way. We'll get them," Agent Holland said with satisfaction.

Leia swallowed hard. *Please let Ben be okay.*

JACKSON FRANTICALLY REACHED for the old man's cell phone burning a hole in his pants pocket. They'd taken his gun but neglected the phone. He had to contact Rand. Let him know what had happened at the pickup sight and, more importantly, what could still happen if something wasn't done quickly before Joe had a chance to spill the beans. Then he remembered that it might be compromised, and raced through the house to his bedroom to retrieve the phone that had been left behind. It was gone, not on the nightstand. Fuck. Was his iPad still safe? Yes, it was password protected and encrypted, but thinking it had fallen into his enemies' hands shook him up. It was gone as well. After their kidnapping the place must have been gone over with a fine-toothed comb. He had no choice but to use the old man's phone.

"Rand! It's Jackson."

"Thank God! Are you all right? You weren't at the pickup."

"Yeah, Hector's men got to us first. I'm okay." He didn't bother to mention the gunshot after what he had just witnessed. It seemed trivial. "We were turned in by an old Mexican guy that recognized Elena for a reward. We're back at Hector's ranch. They picked us up by helicopter a couple of hours ago. But that's not the worst part, one of Hector's men knows about Elena and me."

"What? You've been fooling around with his wife? Piss poor idea, buddy."

"It wasn't like that. But it means I gotta get her out of

here. Hector's capable of anything." His mind flew over what had just happened in the hospital room and he visibly shuddered. "You have no idea."

"That's exactly why we have to nail this guy! Get him off the streets." The zeal in Rand's voice made him pause for a moment. "I meant to tell you this right away! Leia's been found—rescued by a couple of agents who were eating at the same place they stopped at. She's fine. Safe and sound. You can rest assured on that score. She's in protective custody, guarded round the clock. My fucking ex was at the bottom of it. She threw in her lot with that bought off piece-of-shit Kyle Smith—you know—that guy that drove the kids to the facility in the first place. She was even worse than I knew. Sorry Jackson."

"That's good news. And none of it's your fault." Jackson felt all the bones in his tense body relax. His little sister was safe. The world brightened to vivid color with the news.

"And there's something else," Rand began, his voice hesitant.

"Spill it." Now that Leia was safe, he could handle anything. He felt his first twinge of sympathy for Hector at that moment. No matter how it went down, he had just lost his own baby sister and had to be in a lot of pain. Though even that did not excuse his atrocities.

"You asked me to look into the situation about your mother. You know, who she stayed with and had contact with that summer she spent in Mexico."

Jackson's heart constricted. This was it.

"I know this is going to sound crazy—"

"For fuck's sake, tell me! This phone may not be safe for long if at all."

"I think—no I'm pretty sure—that you are related to the Torres family. Hector's family."

"What?" His mind blanked, whirling with white noise.

"I think he's your half brother. His father, Antonio Hector Torres, had an affair with your mother that summer she stayed with her friends from university. Apparently, quite a torrid affair that's burned into local memories. I got confirmation on a number of fronts. I wouldn't bring this to you otherwise. It caused a hell of a scandal because he was already married to Hector's mother. After your mom went back to the states—you were born eight months later."

My middle name is Antonio! His head instantly began to throb in pain. His skull felt too small for his brain, pressed too tightly against it. He slumped down on a chair with the phone clamped so tightly to his ear that it hurt.

What the hell was going on? And what was he going to do? He coveted his brother's wife if Rand was to be believed. Rand had never let him down, never lied to him. It had to be true, as impossible as it was to be believed.

"Jackson, are you still there?"

"Yeah," he muttered, his voice hoarse.

"As crass as this sounds, we can use this. Hector won't kill a brother."

"Yeah, probably not, he's a dyed-in-the-wool family man," he admitted, wiping his mouth with the back of his trembling hand. Did he really share the same blood as that man? The man capable of killing another in cold blood? He was hurt now and Jackson didn't even know how badly. Maybe he was dying over there in the hospital. But he doubted it. It would take more than a few flesh wounds to bring him down.

"We've got to get him back to the states to nail him. It's still all a go if you can keep things together on your end. What's the likelihood that a man who betrayed

Hector is going to come back to share knowledge that will only enrage him further? Most likely a case of 'kill the messenger.' And if something changes, we can send in the troops and get you out fast—with Elena if possible."

"I'm not going without her," Jackson warned. *But what if Joe just picked up the phone and told him, what then?* He didn't say the thought aloud but considered his options. Yes, he wanted Hector in the worst way, even if he was his half brother. Was it wise to wait and continue with the original plan? Probably not. But with so many soldiers protecting Hector and the ranch he had little to no chance of getting Elena away free and clear. Now, with Hector in the states, the ranch would be less guarded, more relaxed with the boss gone. And better yet, what if he brought her to the states? It had been his pattern in the past. It was entirely possible.

"Okay, let's steady the course," he agreed, though his gut roiled with all the unknowns. Was he making the right choice? To hell if he knew. But having the Calvary rescue them right now might just create a bloodbath he didn't want to be responsible for. That could only be the last resort.

"Good. I wouldn't continue this if I thought you were in immediate danger, you know that, right?"

"Yeah."

"Keep your mind on the prize. Hector in jail for life and you going back to your regular life. Well—"

And with Elena if there was any justice in the universe.

Rand had paused and Jackson's interest piqued. "Maybe not so normal a life. There's been a buzz about you around the place."

"What kind of buzz?"

"I've been trying to get a handle on it but it's above

my pay grade. But, if I had to speculate, I would say something to do with your ability."

"Shit."

"Yeah, well, you can wear that white hat full time," Rand joked.

"I never wanted the attention."

"I know buddy, but sometimes you get called up to the majors no matter what."

CHAPTER 26

THE PAIN IN HECTOR'S BODY WAS NOTHING COMPARED TO the pain torturing his soul. He would recover from his physical wounds, but this wound, of his baby sister dying right before his eyes; this would haunt him the rest of his days. Even the thought of a child of his loins being born in a few months could not stem the anguish. The blow had been too severe. He lay prone on the stark white sheets not wanting to get up and take charge of things. He knew his wounds were not serious. That he had gotten off lightly with mere flesh wounds that would heal easily enough according to a doctor on staff who had stitched him up. His listlessness surprised him in one part of his mind while he pondered things with the other.

"Get up, my son," his mama ordered as she briskly entered his hospital room and stood at the side of the bed, confronting him. "This is no time for self-indulgence. You are a Torres, from a proud and noble lineage. And a Torres never breaks, only braces themselves against the winds that blow through everyone's life. What would your papá think? To see you lying down like this," she said the last part with scorn. "Think of all he did to protect this family. Are you going to lie there all day and not get on with all the things that need to be done to help this family flourish? To see your family safely through this storm?"

Thoughts of the sacrifices of his beloved papá made him stir guiltily. He sat up and thrust the covers away. His mamá was right. He should not be wallowing in such silly self-pity. He was a Torres. An ancient lineage. He must take up the reins—everyone counted on him.

"Good. You did what you had to," she said more softly and came closer to help him dress. He looked into her understanding brown eyes and listened as she continued while buttoning his shirt. "Teresa was very ill. It was her time. What you did was valiant—all your efforts to save her life. Do not doubt yourself now. This is the time for strength. We must pull together—now more than ever."

"Yes. I have much to do," he said, thinking of the trip he must take and soon. And a funeral he needed to help his brothers arrange. He was neglecting his duties. Focus on what needed to be done, that was the way. The old way.

"Thank you, Mamá," he said, kissing her once on each cheek. She stepped back and he pulled on his pants buckling the big silver buckle he'd won bull riding in his younger days. It was his favorite from his vast collection. He straightened his shoulders. Gave her a tight smile.

"I will speak with Jesús. We will invite everyone from all the families. See that she goes out with all proper respect. We will build a huge mausoleum in her honor, a place for meditation and reflection."

"You are a good son." She leaned forward and straightened his collar, brushed an invisible speck of dust off the shoulder of his jacket. "You must also be a good husband now. I want my grandchild born healthy and well. Don't push her too hard. Women, we are more emotional when our hormones run amuck as they do when we are pregnant. It will pass, I promise you."

"I cannot imagine you ever letting our father down when you carried me and my brothers and Teresa." Saying his sister's name aloud hurt like hell, but it slipped out defending his mamá before he could hold it back.

"Ah, all women are held sway to it. I was no different though it was a different time with different expectations."

He nodded. "I'll see you later at dinner." He turned back as a moment of clarity struck. "Perhaps it's time to welcome Jackson Banks to our family. Once he knows his roots—that we share a father—he will become one of us. That can only be a good thing, right?" he asked his mamá with all due respect.

"Yes, I agree," she said solemnly as the occasion demanded. "Now is the right time. Tonight, at dinner. We will welcome him to our family. I will see that a special meal is prepared with all your favorites."

This time he made it out of the hospital and walked over to the main house. It was a warm day and the sound of horses in the corral behind the house being put through their paces was soothing to his bruised spirit.

He entered the chapel intent on speaking with Jesús. He spied his brother talking with Alonzo. Hector noticed their reddened eyes and downcast looks. He straightened his spine. His mamá was right, his family needed him.

"Alonzo was thinking perhaps a small service with just family would be best," Jesús said softly.

"No! We will do this up proper—Mamá wants to do our family proud. We'll invite all the families and make a grand celebration of her life. We will send our sister off in the old way."

The pair nodded in unison, bowing to their mother's and Hector's wishes as they always did. They looked relieved to do so to his mind. After cementing plans, Hector excused himself. "I need to check on my wife."

The pair exchanged guilty looks. "What?" he demanded.

"Nothing, nothing," Alonzo said defensively. He always was a poor liar.

"I can see by your expressions it's something. Out with it."

"It's just Aviva said that Elena had moved into the east wing. Soon as she got back." When Alonzo saw the expression on his brother's face he stammered his next words. "Maybe—maybe it has something to do with the baby she's carrying?"

Hector literally saw red. His vision was suffused with the overwhelming color. He shook his head back and forth to dispel the cloying mist.

Jesús placed a hand on his sleeve. "She's carrying your child, brother, a very precious thing. Maybe she is worried about miscarrying and needs to rest. Doctor's orders, perhaps?" He spoke tentatively in his gentle voice that always soothed at wakes and funerals.

Hector nodded. Pretended it was okay.

"I will see you at dinner. Mamá is putting on a special one in honor of Jackson Banks. Tomorrow, I need to go to LA for a couple of days, but I will be back in time for our sister's funeral."

He strode from the room and directly to the east wing, the opposite end of the house from their bedroom. He spied her with the young maid, Juanita. He'd always wanted to fuck the woman. Juanita had that vulnerable prettiness he coveted. But not today. He just looked directly at her and said, "Leave us."

The maid scurried away, dropping her load of clothes haphazardly on the floor.

"You frightened the girl," Elena said, chastising him in a neutral tone of voice. He studied her. She looked different. Stronger.

"I will do more than frighten her," he warned, crossing the room and grabbing her tightly by the upper arms.

She stood her ground. "I need my space. With the baby coming, I will be up at all hours throwing up and having all sorts of pregnant woman aliments. I thought to save you from being disturbed by it all. You need your rest with all that you must do each day. You have heavy responsibilities," she parroted without emotion like a prepared speech she had been hatching.

"Don't think to make this about me. You're the one looking to pull away. I want you back in our bedroom. Now!"

She shook her head. "I can't do that, Hector. Trust me. You don't want it either."

"I can just have you taken there," he threatened.

"You could. But what would you gain? Being stressed is bad for the baby according to my doctor and all the medical journals I've read." She rubbed her stomach for emphasis. "Do you want to be responsible if I miscarry?"

He shook his head with frustration. He could control men with fear, kill without remorse, yet his own wife was an enigma to him. But it was his mamá's words that carried the most sway.

"I can throw a stone in any direction and easily find a woman that would warm my bed better than you, *puta*," he said, curling up his lip in disgust. It was not what he had meant to say but anger seethed in his soul and he wished to wound her.

She nodded, her glance cool. Her lack of caring what he thought angered him further. He reached out a hand and slapped her across the face. Hard. She stood still though tears flooded her golden eyes as she stared him down.

He spun round on his heel and left the room before he did something he would truly regret. This was not the time. Not with his sister lying dead. And not with his family in turmoil.

———

ELENA SLUMPED onto a chair and took a deep breath not even feeling the pain in her bruised cheek. She had won the first round. She was free of the monster invading her bed and her body nightly. Free to think of Jackson and their unborn child. Relief flooded and tingled its soothing way through her system, relaxing her jangling nerves.

Juanita stepped back into the room and began gathering the discarded clothing. Elena watched her for a moment than got up to help her. She needed to keep busy. So much was riding on the next few days it made her head spin. Hector had not shared his plans with her about Teresa's funeral or his intended trip to the states. *If only he would take me.* She longed for that opportunity for she knew back in the states they stood the best chance of getting away unscathed. Perhaps she should have stayed closer to Hector? No. She would not pander to him. Not now. Not ever.

She took a shower and dressed for dinner a few hours later, carefully covering the new bruise with makeup. Layers of pancake did the job. She'd had lots of practice, too much practice. She wasn't going to take it anymore. She thought of the new handgun she had hidden under the mattress that she had begged Juanita to obtain for her earlier in the day. She had traded a very expensive pearl necklace for it and hoped its departure from her jewelry case would not be noticed. She knew she was under surveillance in most parts of the house, and hoped no one had thought to bug the east wing. Pale under her makeup, she looked into the mirror and promised herself, somehow, once this nightmare was over, she was going to become a doctor.

Everyone was already gathered in the library when she entered and slipped into a chair. Jackson looked up and she carefully gave him a cool nod and her mother-in-law a tight smile of greeting as she looked her way.

"Elena, nice of you to join us," Hector's mother said the words with a sharp edge meant as reproof for her tardy arrival. She was five minutes late, caused by a small loosened thread in the hem of her dress. She was all too aware of Mamá Torres impossibly high standards. Perfection was the only option allowed.

Hector gave her a stern look that pierced her armor. Only the thought of the hidden gun gave her the strength to return the look.

"I was about to speak."

She accepted a glass of tonic water from the maid for the toast. Waited.

Hector moved forward in his high-backed chair but did not stand to speak. "The Torres clan has a long-standing tradition of looking out for kin and family. Our grandfathers passed on this torch that we hold blood dearest and protect our own right from the beginning of our legends. We support each other through the bad times, and the good. We believe that family is all. But today we lost one of our own." His voice broke. His mamá laid a steadying hand on his thigh. Hector gave her a grateful look and continued. "Let us toast our beloved sister, Teresa Sofia Camila Maria Torres, may she rest in peace. To Teresa, the finest sister a brother could ask for." He raised his glass and took a sip. Everyone followed suit with a murmured chorus of *to Teresa.*

Hector sat silent for a few moments then stirred himself to speak again.

"But it has also come to my attention that as we say goodbye to Teresa, we are being blessed with a new family member sent to us by the hand of God to ease our suffering."

Everyone looked up with curiosity. Elena glanced over at Jackson who stirred uncomfortably in his chair near Hector's. *What was going on?* Her heart began to beat faster.

"Our father, the great Antonio Hector Alonzo Torres, may he rest in peace, had a son with a woman from America many, many years ago. Until very recently we did not know of his existence. Fortunately, we now know that his offspring, his son, has come home to us. Jackson *Antonio* Banks is our half brother. I want you to raise your glass and welcome him to the Torres family. Welcome, Jackson. Salute!"

Dead silence. Then excited conversations broke out as everyone began to talk at once.

Elena had no idea what to think. Jackson. Related to the Torres family. Given his father's name. It was inconceivable. The knowledge made her stomach roll over. She stumbled to her feet as nausea threatened.

"I must go," she said and rushed from the room.

"Let her go. Elena's pregnant." She heard her mother-in-law explain to the family. Good. She had a plausible excuse. She just made the small powder room around the corner before throwing up.

How could it be? Her reflection in the mirror had no answers as she wiped her mouth with trembling fingers.

She took a sip of water and slumped down on a stool. The walls were closing in and she took a few deep breaths to steady herself. She cleared her mind to be able to look at things logically.

What would this do to their plans? Jackson had known before the announcement, that much was clear. No one had any choice in their parentage. Jackson was no different in that regard. She may hate that some of the Torres blood would run through her child's veins, but it was the least of her worries. For the clan wasn't known for letting one of their own escape their clutches. Would all this come back to haunt them? Yes, most likely it would. Did it stop them from trying? No. It did not. *It might benefit us on one level.* Surely they would think twice about killing him now?

She got up pushed a few strands of hair that had escaped her bun back into place before the mirror. She needed to keep her feelings in check and help Jackson. That was all that mattered.

———

JACKSON KEPT a close watch on the doorway through which Elena had disappeared. Was she all right? Having such news dumped on her had to be bad. Would she think him a monster with Torres blood running through his veins? The thought filled him with dread. He tried to pay attention to the history lesson of the Torres family lineage from Alonzo's wife Aviva, who had taken it upon herself to produce an old family photo album and now sat at his side busily turning the pages, but found his mind incapable of taking it in. Who cared who his great-aunt and uncle were? Maybe one day, but not today.

"Aviva, put that away until later, it's time for dinner," Hector's mother interjected, and for once he was glad for her bossiness.

"Shouldn't we wait for Elena?" Jesús asked, looking up from texting on his cell phone.

"She'll join us when she's ready," his mother answered crisply and stood up to lead the parade into the dining room.

"Jackson will sit beside me," she announced with satisfaction as they spaced themselves out around the table.

Corralled, he had no other choice but to sit down where she indicated. He winced at the twinges of pain in his side. Pain medication would have helped but he was reluctant to take any, wanting all his facilities sharp. Hector sat on his other side and soup was served. A couple of minutes into the meal Elena joined them, and Jackson's appetite came back.

"I'll be leaving in the morning and will be away for a couple of days," Hector said as he waited for the servant to remove his soup plate and replace it with the main course.

"I would like to go with you, Hector," Jackson interjected quickly.

"You need your rest," the matriarch argued, giving him a look of concern.

"I'm fine. I've had worse wounds." He shrugged. "And the scars to prove it."

Hector gave him an assessing look from his dark unfathomable eyes. The man would make one hell of a poker player. The fortress was too heavily guarded for him to whisk Elena away, eyeing the pair standing just at the doorway studiously ignoring the family eating dinner, but with telltale bulges under their jackets. Since his and Elena's kidnapping, Hector had doubled his security. Hell, even his house had a detail assigned to it though the men had stayed outside and guarded the perimeter.

"You have suffered much, my brother. And with much suffering comes great wisdom. I could make use of your wise council. We leave early—at six in the morning."

Jackson could feel Elena's gaze on him. He wanted to ask but held himself back, knowing it would not help. His gut roiled. So much hinged on the next couple of days. What or who would be left standing when this was all over? He shook his head, exhaustion was playing tricks with his mind. He reminded himself she would be safe as Hector would not harm the mother of his child. He had to believe that.

Back in his house Jackson took a quick shower. He poured a stiff bourbon and went outside to sit on the porch. He needed time to think.

The security detail had moved off and in the darkness; he couldn't see them as they patrolled. So much the better. Having eyes on him gave him the creeps. He wondered idly how prisoners withstood such a stripping away of their privacy as he took a large swallow from his glass. No choice. The one thing he had always promised himself was he'd never go to prison. He'd always tried to be an upstanding citizen to keep the whiff of crime from him. And here he was right dab in the middle of illegal activities. Sure, the government was behind his activities. The reminder sent his mind off on a different tangent. Would they want to exploit his unusual ability in the future? Most likely. Was it time to step up?

He heard soft footfalls in the darkness and sat up straighter.

"Just me, Jackson," Jesús called out from the edge of the yard as he came into view, his hands stuffed in his pockets.

"Jesús," Jackson said with some surprise and then realized he was related by blood to this gentleman.

"Mind if I join you?" he asked.

"No, of course not."

"You couldn't sleep either," Jesús observed.

"No. Can I get you a drink?"

"Thanks, but no. But I will sit for a bit if you don't mind?"

Jackson nodded toward another high-backed Algonquin chair. "Sure, join me."

"I like to walk at night. Best time to think and ponder," Jesús said as he sat down in the chair and clasped his hands in his lap.

"Strange to think we're related," the man murmured, getting right to the matter that was obviously uppermost in his mind.

"Yeah, I was shocked as well. Are you okay with it?" Jackson thought to ask as he suddenly realized how much it changed things for all of them. In ways they couldn't comprehend as yet. He felt a stab of remorse for the ill will he held this man's brother. The irony was that Jackson had always wished for a brother. Now he had three.

"Talk about not being able to choose your relatives," Jackson joked to lighten the load.

"Hector trusts you and speaks well of you. That's good enough for me," he said simply.

"Hector's good to his family." Jackson gave the devil his due.

"Thank you. Hector loves his family. I know that he sometimes carries that love too far, but he means well. He'd do anything for any one of us. It is truly us against the world for my brother—our brother. Has he shared the history of our father with you? How he came to be killed?"

Jackson nodded. "Yes, I am sorry for your loss." Then

he realized it was his loss as well. He wasn't sure how he should feel about that. Too soon.

"Hector was very young when he felt the burden of stepping up to be the father of our family. It changed him —made him the man he is today. He never got to be a child."

"It's a lot for a child to handle," Jackson agreed. "Was the Torres family always involved with the drug trade?"

"You don't approve?"

"Not exactly a legal business."

"There's a long tradition of it in our country. Long-standing roots that can never be pulled from the land—they go far too deep. It's not an immoral trade, Jackson Banks, but a business. The choice to use or not to use is made by the people themselves. Should they not have a choice? Is each person so weak they don't know their own minds?"

Stymied, Jackson sat and sipped at his bourbon. The Torres family thought differently from the people he knew back home. They weren't bad people, just raised in a different culture. Who's to say if he hadn't been born there, he might have been sucked into it? The thought startled him. What if his father had insisted he be raised right there with his brothers? What then? How would his life have been different? The idea was mind blowing in ramifications. He would probably think a lot more like the brothers he was now getting to know. Uncomfortable with his thoughts, he frowned into the bottom of his empty glass as he composed his next words.

"The collective good is important as well. Perhaps a government needs to step up and stop such activities if the people cannot or will not act. Just look at the results of the drug trade. Families torn apart, not to mention the violence of those looking to get ahead. Many people have died violently at the hands of rival cartels. You cannot deny a lot of blood has been spilled, Jesús." Jackson let his passion spill over in his voice.

"No, you're right. The violence is more than tragic," Jesús admitted in a quiet tone as he stirred in his seat and crossed his legs.

"And unnecessary if a different path is chosen."

"Well, if only that were true, we wouldn't be having this conversation."

"Would you go legitimate if the choice was offered to you? Sell your coffins to the United States without trying to smuggle drugs aboard?"

"Perhaps, if the choice was there, but it is not remotely possible as things stand, so why waste time thinking about it? My business brings in a pittance compared to Hector's, though Alonzo's horse trailers sell well. I would need to expand my operations—hire and train men and find more places to sell my goods. No point in spending time planning for what can never be."

"You yourself said that people have a choice in whether or not they use drugs," Jackson reminded him.

"Yes, but the family one is born to, the country one is born in, not much choice in that, my brother."

"No, not much choice in that at all," Jackson admitted as he considered how he could help the man.

A lonely yip of a coyote echoed in the distance.

"I should be getting back," Jesús said and got to his feet.

Jackson followed suit. He was surprised by the man turning and embracing him, though he readily returned the hug.

"Perhaps you are just the man to lead us in a new direction. I look forward to getting to know you better," he said, surprising Jackson further.

Did Jesús really mean it? Would he consider doing things differently if the choice was offered to him?

He watched his brother walk away in the darkness until he disappeared from view. Melancholy overcame him. Was this the only and last time he would speak with the man openly? Did he have a duty to help him in some way?

Confused, he rubbed his aching head and became aware of the pain throbbing in his side and realized it had been trying to grab his attention for some time. He needed to sleep. Allow his body time to heal.

He went inside and locked the door knowing it would do no good if someone wanted in. He lay down on a bed in a back bedroom and winced at the pain, staring at the ceiling, going over the conversation with his brother. The world was changing far too quickly. He dreaded what tomorrow might bring. How did he really feel about bringing Hector down? How much was this going to hurt his brothers? His new family?

He lay in the dark, not awake, not asleep. Suspended. No answers forthcoming during the long endless night.

When the sun rose, he rose as well. He showered, packed, and was ready to leave when a knock sounded at the front door.

"Morning," he said, greeting the soldier sent to fetch him. He noted another pair on foot patrol around the property and felt the odd sensation of escaping prison.

The man just grunted and led the way to the Jeep. They sped off to the landing strip where a small five-passenger Cessna 310 twin-engine plane painted white with red trim awaited them.

"Morning, Jackson. You're right on time. We're ready to go," Hector greeted him with enthusiasm, clapping him on the back. Jackson's bag was quickly loaded, and he climbed up the stairs behind the wing and into the compartment. He ignored the pain he experienced and looked around to see who else was going when a trap-door opened up in his stomach and he realized Elena was not on board. It was all he could do to stay in his seat and not rush off the plane to see if she was safe after all he had promised her. With pure strength of will, he remained seated, grinding his teeth so hard they ached. Was this the best course? Putting Hector in prison first and then coming back for her? For the first time in his life he truly wished he could see into the future. Why had he not been given that gift instead?

He watched Hector take the controls. Alonzo sat down across from Jackson. It was just the three of them then. Why not Elena? There was plenty of room. He forced himself not to ask and stared out the small window with longing in his heart, the barren beauty of the land lost on him as he tilted his baseball cap forward to shade his eyes. He sunk deeper into his seat. It would be about a five-hour trip to LA, give or take on a Cessna 310, far too much time to think. Fortunately, he was so exhausted he drifted off, the perfect blue skies producing a soft cushion of air current around the plane suspending it effortlessly while the endless drone of the twin motors lulled him.

He woke as the plane landed on the tarmac. Rubbed the sleep from his eyes.

"I'm thinking Sweet Valentine's tonight, what do you say?" Alonzo asked with a salacious grin as he noticed Jackson was awake.

"Not till this wound heals," Jackson said, coming up with a viable excuse.

Alonzo grunted. "Your bad luck, but I would imagine a blow job wouldn't hurt much, but I know what I've got planned and it involves *plenty* of action, if you know what I mean. A night away from the old ball-and-chain doesn't happen every night. How about you, Hector? You up for it?"

Hector finished speaking to the tower and gave his brother an affirmative leer. "Sure, I'm always game."

"Are we checking out the can today?" Jackson asked, his heart rate immediately increasing at the thought that zero hour rapidly approaching. He didn't know how he felt about the fact that the raid would now nab two of his brothers. He was relieved that Jesús hadn't come with them feeling an affinity for the earnest young man after their revealing conversation.

"No rush, I got some people to see first," Hector said as he took off his black headset and lay it on the instrument panel. They disembarked and grabbed their bags from the plane's cargo hold, then walked across the tarmac to the waiting black SUV. George was behind the wheel, Thomas seated next to him.

"I've booked us into the Fairmont," George said as he started the vehicle's ignition as the three men got into the back.

"Good," Hector said.

"You can drop me anywhere and I can take a taxi to my place," Jackson suggested.

"I won't hear of it. You're our guest at the Fairmont as well," Hector said, concluding the matter.

"Okay," Jackson agreed. This close to his goal he was prepared to see it through. A couple more days wasn't going to change things for Leia and she was safer where she was. But the thought made him realize Hector hadn't brought up that development with him. Did he know? He must. There was little that this astute man didn't know about. Did he blame Jackson for it? The agents coming across the kidnappers had been an accident, not planned. That should let him off the hook. But without leverage, how did Hector see the relationship with him? Did he trust him enough to let him tag along to the warehouse? *Hell, do I even want to be there for the final takedown?*

Jackson picked up the phone and punched in Rand's phone number soon as he walked through the hotel room door.

"I'm at the Fairmont with Hector and three others," he said. His voice terse. *Calm the fuck down.*

"How are you doing, buddy?"

"Getting by. How are things on your end? Leia still safe?"

"Yeah, of course. When are you headed over to the warehouse?"

"Not till tomorrow, by the looks of it. Everything in place?"

"You bet. We just need the time. We're down to the short strokes now, buddy, hang in there."

Rand sounded a little too upbeat.

"Everything okay?"

"A little fucking nerve-racking, but yeah, I'll manage. Could we meet? Later?"

"Sure, Hector and his minions are headed to that Sweet Valentine's club on Ellice. How about we meet at the Denny's around the corner—say in two hours."

A knock resounded at the door. "I gotta go. Just one thing, promise me you'll look out for Elena if anything happens to me, Rand. This is important," he added as it went quiet on the other end. "She's carrying my child."

"Okay. You have my word."

"Thank you, that means a lot to me."

Hector stood in the doorway, a bottle of Kentucky bourbon clutched in his right hand. "Thought you might like a drink before dinner," he said as he walked in uninvited and over to the bar. He pulled the cork from the bottleneck and poured two stiff drinks. He sat down at the round table near the window, gestured for Jackson to do the same.

Jackson sat down across from the man and took up his glass.

"Salute," Hector said and took a big swig.

The bourbon was more than fine and flowed down Jackson's parched throat like golden nectar from the gods.

"Good quality."

"Nothing but the best for the Torres brothers."

Jackson stirred uncomfortably.

"Sure you don't want to join us at Sweet Valentine's?"

"I'm sure."

Hector finished his drink and poured them another. Jackson drank it slower this time. He needed to keep his head.

"Let's you and I take a ride," Hector said, getting to his feet.

"Now?" Jackson stalled.

"You got a problem with that?" Hector turned on him.

"No, it's fine. But I warn you, I intend to call it an early night. Still got some healing to do."

"I'll have you back in plenty of time for your beauty rest."

Jackson followed his brother down to the garage where George had parked the SUV. Alonzo and George were already there in the back seat, raising his suspicions even more while Thomas was at the wheel. He got in the back, Hector got in the front, and Thomas sped off. They drove for a few minutes in silence, while Jackson's heart rate sped up again. If he hadn't had a fucking heart attack before now, his body must be sound.

They pulled up at the intersection and turned onto the I-110 that led to the Port Authority and the warehouse. Shit. He should have seen this coming. Hector was being smart, hitting the place tonight instead of tomorrow. The man didn't trust anybody. Jackson felt a stab of guilt. His mistrust was justified.

"Thought we were headed out to dinner?" Jackson said in an effort to make conversation.

"Sure, later. What do you want? Mexican, Chinese, Italian? I've got a hankering for a good steak myself." Hector turned around to give him a questioning glance.

"I could go for a steak. In fact, I'm starved. We couldn't eat first?"

"This won't take long. Got to meet a guy."

Jackson raked his brain for another idea of how to get the thirty seconds necessary to call Rand.

"The bourbon's pressing on my bladder. Need to take a leak."

"Could you hold it a few minutes?"

"Afraid not."

Hector cursed but pulled into a parking lot of a fast-food joint hitting the speed bump so hard the vehicle bounced and their heads nearly hit the roof. As Jackson was climbing out Alonzo joined him.

"Gotta go too."

Feeling like he was under surveillance, Jackson made his way into the building, the odor of fast food making his mouth salivate. He really was hungry. He hurried to the back and pushed the men's room door open, and rushed into the one available stall. If he hurried, he might get a moment to give a clerk Rand's number and get him to pass on a message. Inside the stall, he pulled out a pen and wrote the number on a piece of tissue. He tucked it back in his pocket and then hurried to piss to allay any suspicions.

Alonzo was still at the urinal as he left. *Just give me two seconds*, he prayed. He headed right up to the counter and was about to speak to the server when Alonso appeared at his side.

"No time for this right now. Let's go. Hector doesn't like to be kept waiting."

Jackson bit his lip, but he had no choice but to follow his brother from the restaurant.

They settled back into their seats. Buckled up. Twenty minutes later, they were pulling up at their destination. He exited the SUV with the men, the surreal moment making each second feel stretched into slow motion.

He followed the crew to the warehouse's side door where Hector produced a key from his suit pocket. He stood and waited, his throat dry as dust. The key stuck in the lock and it took a couple of noisy thumps with Thomas's broad shoulders to jar the door loose. Inside the warehouse, large shadowy shapes loomed in the dark until George found the light switches and turned them on bringing everything into sharp focus.

Hector nodded at Thomas. "Wait outside for them," he instructed. "They should be here shortly."

"Sure." The bodyguard obediently went back through the doorway.

Hector strode ahead of the pack right up to his container, one of the few items the building housed. Normally cargo containers were parked outside, but this one had been given special privilege. It was parked near the front entrance with its row of huge overhead doors, ready to be hooked up to a trailer. Kept out of view until now.

His brother grunted as he pulled out a Leatherman utility tool from his suit pocket and cut off the plastic tie that sealed the door shut and unlatched the back door, swinging it open. It emitted a loud squeal of protest. A dismal arid smell instantly permeated the space. Jackson winced. He wished he could change his story at that moment to it being cinnamon that could cover up the odor of cocaine.

"Whew, stinks, brother. What if it's polluted the drugs?"

"That's what we are here to find out." Hector climbed up the back of the container and opened the lid of one of the coffins. He pulled back the silk lining and packages of vacuum sealed cocaine fell out. He picked one up and walked back to the edge and stepped down.

He stabbed the package with the penknife on the Leatherman and drew out a bit of the white powder. He sniffed at it. Assessing.

"Smells all right far as I can tell."

"Hector!" a voice called out, and everyone's head turned. "Your company's arrived," Thomas said, waving from the doorway.

"Good."

Package in hand, Hector strode over to join Thomas and the two men just coming in behind him.

"Johnny, Luis, good to see you both," Hector said as he greeted them like old friends.

The pair had eyes only for the coke.

"Nice. May I taste?" one of them asked, his eyes alight with greed.

Hector acquiesced, his expression one of graciousness as he played host to the pair. Jackson figured the men had to be an important part of the supply chain and wondered if Rand had any knowledge of their where-abouts, or if perhaps they were being followed by his men. If only he could have called his friend. But he had to admit another part of him was relieved and that part he was trying his best to ignore.

"Of course."

The man touched the powder spilling from the small cut with a dampened forefinger and brought it to his mouth. Tasted it carefully with the tip of his tongue. He nodded.

"Exactly as promised. To say I'm impressed is too small a word, *padrino*," he said with respect, laying it on a bit thick in Jackson's opinion.

But Hector just smiled a wide smile of satisfaction.

"We Torres are men of our word. Now I would like you to meet the newest Torres, my brother Jackson—"

"DEA! Get on the ground! Get down!" shouted orders came from the entrance as black-garbed men burst through the side door like an army of giant ants in their tactical SWAT gear.

The world sped up. Spun out of control. For instead of Hector and Alonzo doing what they were told they both pulled guns from their underarm holsters and dived away. They turned and fired in unison at the armed men from their new position on the floor catching the DEA agents by complete surprise. Hector screamed at Jackson, "Use your power! Now, bro!"

Before he could react, Jackson was grabbed from behind by Thomas. The sudden movement sent a stabbing pain deep into his gunshot side. It took him less than a split second to realize he was being used as a human shield against the lawmen who were now returning fire against his brothers. His heart squeezed with fear. He wanted the bad guys captured. Not dead. Unable to look away, he saw at least one bullet hit Hector in the thigh before his head was jerked backward by his hair.

"Pull back or I shoot this man! He's an American," Thomas barked loudly, his handgun pressed painfully against Jackson's temple.

"Don't think you can give me a fucking heart attack before I take you down. I promise you, you'll die first, asshole. I never trusted you," Thomas growled in his ear.

Thomas jerked him away from the line of fire and toward the front of the warehouse, moving backward to keep Jackson's body between the intruders and himself. He punched the big red start button with the back of his closed fist making the electric motor start up with a noisy grinding sound to lift the heavy steel doors upward. The outside world came sharply into focus as the sunlight streamed in the rapidly enlarging opening until it loomed well above their heads.

Jackson had no choice but to be dragged outside. Bullets were flying in all directions. His spirits plummeted. Would anyone be left alive? *What had he started?*

"Keep fuckin' moving!"

Around the side of the building and toward the SUV they inched, their footfalls crunching on the loose gravel. Jackson stumbled and was brought up short by Thomas who grabbed him tightly around the neck this time. Barely able to breathe, he kept focused on staying on his feet. Suddenly there was movement to the right. Thomas shouted at the man, "Stay back! I'll kill him!"

The vehicle loomed closer. Thomas slammed open the driver's door, keeping the vehicle between himself and the man holding the gun.

At the last possible second he hit Jackson hard over the top of his head with the butt of his gun, hard enough he heard a sickening sound that sent acute pain instantly ricocheting through his head.

"There, asshole. Try giving me a heart attack now!"

The last words he heard before his vision shattered. He slumped to the ground. Gone.

CHAPTER 27

"There's a hairline crack in his skull and a small hematoma. Until he wakes up, we have no idea if there will be any impairment. He needs time to heal." The doctor had shrugged when he'd shared the information yesterday, his expression grave enough to make Rand swallow hard against his fear. He hoped that was the man's usual delivery when dealing with the family.

He felt helpless. His best friend lying pale and wan on the hospital bed ate at his soul. A good man, this just wasn't right. It grated at him how much Jackson had gone through in his life. A shit of a stepfather, the horrors of beings struck down by electricity, and now this. It was the old adage, bad things happen to good people. It fucking sucked. Big time.

There was so much he wanted to tell him but couldn't. He sat down and stared at his friend.

"Hey, bud. How's it going?" he said out loud with a cheerful a voice as he could manage. The doctor had said to act as if Jackson could hear him and he felt pretty certain the past twenty-four hours that he could what he was saying to him.

"You know. You didn't have to go it alone. I would have backed your play sooner if you'd called me," he chided him.

A slight noise at the door alerted him to another visitor. Leia's worried face popped around the corner.

"Hey, Rand," she said as she joined him. "Any change?"

"I think he's better," he said with false bravado.

"Yeah?" she asked doubtfully.

"Doctor says it's just a matter of time. He'd been through worse."

"Rand…Leia…"

They both swung their heads toward the bed.

"Jackson!" Rand said. Excitement pounded through his body.

Leia moved and grabbed her brother's hand.

"Don't speak, just rest," she instructed.

Jackson nodded, his eyes blinking rapidly against the intrusion of light.

"Call the nurse!" Leia exclaimed while she continued to stroke her brother's hand.

Rand rushed out of the room in pursuit of medical aid. At the nurses' station, he shouted, "Come quickly! He's awake."

The next few minutes were filled with excitement and tension as Jackson was thoroughly checked out by the doctor and nurse in attendance. Rand and Leia had been pushed aside by the medical personal. They waited unspeaking, watching the proceedings.

"Well, you're one lucky man, Jackson Banks. Your eyes are tracking properly and you seem to have your faculties about you. Barring more tests, I'd say you look like you will recover fully."

"Got anything for this monster headache, doc? You'd think someone clobbered me with a fucking pistol the way it's throbbing," Jackson deadpanned as he rubbed his forehead. He gingerly touched the top of his head and located a row of stitches on his scalp buried underneath his hair.

"Of course." The doctor chuckled. He turned and gave instructions to the nurse for the medication.

Rand drew his first real breath since the incident. His friend was back, and he was going to be just fine. Life made sense again.

————

JACKSON LOOKED at Rand and Leia as he winced from the pain in his head. "Hey, what's up? Did you guys lose your best friend or something?" he asked.

"Shit, Jackson, you gave us a hell of a scare," Rand pounced on him.

"Yeah, me too," Leia said in a quieter tone.

The nurse came in and offered him the pain medicine he'd requested. He swallowed the pills down with a few sips of water. "Good ole Kentucky bourbon would taste better than this," he said to the nurse who gave him a frown in return.

"Alcohol's not allowed," she warned sternly before leaving.

"Okay, I need to know some things," Jackson said, getting serious. "Like what the fuck happened? Spill."

"I got bad news, buddy. Hector's wounded, one of our men took a bullet, but I'm afraid that Alonzo took a head shot and died at the scene. I'm sorry."

"The way the bullets were flying—" Jackson swallowed his anguish. He hardly knew the man, but he was his brother, and now he never would get to know him. He felt the loss churn in his gut.

"Everyone was wearing bulletproof vests and gear.

Only places to hit were either non-life threatening or like what happened to Alonzo."

"I wish it could have turned out differently." Jackson shook his head in frustration and thought to ask, "How did you end up there? You were there as well, right?"

Rand nodded. "Yeah, after we talked one of my men said he just couldn't see Hector waiting on it. Said his gut was saying it would happen sooner rather than later. I owe him breakfast for figuring it correctly. And my boss for buying into the overtime. Also, I won the bet that your skull was too hard to break." He said the last part with a rueful glance at him, and if Jackson wasn't mistaken, a hint of tears shone in his sleep-deprived, red-rimmed eyes.

"Glad I could help you win something. You owe me a bottle when I get out of here." Jackson took a deep breath. "What about Elena? Is she safe?"

"Not good news on that front, I'm afraid." Rand ran his hand through his hair, obviously agitated. "The department felt that a kingpin's wife just didn't justify a full-court press. You know, since they just got married, she wouldn't know much about his operations and they already had him dead to rights. I'm sorry, buddy, I guess what I'm trying to say is she's still in Mexico."

"Fuck." Jackson moved to sit up and pull out his IV line. "I gotta go there. She may be in danger."

"Stop! You can't do that! It's too soon. You need to recover for a few days first."

"Please, Jackson, you have to stay in the hospital," Leia chimed in.

"No, I can't. If anyone finds out she's carrying my kid, she's going to be in mortal danger," he said as he swung his legs over the side of the bed. "Okay, who's going to help me get dressed?"

Leia gave him a stunned look. "You got someone pregnant?" she finally managed to squeak out.

"Yeah, it wasn't planned or anything. But we got to get out of here now before they let the authorities know I'm alert for questioning, otherwise it will be all red tape. I'll tell them what I know when we get back. Not before that."

"No kidding; there's going to be hell to pay," Rand said. "I'll get your clothes."

Jackson watched him as he pulled the items from the small closet wincing at the sight of the dried blood on the shirt front. "How about I go and see if I can buy you a tee shirt at the gift shop?" Rand said.

"Good idea."

Twenty minutes later he walked out of the hospital under his own steam albeit a tad slower than usual.

"I've arranging for transport. A friend owes me a favor. You're not going it alone," Rand said as he used his cell phone to complete the task.

"Fine," Jackson said after glancing at his friend's determined expression. "But I warn you, it could be dangerous."

"Dangerous! Jackson, you can't go there," Leia wailed by his side, tugging at his arm. He was relieved her eyes were clear of the drugs. He'd do his best to see it stayed that way. Keep her close. Make her live with him and go to school.

"No choice, sis. Elena needs me. Don't worry. I'm a tough nut to crack as I've just proven. And I got help this time."

"Okay. All set," Rand said with satisfaction as they walked across the parking lot to retrieve his vehicle. "We leave tonight. That'll give us time to prepare. And I've got some ideas about that as well."

"Thanks, Rand, means a lot to me," Jackson said, trying not to choke up but failing miserably.

"No sweat."

Jackson struggled with his old wounds and his fresh ones for the next few hours as the pair prepared. But something more than the mere physical was driving him forward, something that made every second of pain worth the trial. Elena. Her vision followed him everywhere, haunted him, kept him upright.

"Do you think it's enough?" Rand asked.

"Yeah, I think you've got it more than covered," Jackson said as he took in the arsenal his friend had pulled together on the tarmac ready to be loaded into the cargo hold of the small plane. "We may not need any of it if they're as fractured as I'm expecting with Hector hurt and in custody. Jesús is the only brother still standing, and he's not like the others—much more reasonable and I think ready to make a change. The matriarch probably poses more of a problem than anyone. Tough old bird."

"What about his lieutenants?"

"The only one I met was George and he got busted at the warehouse. Thomas was Hector's personal bodyguard, the *bastard* that used me as his hostage. I owe him big time for that one." The world tilted as the headache throbbed, reminding him of his recent wound. He gritted his teeth and thrust the sensation away, forcing himself to stay focused on what was right in front of him. Lots of time for healing later.

"There are at least a dozen soldiers patrolling the grounds and guarding the house. I'm going to try to get my brother Jesús to help us. Maybe it would be best if you waited far enough away no one's aware of your being there, then I can get to him first."

Rand turned to look at him with disbelief, stopping in the act of stowing another duffel bag full of ammo and weapons. "You think you're in any shape to walk a couple of miles? No way, bro. I say we land right there under cover of darkness and go in strong. A 'hand her over or else' kind of scenario. Catch them all by surprise. It's a tactic that's worked many times before for us on drug raids. Bust in their front door with a breacher."

Sirens whined in the distance drawing both their attention. The night he'd rescued Leia and Ben came to Jackson's mind.

"We'd better hurry," he said. "We'll finalize plans on the plane."

Rand's buddy Seth, a big burly guy with ginger hair, called out from the cockpit of the plane.

"You about ready there?"

"Yeah, just about," Rand raised his voice and loaded another bag. Jackson had been floored at learning Rand had saved Seth's life in Afghanistan while he'd been in Iraq for his second tour. Just like his friend not to mention it. It seemed appropriate that his last name was Givens. Unassuming and as loyal as they come. Was he doing the right thing bringing his friend into the fray? Maybe he should make them turn back—find another way. Stuck in a mental quagmire he spotted a group of five men running toward them across the runway. *Now what?*

"FBI! FBI! FBI! Get down! Get down!"

"Fuckfuckfuck!" Rand let the expletives fly.

Jackson looked frantically at the men closing in with the prominent letters FBI blazed on their flak jackets and then back at the plane. So damn close.

He winced as he dropped to the ground, Rand at his side, arms spread wide.

"Go easy on him," Rand barked as one of the men stepped up to pat Jackson down. "He only just got out of the hospital."

The man just grunted as he found the handgun

Jackson had used to rescue Leia. It seemed like a thousand years ago.

"Okay, they're clean." The agent handcuffed the pair and hauled them back to their feet.

"You know I could drop you all right here, right?" Jackson warned, his thoughts dark and troubled. His words sparked a chain reaction as the men first looked more confused than angry.

"But I won't. I'm one of the good guys. But if you help me to rescue Elena Torres, I'll help you. Do whatever you want."

"You think you can take on all of us," the agent in charge mocked, appearing more interested in disputing his ability than making any kind of trade-off. "That's a pretty tall order, buddy."

"Jackson saved my life by restarting my heart after I was hit by enemy fire. He's a good man, just like he says. And you should all be helping him. And thanking him for helping take Hector and Alonzo Torres down. And taking a shit load of cocaine off the streets."

"You don't need to defend me, Rand, but thanks. I hope I haven't landed you in the soup here," Jackson apologized, realizing this could cost his friend big time. The bitter taste of defeat filled his mouth.

"That was you?" the agent's tone changed as he peered closer at Jackson. "You guys helped with that Los Knights sting?"

"Yeah, he was the guy who made it all happen. Singlehandedly fooled the cartel into moving drugs across the border. Now Jackson wants to finish it. Rescue his woman before she's harmed by the thugs. She's carrying his kid, for Christ's sake! You'd think someone would help him for a change."

"You the guy who got all those Mexicans to pee on wood to mask the odor of cocaine in the can? And then sent those fake drug dogs from the pound to make the case? Brilliant maneuver, by the way. Be happy to have you on our team."

Jackson nodded.

"Hell man, you're the stuff of legends!" The men broke out into laughter. "Funniest story I've heard in a long while. Okay, let me call this in. See what I can do." He nodded at one of the agents. "Take off the handcuffs for heaven's sake."

Jackson didn't dare let his hopes rise as the agents around him asked him more about the specifics of the operation. He just kept focused on answering the men. It seems another thousand years before the agent returned.

"Sorry, buddy, but headquarters wants you to come in first. But, and it's a big but, they are talking about doing something. I persuaded them it would ensure your full cooperation. Apparently getting you onboard is a big deal. By the way, what's your special ability that's got them so all fired up?"

Jackson swallowed his despair. He knew his body was beyond depleted with no chance of using his ability on these men. Not to mention the agents were innocent and undeserving of such a thing. He could not have done it even if he was at a hundred percent.

"He can make you think you're having a heart attack. He can drop men to the ground in a matter of seconds." Rand's voice was grim. Jackson realized he was also disappointed in not following through with their raid on the Torres ranch. Rand had his back. Always.

"For real? That sounds more than bat shit crazy," the agent observed.

"Yeah, I know. I've lived with this craziness and I still have a hard time believing it. Feels a lot more like a fucking curse," he muttered.

"Well, they want us now. Time to move."

Seconded in the back of the Suburban, Jackson felt the seconds slipping away, thinking they would have been airborne by now and headed across the border. Why was this happening? There would never be a better time to rescue her than when the Torres family was in shock. He turned his mind away from how deep a swath the pain would cut with Alonzo's death and Hector's arrest.

The briefing room was housed in a garage of the special operations structure of the FBI office in West-wood, just down the hill from UCLA. Jackson faced a trio of men while Rand had been escorted elsewhere. He sat on chair across a wooden table from the agents. They eyed him suspiciously while they shared a dossier on the operations to bring the Los Knights cartel down supplied by the DEA, a separate agency from the FBI. Jackson recognized surveillance maps of Ojinaga and the surrounding area.

Finally, after an uncomfortable twenty minutes of shuffling papers back and forth the men sat back and looked at him. None of them had much of an expression on their faces though he could see the wheels turning inside. They didn't bother to introduce themselves.

The guy in the middle with a bristly salt and pepper haircut appearing to be in charge tented his fingers. He twisted his lips in a grimace and spoke first. All the men were dressed in uniformly dark suits. "Why do you think you're here?"

"I would imagine because of my involvement with the recent raid on the Los Knights cartel and the taking down of Hector and Alonzo Torres?"

"Wrong. Guess again." The man leaned forward, the chair protesting at the shifting of his weight.

"Then that just leaves the curse to make a man think he's having a heart attack."

"You'll excuse us if we say we're having a hard time

believing it's even possible," the man said with deep skepticism and sat back now that the trump card was on the table.

"In fact, you could say we're more than a little skeptical," the man on the right with the steely blue eyes of Mel Gibson's Mad Max sent a dagger of apprehension slicing into Jackson's body. These men were not to be fucked with.

"No one wishes more than me that it wasn't the truth. It's caused me nothing but grief." The stark image of his mother and the fire came to mind and he closed his eyes, swallowing the instant bile that rose in his throat. At least the bastard who had ended her life was dead.

The third man's eyebrow rose at his reply while the center man ran a hand over his bristly head. He grimaced again. Was it for his benefit or for his men that he was acting so hard-assed?

"We know you have just gotten out of the hospital or we'd ask for a demonstration right here and now."

"Like I told the agents at the plane, you're not going to get any cooperation from me until Elena Torres is rescued."

The supervisor's eyes darkened while his fingers drummed on the tabletop.

"You compromised your op by getting involved with the wife of the drug kingpin?" It wasn't a question but an observation and Jackson knew enough to stay quiet.

"Until you've proven to us you have this ability, I will not authorize any of my men to undertake the Torres woman's rescue. Too risky."

"Fine. I'll do it right now. You want to be the first?" Jackson's ire rose as he challenged the man.

"Hardly the way to gain my cooperation," he observed dryly. His eyes narrowed to slats as he turned and conferred with the other men in a quiet whisper.

The *Mad Max* character got up and left the room. A few uncomfortable minutes later and he came back with another man dressed in a black flak suit with the prominent FBI emblems blazing front and back. It was one of the men from the plane. It didn't sit right with him that the man had been asked to be a victim of pain. Even if it was only temporary.

"I would prefer a guy who's done something wrong —" he began to protest.

"Don't worry," the guy joked. "I think I can handle it!"

"Are you sure?" *Did he have the juice left?*

"Come on. Give it your best shot. Give me something to brag about—that is if it works."

"Oh, it works all right," he muttered, hoping he would be able to pull it off. Elena's life hung in the balance.

He reached inside himself, inside the weakened physical vessel that his body had become from sustaining too many injuries. Found a small reservoir that was more strength of spirit than anything else and pulled on it, rolled it uphill to the surface, forcing it to bend to his will. Nausea threatened. He had only a few precious seconds to act. With a tremendous burst of willpower he scraped the last dregs of energy out of himself and flung it at the volunteer who faced him with far too little concern for his own plight. He prayed he'd released enough to do the deed before he passed out. And that the guy would forgive him.

———

JACKSON CAME BACK to consciousness on a cot in a small room. He was alone. He tried to sit up but his head spun dizzily making him reel back onto the cot. The sensation passed as he impatiently waited until he found the energy to sit up. *Where am I?* He found bottles of water on a small table near his bedside and unscrewed the lid of one. Downed it in a few gulps. Had the test worked? Antsy with concern, he stood up and checked the door to his room. Locked. Fuck, this was bad. Now they didn't trust him. It must have worked. He looked around and spotted a camera high on the wall. Someone must know he was awake. The clock on the wall reminded him he had lost precious hours.

He banged on the door. "Let me out!"

He waited and finally heard footsteps approaching.

The door opened and Mad Max confronted him. "Okay, I see you're back in the land of the living. Doctor said you needed rest."

"Am I under arrest?"

The guy cracked a smile from a closely guarded vault and shook his head. "No, we want to encourage you to consider training to work with us."

Jackson took a deep breath. "Thought maybe taking a guy down was a criminal offense."

"Not likely. More than a few of us on staff would like your ability, especially during an interview when you're ready to shake some sense into some asshole. We got a lot of questions for you, but they can wait. You need to go home and rest. Why you left the hospital so soon…" His voice trailed off as he escorted him back through the building.

"What about the mission to rescue Elena Torres?"

"Hmm, all I can say about that—it's classified." The man evaded his eyes. A bad sign.

"Fuck classified! If you think I'm going to leave her in harm's way in Mexico—"

The man held up a hand. "Calm down. It's being

taken care of as we speak." He sounded pissed to be having to say even that much.

"Where's Rand?" Jackson looked around frantically.

"Gone. He'll contact you. Later this evening most likely."

It was a lightbulb moment. "Fuck! I wanted to go with him."

"You were in no shape to do that. Go home. Wait there. Agent Romero will drive you. We'll talk in a couple of days. Here, take this." He handed Jackson a white card. James A. Sterling was embossed on it along with his rank and information. A supervisor and important SOB by the look of it. Jackson was too upset to be impressed.

The agent in question joined them. "Ready?" he asked.

Jackson nodded.

Agent Romero pointed at one of the black Suburbans lined up in the car park. "We're over here."

Frustrated, he had no choice but to follow him, their footsteps echoing on the dingy cement garage floor.

Strapped in the seat belt, the agent gave him a curious look. "Heard you gave Wilson quite a jolt. That true?"

"Yeah, no choice. Tell him I'm sorry about that."

"He's pissed about it all right." He chuckled. "I'd watch your back around him for a while. Give him a chance to calm down."

He started the vehicle and headed out of the compound. "How do you do that anyway? I saw the tape. Un-fucking-believable! The guys will be talking about it for years to come."

"Got hit by electricity and it left me like this." A simple truth had fucked his life. He still remembered as if it were yesterday. The acrid stench of the electrical smoke that seared his nostrils, the flood of sulfur in his mouth as he had chewed his tongue to bits, the sharp, burning needles of blinding pain that had blossomed in the hollow of his skull like a whirlwind had blasted a thousand hornets to drill unceasingly into his vulnerable brain. An instant taste of death. It had been months before he had fully recovered all his facilities and he knew he was one of the lucky ones. A survivor.

"Do you always pass out? Because that would be a bit of a handicap on an operation in the field. Just sayin'." The man turned to look at him, curiosity plain on his face.

"No. This was a first. I'm just exhausted. Recent bullet wounds and being hit over the head by a guy too free with his pistol will do that. Normally I'm fine when I'm functioning at a hundred percent."

"Going to join our team?"

"Maybe. Depends if they want me after what they saw today."

"Oh, *they want you all right*. My best guess is a hush-hush group no one is supposed know about. I only know of its existence because of a personal connection. Anyway, its members are an awesome group of men—all with special abilities. You'll feel right at home. But you didn't hear it from me; well above my paygrade."

Romero turned onto Jackson's street and pulled into the driveway before he realized he hadn't even given him the address. The realization sunk in that his entire life was now an open book to the FBI. Chilling. Would his connection with a convicted death row inmate lesson his chances of entering this new world? Becoming an FBI agent was a really big deal. All he knew was that many applied and few got in. If they did accept him, he'd consider himself lucky. Maybe Romero was right. They might want him enough to overlook his past.

"Thanks for the ride." He got out and was about to shut the door when Romero spoke up. "Mark my words.

I'll be seeing you sooner than you think." Jackson watched him back up down the driveway and onto the street before driving away.

He noticed his sunburned grass was badly in need of cutting as he navigated the narrow sidewalk. He'd been so busy that common tasks were slipping by the wayside. No time to worry about it now. He hurried into the house and slammed the door. He needed to contact Rand.

CHAPTER 28

RAND TOOK A DEEP BREATH. HIS TEAM WAS AT THE STAGING area. It had been a long trek with fifty pounds of gear that included a Kevlar helmet and tactical boots. He checked his lighted watch while hiding behind the cement wall that surrounded the property. 3:12 a.m. Good. Right on time, best hour of the night for a raid. The team of twenty agents was still under code yellow which meant cover, but it was nearing the end. Soon as they breached the wall they'd be in plain view. He watched his second in command out of the periphery of his vision as he scanned the area, waiting for the signal to move out and scale the wall. He'd checked his equipment and weapons on the fly in. Ready.

They'd left the choppers two miles back, agents at the helm ready to squire them away soon as they had Elena Torres in their clutches. He prayed they could pull this off without any loss of life. Anyone died here in Mexico and he knew his friend would be in pain the rest of his life. He didn't deserve that. Not after all the shit he'd waded through and somehow managed to wash off.

He activated the push-to-talk switch on his Motorola radio to speak into his throat mic, the wire connected to a receiver in his ear, a black Velcro strap holding it in place. The regulation gear ran on batteries which allowed them to communicate anywhere in the world. "Green light," he said, giving the instruction to move out.

He launched the grappling hook over the wall, tugged on the line to make sure it was secure, and braced himself to scale the ten-foot-high structure. All the agents were over the wall in a matter of seconds and working their way toward the main house, rifles at the ready. Rand noted an unfinished structure on his left and knew it must be the hospital under construction Jackson had told him about. He shuddered at the memory of what had gone on there and continued to advance. The man was going to pay for his sins and pay dearly.

The mansion was in darkness, but its perimeter was lit with pot lighting. Not good. They would be exposed for a few precious seconds getting inside. The agents spread out and he got into second position behind the agent with the breacher, the one-man ram assigned to knock down the front door. Or, as Rand liked to think fondly, the master key. Two men had carried the three foot long, five-inch diameter, concrete-filled steel pipe in shifts over the distance. They would not have access to the hydra ram on this in-and-out mission, a mini version of the Jaws of Life. Without a support vehicle to carry it or everyone's personal favorite, a strong hook and chain connected to a truck, there was no way to get it here. The ram would have to be enough and would be barring a residence with a steel reinforced vault door. Two other agents carried fire extinguishers for aggressive guard dogs.

The breacher stood ready, waiting for the final command. Rand nodded. With a mighty backswing of the device, he hit the door in a perfect arc and blew it to smithereens. The team surged through the opening. Some raced across the titled floor while others ran up the curved staircase. Rand was in the lead up the stairs. Hit the second floor in seconds.

A groggy woman in a robe, most likely a maid, wandered into the hallway rubbing her eyes.

"Elena Torres! Where is she?" Rand barked.

The woman pointed further down the hallway with a shaking hand, her eyes wide with concern as she took in the men dressed in black tactical gear, weapons drawn.

"At the end of the hallway, señor," she whispered.

The men streamed down the hallway. All the other doors remained closed. At the last door, Rand stood to one side and the other men on the other. He tried the knob. It turned under his hand. He nodded at one of the men.

He thrust the door open so hard it slammed against the wall.

"FBI. Show me your hands!"

A woman sat upright in the bed. Alone. Her hands were visible and she spoke out, "Don't shoot. I'm not armed."

Rand checked out the corners before he entered the room to be certain she was alone before entering the room. He hurried to the bed.

"Are you Elena Torres?"

"Yes." She was as beautiful as his buddy had said. His heart squeezed at realizing what Jackson had found in her. Lucky son of a bitch.

"I'm Rand. Jackson Banks sent me to rescue you."

"Is Jackson all right?"

"Yeah, just took a bump on the noggin, is all. Don't worry—he's got a thick skull. It would take more than a single hit to break through that sucker!" he joked to reassure the young woman before adding sternly, "You need to get up and dressed. *Fast.* We're taking you out of here."

Rand turned his back as she leaped from the bed and hurried to do as he ordered. He heard drawers being opened and closed as he waited.

"Okay," she said. He nodded his approval. Jeans, a blue sweatshirt, lightweight jacket tied around her waist and sturdy hiking boots, hair pulled into a tie.

"Good, let's go."

They made the hallway, the team gathered around Elena in the protective boxed in stance they had practiced to keep civilians safe. They advanced through the hallway and down the staircase without incidence.

Gunshots rang out.

Rand looked into the other men's eyes and saw the tension driving them. He nodded. Everyone kept their weapons at the ready. They continued as a group across the foyer floor to the broken front door.

"Elena! Where are you taking her?" a male voice alerted him to possible conflict. Trained response. He scanned the young man for weapons. No weapons in view.

"Show your hands!" Rand barked.

"Jesús! I'm fine!" Elena spoke up as the man lifted his hands palm upward to show he had nothing to hide. "These men are here to help."

"Help? What's the meaning of this?" The man looked more confused than anything as Rand recognized the man from Jackson's physical description.

"They're taking me to see Jackson."

"But why?"

"Because I love him," she said. The truth shone in her amber eyes.

"*Puta!*" The word came from an older woman dressed in a robe, who came scurrying up to them, her long graying hair tied into a braid and snaking over her shoulder. "My son should never have married you!" The woman spit on the floor at Elena's feet.

"And I would not have married him if I hadn't been forced!" Elena's eyes sparked with outrage. Her mother-in-law lunged at her. Rand reacted instinctively and moved forward to intervene. Another agent grabbed the older woman and pulled her away.

"You are no longer welcome in my home, *puta!*" the woman screeched, her body rigid with anger as she was held firmly by Rand's man.

More gunshots outside.

Rand turned to confront Jesús. "Do you have access to the outside lights? Can they be turned off from inside?" he asked.

"Uh, yes, of course. I have the access code." The young man with the dreamy look in his eyes scurried over to the wall and began to punch in numbers to the large electronic keypad.

"Don't you help them!" his mother warned, still needing to be held firmly by the nonplussed agent.

"I can't let them kill Elena," Jesús said over his shoulder. It took a few more precious seconds and the foyer was brightened with overhead lights before it too was plunged into darkness and all the outside lights were switched off.

"You don't have long before the generators are switched on and the lights come back on. Just a minute or so," the young man warned as he rejoined them. The dimmer light was comforting for it meant no one outside could see them.

"Come with us, please, Jesús, you can make a better life in America," Elena pleaded.

He shook his head, his expression solemn. "No. My

place is here." He went to his mother's side and took her into his arms, setting the agent free to leave.

"Let's move," Rand said, gathering his men. He ignored Elena's stricken face. He had no orders about taking any other family member. One brother should be left free to look to needs of the family. Perhaps it was wrong, but he felt compelled to leave Jackson's last brother alone for now, and maybe he would catch hell for it. But maybe too Jesús would straighten up his act and get out of the drug business altogether. He had a second chance now.

Rand nodded at his men. Time to move out.

The team moved as a unit to the open doorway and into the night.

Rand was on high alert. His eyes continually scanned the area looking for any movement.

Acutely aware of the danger staying in a group posed, he increased the pace. One of their men rushed up to the group. He recognized Agent Malcolm as the man gave his report, "One man hurt. But we got the bastards shooting at us."

"How bad?" Rand asked.

"Shoulder. Jacobson. He'll be able to walk."

"Good. Tell the others to pull back. Head for the chopper. We've got our target."

"Copy." Malcolm vanished into the darkness. Rand was grateful for the moonless night as they made the wall safely. Elena moved forward, the team still shadowing and protecting her, and operated the electronic switch to open the fence. The men hurried through it.

The warm humid air surrounded the agents as they rushed through the darkness, their boots crunching on the rocky ground, the weight of their packs making them sweat profusely inside their clothing. It would be a long trek back to the chopper on high alert. Rand would not inform his friend until they were safely off the ground. No point in tempting fate.

A screech owl hooted eerily in the night from a tree close by. He started in his skin and began sweating even more, his mouth gone dry. He felt so responsible this night, filling in for his friend who he knew would give *anything* to be there in his place. He held the lives of Jackson's family and future family in the palm of his hands and he did not take that lightly. He prayed for it to be over even as he embraced the adrenaline rush that all missions brought forth. It was why he did the job. A chance at getting the bad guys and making the world a little safer.

The first mile behind them, Rand breathed a little easier.

There had been no more gunfire. He prayed, *please let everyone make it back to the chopper alive.*

He glanced at Elena. He had to admit she was a trooper as she kept up with the swift pace he'd set. She appeared in good physical condition as she half ran inside the circle of men due to her shorter stride.

Less than a quarter mile to go.

All senses on high alert, Rand could hear the strenuous sounds of men breathing hard around him, bodies pushed to the limit straining for oxygen. He swiped the sweat from his forehead, his helmet too tight, his skin swollen from the excessive heat.

One thousand yards.

Hope flared.

He could hear other bodies moving around them in the darkness and he prayed they were friendly, striving to get to the chopper for the ride home.

Five hundred yards. One hundred yards. The chopper was in sight.

Fifty feet. So close he could taste it.

A loud explosion rocked the night. Bright as day in a flash, so intense it blinded him in an instant.

"What the fuck! Get down!" he ordered.

Everyone dropped to the ground. He turned and threw himself over Elena, pushing her beneath him. No way was anything happening to her on his watch.

"What's going on?" he spoke into his radio attached to his collar. He could feel Elena trembling beneath him as he covered her as best he could.

"They launched a shell from a machine gun. No one's hurt. Thank God it missed the chopper or it would have blown it sky high. Those suckers can blow holes in armored cars. Lucky and Davis have them pinned down. They'll give us cover."

"Okay, we'll make a run for it. Hope their aim's as bad the second time if they get one off."

He turned to his men as everyone scrambled to their feet. "Let's roll!" They began moving with calculated precision.

The last twenty feet were the worst. Time slows. Sound stops. Each split-second an agony of apprehension. Any moment a bullet could enter flesh. End a life. The whirling of the chopper blades sent the dust and debris flying into a pulsating smokescreen of grit and debris. It stung the skin and burned the eyes as they clamored into the belly of the V-22 Osprey Blackhawk helicopter. The pilot lifted off before the men were strapped in, lurching into evasive maneuvers that roiled the stomach and knocked equipment about, the noise of the engines deafening. The Osprey were known for their speed and versatility, and a god-awful sound like it always needed an oil change to ease the gears. They'd all need to put on headphones to keep from going deaf.

"Any word on the other chopper?" he tersely shouted at the crew pilot as soon as he had a moment to talk. His stomach would be in knots until he knew all the men were safe.

"Yes, they're in the air and headed for home." The wide grin and thumbs up signal said it all as his words were nearly drowned out.

It took another ten minutes of flight before Rand drew a free breath. They had made it. Lucky and Davis were as much to thank as anyone and he made a mental note to give them a written commendation for their efforts when he reported back to the bigwigs. He sat back with a satisfied smile and gave Elena a reassuring smile.

"Jackson's going to be happy to see you," he said loudly and was rewarded with a happy though strained look. Not surprising considering all she had been through.

"I hope so," she shouted over the din. "My life—well, that's all over. I can bring little to the table but my love and support." Her golden amber eyes were arresting, reflecting somber reflection as she pushed thick strands of loosened hair back from her face and behind her ears.

"I know so. He thinks the sun rises and sets on you," he said emphatically. Elena had a sweetness of spirit that was refreshing, but he could also see the underlying strength under the beautiful smooth surface. A true steel magnolia. Another stab of envy entered him that he pushed aside. He had to believe his turn would arrive. Someday. If he got lucky.

"Tell me how he is—really?" she demanded, her glance locking with his.

"I promise you, he's going to be fine. He would have come if he could have."

"I know. He's a white knight, just like his buddy," she remarked, her mouth twisting in a wry smile, but her eyes spoke more of the love she bore him.

"Yeah, well, we aim to please, ma'am." He felt off-kilter talking with Jackson's woman. His friend had never been serious about a female before. In fact he's always been shy around women, probably not helped by his multitude of scars.

"*Ma'am!* I'm not a hundred years old!" she struck back. She chuckled, softening the blow.

"You want to talk to him?" he shouted.

"Could I? That would be great!" She sat up straighter, her eyes shining with a thousand megawatts of enthusiasm.

"Sure." Rand pulled out his cell phone and brought up Jackson's number and waited while it rang.

"Hey, buddy. Got someone here you actually wants to talk to your sorry ass."

"Rand! Is that you? How are you? Is everyone okay?"

"Yeah. We're all safe in the air and headed back to base. Now, do you want to talk to your woman or not?" Rand smiled into the phone.

"A thousand times yes! Put her on."

He handed the cell to Elena who grasped at it with eager fingers.

"Jackson! How are you? You had me so worried!"

Silence except for the noise of the motors as she listened intently to his response.

"Fine, now that I can hear your voice."

He couldn't take the love bouncing between the pair and pulled on his headphones to give them their privacy, turning up the music to high volume.

A few minutes later Elena nudged him to take back his phone. He pulled down his headphones leaving them looped around his neck.

"He wants to talk to you."

"Hey, what's up?" he asked as he put the phone to his ear and cupped his hand over the other side of his head in an effort to hear.

"I need to say something, so listen up."

His friend's voice sounded husky and he sat up straighter, wondering what was going on.

"I owe you big time, my friend. What you just did—it means everything to me. Getting Elena out safely, I almost don't know *what* to say except it means the world to me. Anything you need, anytime, I'm your man. I love you, buddy."

Rand swallowed hard, and his throat constricted. He cleared his throat; his skin felt too warm.

"Hell, you'd so the same for me. I know that, but, yeah, if you insist, sure, you owe me big time! And don't worry, I intend to collect. Make you listen to all my bad jokes come hell or high water," he joked.

"Good. See you soon. I'll be waiting."

"You bet," he grunted and hit end to terminate the call.

Elena smiled at him, a fellow conspirator.

"I see a lot of dinners and evenings spent at our place in the near future," she remarked.

"I warn you, I have a legendary appetite. I could eat you out of house and home."

"You can try! I'm a legendary cook."

Christ, was there anything this woman couldn't do. A third stab of envy.

The good humor between them died as she looked away for a moment and then gave him a level look stripped of emotion. "You know he's *never* going to let me go right—not as long as he's alive," she said, chewing on at her lower lip. She didn't have to say the name. Rand knew who she meant. "I should make you take me back to the ranch right now; if I had the courage. Leave Jackson safe to live his life. Hector has a long reach and he's not a man who will just let this go." She shook her head sadly as if all the burdens of the world lay on her slender shoulders.

Her words took Rand by surprise. "You don't look to me to be a woman without courage. And Jackson, well, he's a big boy, he knows what he wants. Besides, Hector will be going away for a long, long time. You're safe now, trust me."

CHAPTER 29

Three months later
The SHU, Maximum Security Unit, Pelican Bay "Supermax"
State Prison

"CONSIDER YOURSELF SERVED," THE PRISON OFFICIAL SAID thrusting a manila envelope through the slot in the steel door. It was designed for minimal interaction with prisoners and was mostly used for meals and any correspondence that came their way. The inmates in the maximum wing spent nearly 24/7 inside their cells, only allowed out for two hours in the exercise yard every second day alternating days with showers and a day of zero programs on Wednesdays. It brutally sucked.

Hector ignored the man and the envelope landed on the floor of the six by eight precast cell with a slight whooshing sound, face down.

There are two kinds of people in this world, bro. Those you can count on and those you can't. Being in here separates that herd. Ain't but two kinds of men are on the inside too: inmates and convicts. Inmates follow the rules; convicts are mean moth-erfuckers. You gotta decide how you're going to be on the inside no matter what you stood for on the outside. Me, I'm too old to change. Been a mean motherfucker all my life. The words of a fellow prisoner came back to him as he picked up the envelope and turned it over, wincing at the residual pain in his leg. It was healing from the gunshot that had pierced the thigh bone and left him what he was worried would become a permanent limp. Lousy fucking medical care.

The last few weeks had been a hell of an adjustment. The lights stay on in the SHU nearly twenty-four hours a day only dimming a little at night making sleep damn near impossible. Like a fucking Las Vegas casino that makes time vanish into nothingness. Caged like a fucking animal, he had to get out of there. He'd been using his time wisely, observing patterns and sifting and sorting all the information that flowed sporadically his way. Just about time to act. The exercise yard held the key.

He tore open the end of the letter and pulled out the sheath of papers and scanned the five-page stapled docu-ment, turning each page over with increasing agitation as he absorbed what they meant.

"*Cocksuckers!* If they think they can get away with this bullshit—" He threw the papers back on the floor with disgust, unzipped his fly, and pissed on the papers. The actions reminded him of the day when his soldiers had drank beer in the hot sun and pissed on the camphor wood. A ruse by a man he had been beginning to trust—to like. A betrayal that ate away like a raw canker sore pressing deeper into his soul each day with too much time for thinking. It could only be eradicated by taking Jackson Banks down. The man who had left their brother to bleed out on a warehouse floor. A brother and sister he was not allowed to see properly buried. He bit down on the inside of his mouth to stem the pain oozing from his soul at the memory. The only way he could get some relief from the disgrace and shame the man had brought onto his family was to take him out permanently. The man had been offered a chance at being a Torres. And *this* was how he repaid him? His flesh overheated with indignation and he had to force himself to calm down. The doctor had warned his blood pressure was too high—in the danger zone.

And now, with the arrival of the divorce papers, he added Elena to his ever-growing hit list. The fucking bitch would not get away with this desertion. Leaving his mamá to fend for herself during her time of greatest need. The loss of another child. She truly was the *puta* his mamá claimed she had been all along. Why had he not seen it? Blinded by her beauty and sweetness, a smokescreen hiding her disgusting lack of character. *Puta*. And after all he had tried to provide for her. His disgust made his stomach squeeze in pain and he reached in his pocket for an antacid tablet to relieve the stabbing discomfort, unrolling the silver foil and popping the white pill in his mouth. He added a second one for good measure.

"You clean that up, Torres, or so help me I'm going to beat some sense into that lazy ass," a guard said as he stood at the door to his cell and peered through the small opening.

Hector ignored him, knowing the large sums of money he paid for protection kept the system from biting his ass, and lay down on the mattress, head propped on his arms. Time to go over his plan one more time. There was no room for error. And soon, very soon he would be free to unleash hell.

———

JACKSON TOOK A DEEP BREATH, swiping the sweat from his brow with the sleeve of his shirt that clung wetly to his back, drenched in perspiration. Eyes stinging, he reached for a bottle of water on the side of his pack, downing it in a few large gulps. Training with sixty pounds of tactical gear on your person was daunting under the brutal desert sun though it was getting easier after weeks of training. He eased his sore muscles by stretching back and forth at the waist while watching his fellow candidates being put through their paces.

As always, Maxim had taken the lead, his agility and strength already legendary in their class. Every year the men and women in the FBI had to commit to fifty days of training. If he proved his medal and passed all the tests, both physical and mental, he would be joining their ranks. He noted that the easygoing Sangster was letting Maxim set the pace. But Jackson had learned not to underestimate the man when he set his mind to do something. Sangster became a ruthless machine.

He'd found a home with these men and women in these past weeks and now felt a part of the tightknit group that strived and pushed so hard to become special agents. He knew some would muster out, that standards were set high, but hoped that most would be working with him to aid the United States government in keeping the country safe for many years to come.

He'd stepped up even though he had been warned by his handler at the FBI that he would be asked to do very unorthodox missions that would test his abilities to the limit. He needed to do this now. To make up for all he had been recently blessed with, thinking of Elena, his-soon-to-be-wife, and the upcoming arrival of his baby daughter. And the continued good health of a drug-free Leia. Yes, he was a lucky man. But still, something was worrying him, something he couldn't admit to out loud—not yet. It would spoil his new idyllic life if he said it aloud. Make it too real. A text had arrived on his phone last night.

Terse words all capitals: A TORRES NEVER FORGIVES.

And instead of an emoji of a smiley face after the words there was a big red X.

The number was blocked but he was certain the roots lead straight back to Hector. It made him want to scream with frustration. Was the man going to come after him? Send someone after him? He was in a maximum-security prison cell for fuck's sake. Surely he was locked up for good and out of touch with the outside? But a niggling doubt had been planted and took the shine off his newfound happiness. Anything was possible. He knew that now.

He straightened his shoulders still watching the men and women on the obstacle course. Fuck. Hector. He now had his own family and he would fight to the death for them. But he had one last stop to make to finish with his old life and get on with it. He felt strong enough now to handle it.

"Banks, Chief wants to see you." He turned at the loud sound and nodded at the messenger who was out of breath from hurrying across the field to find him.

"Sure thing." He strode back to the main office. Knocking on the office door he waited until a voice inside answered.

"Come in."

Supervisor James A. Sterling, or Mad Max as Jackson still liked to think of him, sat at his desk. Another man was sitting in one of the two chairs placed squarely in front of the desk. He slid into the empty seat and waited. Both men looked so serious he felt his stomach clench before he told himself to calm down. It didn't automatically mean bad news.

"Jackson, this is John Whitmore from the National Human Genome Research Institute—NHGRI. He's a scientist working on the human genome project in Bethesda, Maryland."

Jackson nodded at the man and shook his hand. The scientist was looking at him with such intense interest in his eyes that he shifted uncomfortably in his chair and glanced back at the commander to see if he was in on the joke. The guy looked too much like he should have his photo in the dictionary. Even the plastic placket in his pocket to house his pens screamed nerd.

"What's this about?" he asked.

"What do you know about the human genome, Jackson?" the scientist asked before Sterling could answer him.

He shrugged. "DNA? Not much. Just that it's what makes us who we are and that it is unique to each one of us. Useful in proving someone innocent or guilty of a crime. Why?"

John nodded. "Inside each of our cells are twenty-three pairs of chromosomes that contain the entire genetic program for a specific individual—it is indeed what makes us unique. What you, and most people for that matter, are unaware of is that much of this code is not turned on, in fact, appears switched off. Only approximately three percent is currently functioning in homosapiens with long sequences not operating in between—junk DNA if you may. Biologists have long wondered what human abilities could be hiding in these dormant sequences. That's why we tested your DNA, hoping to find an explanation."

He took a quick breath, his eyes shining with a reverent zeal before continuing, "And we discovered something so startling that I will just come out and say it. Your code is beyond *anything* we have ever seen before. We can only postulate that somehow the jolt of electricity you experienced led to a spark in your cells that turned on some of these sequences. It's what we theorize must be giving you your unusual ability. Of course, we will need to do more testing."

"Really?" Jackson sat up straighter. "So there's a reason for my being this way? My cells were basically changed, charged up by the accident."

"Yes. Quite frankly, we have never seen such a thing before. It's beyond the inexplicable. Beyond the scope of our understanding. It defies everything we know about the human genome. You are most definitely a one-of-a-kind human being, Jackson Banks. You should be cloned." The scientist sat back with supreme satisfaction, tenting his fingers, and beaming as if he were the God who had made him this way.

"Just so you know, I refuse to be anybody's fucking guinea pig. What kind of investment of my time are we talking about here?"

John glance shifted between his and Sterling's, his eyes revealing that he was less than pleased that Jackson wouldn't jump right in with both feet.

"We thought you'd be pleased to discover more of what has made you this way—"

"Don't get me wrong. It's good to know. But I have a job to do now. Get through the academy and help the American people."

"I think you can do both, Banks." Sterling did what he was best at, oiling the waters. "We can let you go to Maryland—say, for two days a month."

The frustration in the scientist's eyes was obvious. "We expected—"

"You can have him for a couple of days right now, if that helps?"

"Yes, of course. But I had hoped for a little more cooperation," John wheedled. "This is a once-in-a-lifetime opportunity."

"For you, maybe," Jackson shot back. "Now, if you'll both excuse me, I have somewhere I have to be."

———

EVERGREEN CEMETERY'S stone arches and wrought iron decoration stood silent sentinels as he drove the GMC through the open gates. Though it had been years—too many consumed by the guilt that had stalked him—it still looked just the same. A quiet place to lay the dead to rest. Forever. The beautiful clouds floating against the perfect blue skies seemed at odds with reality of the place, but helped give him heart as he parked the truck and stepped out, a bouquet of white roses, her favorite, clutched in his hand.

His memory did not fail him and within a few minutes he had located the gravesite. He leaned down and touched the headstone, running his fingers over the lettering: *In Ever Loving Memory, Sarah Elisabeth Banks. 1960-2001. 'Til we meet again.*

Now, just maybe, he could face her once more when they met on the other side, his conscious clear. Her murderer was gone, sent straight to hell. *If there was justice in the afterlife.* But more importantly, he was moving on. Having the life she had always hoped for him.

It had been a long road to this place. A road of endless searching for redemption. Elena had helped give him that peace, put him on the right path with his need to help her. And funny how she had ended up helping him more.

But he had also helped himself by accepting his strange ability as part and parcel of who he was now. And he intended to spend the rest of his life proving it, using his gift for good. He laid the white roses on top the grassy mound and spoke a silent prayer, a winged bird flying overhead the only witness. *Rest in peace, dear mother, rest in peace.*

A LOOK AT: CITY OF LIES

A Gripping Tale of Identity, Crime, and Survival…

Claire Preston, a script reader for a Hollywood movie studio, has recently lost her mother. Discovering she was adopted as a baby, she goes on a perilous quest for her true identity.

Assisted by her mentor, the seasoned private investigator, Jake Sterling, Claire delves deeper into her past, only to unearth a labyrinth of secrets more daunting than she ever envisioned. Soon, she finds herself in the crosshairs of a ruthless serial killer —an ex-Nazi fugitive evading justice for decades.

As Claire confronts her heritage, grapples with danger, and races against time to evade the clutches of a deadly predator, she finds herself wondering: Is uncovering the truth in a city of lies even possible?

AVAILABLE NOW

ABOUT THE AUTHOR

January Bain is an award-winning author who firmly believes that stories unite us, that good stories help us to discover the commonality of the human experience by supporting values, empathy and understanding. She writes with her heart, mind, and soul, hoping that her novels will touch your life, giving you moments of freedom as you fly with her to other worlds.

Bain has had the pleasure of select novels being turned into games, and her work is also available in different languages.

January and her husband live in rural Canada on peaceful acreage where a variety of wildlife comes to visit regularly and expect to be fed and paid attention to.

www.ingramcontent.com/pod-product-compliance
Lightning Source LLC
Chambersburg PA
CBHW010727250626
47155CB00011B/3581